THE WORKHOUSE ORPHAN'S REDEMPTION

RACHEL DOWNING

CORNERSTONETALES.COM

PART I
THE CRUCIBLE OF YOUTH

Let no man despise thy youth; but be thou an example of the believers, in word, in conversation, in charity, in spirit, in faith, in purity.
  – Timothy 4:12

WHISPERS ON BRICK LANE

The gas lamps flickered to life as dusk settled over London, casting long shadows across the cobblestone streets. Emma Grace Redbrook clutched her father's hand, her wide hazel eyes drinking in the sights and sounds of the bustling city. The clip-clop of horses' hooves mingled with the shouts of street vendors, creating a symphony of urban life that both thrilled and overwhelmed the ten-year-old girl.

"Papa, look!" Emma tugged on John's sleeve, pointing at a peddler balancing an array of shiny pots and pans on his shoulders. "How does he carry all that?"

John chuckled, his laugh lines deepening. "Years of practice, I'd wager."

Mary placed a gentle hand on Emma's shoulder, steering her away from a passing carriage that splashed muddy water onto the pavement. "Mind where you're walking, love."

Emma nodded, but her attention was already captured by a group of street urchins huddled around a storyteller, their faces alight with wonder. She longed to join them, to lose herself in tales of far-off lands and daring adventures.

As they turned onto Whitechapel High Street, Emma

noticed a change in the air. The excitement of moments before gave way to a palpable tension. Hushed whispers passed between shopkeepers as they hurriedly shuttered their windows. A crowd had gathered around a wall where a man was nailing up a notice, his face grim.

"What's happening, Mama?" Emma asked, pressing closer to Mary's side.

Her mother's grip tightened. "Nothing to worry about, my dear. Just some city business."

But Emma couldn't shake the feeling that something was very wrong. She caught snatches of conversation as they passed:

"...another case on Brick Lane..."

"...closing the pump on Broad Street..."

"...cholera's back, God help us all..."

The word 'cholera' sent a shiver down Emma's spine, though she didn't fully understand its meaning. She looked up at her parents, noting the worry lines etched on their faces, so at odds with their reassuring smiles.

Emma's heart raced as her father's cough echoed through the narrow street. She glanced up at him, worry creasing her young brow. John's face had gone pale, his shoulders hunched as he fought to catch his breath. Mary's hand tightened on Emma's shoulder, a silent comfort that did little to ease the knot forming in her stomach.

"Perhaps we should hurry home," Mary said.

As they neared their modest dwelling, Emma's eyes darted to the small bakery on the corner. The warm, yeasty smell of fresh bread wafted through the air, momentarily chasing away her fears.

"Mama," she said, tugging gently on Mary's sleeve. "May I fetch some bread? And... perhaps a bit of honey?"

Mary hesitated, her gaze flicking between John and Emma. After a moment, she nodded, fishing out a few carefully hoarded pennies from the pocket sewn into her apron. "Be quick about it, love."

Emma clutched the coins tightly, their edges biting into her palm as she hurried into the bakery. The shopkeeper's smile didn't quite reach his eyes as he wrapped a small loaf and dolloped honey into a twist of paper. Emma thanked him, cradling her precious cargo as she rushed back to her parents.

The climb up the narrow staircase to their rooms seemed steeper than usual. Emma's breath caught in her throat as she pushed open the door to find her mother helping her father into bed. His cough had worsened, each ragged breath sending a shudder through his frame.

"Papa?" Emma's voice quavered.

Mary turned, forcing a smile. "Your father just needs some rest, dear. Why don't you read to him for a bit? It always soothes him so."

Emma nodded, setting aside the bread and honey. She retrieved her most prized possession – a small, well-worn Bible – from its hiding place beneath a loose floorboard. Settling into the chair beside her father's bed, she opened to the Book of Psalms, his favourite.

"The Lord is my shepherd," Emma began, her young voice steady despite the fear coiling within her. "I shall not want..."

PARTING GIFTS

*E*mma's voice faltered as she read the familiar scriptures, her father's laboured breathing growing more pronounced with each passing moment. She glanced up from the Bible, her heart clenching at the sight of her father's ashen face. His eyes, once warm and twinkling, now gazed at her with a mixture of love and sorrow.

"Emma, my sweet girl," John whispered, his voice barely audible. "Come here."

She set the Bible aside and moved closer, her small hand finding his. Mary sat on the other side of the bed, her fingers intertwined with her husband's.

"I want you both to know," John said, each word a struggle, "how much I love you. You've been my greatest joy in this life."

Tears began to form in Emma's eyes, but she blinked them back, determined to be strong for her father. "We love you too, Papa," she said, her voice quivering.

John's lips curved into a faint smile. He looked at Mary, his gaze filled with unspoken words. Then, with a final, shuddering breath, he closed his eyes.

The room fell silent, save for the muffled sounds of the

street below. Emma stared at her father's still form, unable to comprehend the finality of the moment. It wasn't until she heard her mother's choked sob that the reality crashed over her.

In the days that followed, Emma moved through a fog of grief and disbelief. She went through the motions of daily life, fetching water, preparing meagre meals, and tending to her mother. But the world had lost its colour, its vibrancy.

It was on a grey morning, not long after they had laid John to rest, that Emma noticed her mother's flushed cheeks and glassy eyes. Mary tried to wave off her daughter's concerns, but Emma saw how she gripped the edge of the table for support, how her steps faltered as she moved about their small room.

"Mama, please," Emma pleaded, guiding Mary to the bed. "You need to rest."

Mary acquiesced, her usual strength seeming to drain away as she sank onto the thin mattress. Emma's hands shook as she wrung out a cool cloth and placed it on her mother's forehead. She tried to recall everything she'd seen the neighbourhood women do when tending to the sick, but panic clawed at her chest.

EMMA SAT by her mother's bedside, her small hands clasped tightly around Mary's fevered fingers. The room felt suffocating, the air thick with the scent of illness and fear. Outside, the bustling sounds of London continued unabated, oblivious to the tragedy unfolding within these four walls.

Mary's eyes fluttered open, her gaze unfocused at first before settling on Emma's face. A weak smile tugged at her lips. "My little darling," she whispered, her voice hoarse.

Emma leaned closer, her heart pounding. "I'm here, Mama. I'm right here."

With trembling hands, Mary reached for the chain around

her neck. Emma watched, confusion mingling with dread, as her mother fumbled with the clasp.

"Help me, darling," Mary murmured.

Emma's fingers shook as she undid the delicate fastening. The silver cross necklace slid free, catching the dim light filtering through the grimy window. It was beautiful in its simplicity, a treasure Emma had admired countless times as it rested against her mother's chest.

Mary closed her eyes for a moment, gathering strength. When she opened them again, they shone with a fierce love that took Emma's breath away.

"Emma, my sweet girl," Mary said, her words slow and deliberate. "This necklace has been in our family for generations. It's carried us through joy and sorrow, through plenty and want."

She pressed the cross into Emma's palm, curling her daughter's fingers around it. "Now it's yours, my love."

Emma felt the weight of the necklace, so light yet so significant. "But Mama—"

Mary shook her head, silencing Emma's protest. "Listen to me, Emma Grace. No matter what happens, no matter how dark the world may seem, you must always keep your faith. This cross isn't just silver and metal. It's a reminder of God's love, and of our family's strength."

Tears spilled down Emma's cheeks as she clutched the necklace to her chest. Mary reached out, her touch cool against Emma's flushed skin.

"Promise me," Mary whispered, her eyes intense. "Promise me you'll always keep your faith, no matter what."

GRIEF'S EMBRACE

*T*he dim light of dawn seeped through the grimy window as Emma's eyes fluttered open. For a moment, she lay still, her small body curled against her mother's side. The room was quiet, too quiet. No laboured breathing, no fevered murmurs. Just silence.

"Mama?" Emma whispered. She squeezed her mother's hand, the one she'd been clutching all night. It felt cold, unnaturally so.

Emma pushed herself up, her heart pounding. "Mama, wake up," she pleaded, shaking Mary's shoulder gently. But Mary didn't stir. Her face, once flushed with fever, was now pale and still.

The truth crashed over Emma like a wave, stealing her breath. She stared at her mother's lifeless form, her mind refusing to accept what her eyes were seeing. This couldn't be real. It couldn't.

A sob bubbled up in Emma's throat, raw and primal. She threw herself across her mother's chest, fingers clawing at the threadbare nightgown. "No, no, no," she wailed, her cries echoing in the empty room.

Hours passed, or maybe it was minutes. Time lost all meaning as Emma clung to her mother's body, her grief too vast to be contained by her small frame. When she finally sat up, her face was blotchy, eyes swollen and red.

With trembling hands, Emma smoothed her mother's hair, arranging it just the way Mary had always worn it. She straightened the blanket, tucking it around her mother's shoulders as if to keep her warm. These small acts of care were all she had left to give.

Reality began to set in, cold and unforgiving. Emma knew she needed to arrange for her mother's burial. But how? They had no money, no family to turn to.

Wiping her tears with the back of her hand, Emma stumbled out of the room. She made her way to the local church, her legs shaky beneath her. The priest, a stern-faced man with greying hair, listened to her halting explanation with growing impatience.

"I'm sorry, child," he said, his voice devoid of warmth. "Without payment, we cannot provide burial rites."

Emma's heart sank. "Please, sir," she begged, her voice cracking. "She was my mama. She deserves a proper burial."

The priest shook his head. "Many deserve what they cannot afford. That's the way of the world."

Stumbling out of the church, Emma's small frame shook with each ragged breath. The priest's words echoed in her ears. She leaned against the rough stone wall, her legs threatening to give way beneath her.

The bustling street before her blurred as fresh tears welled in her eyes. People hurried past, their faces a snear of indifference. Emma clutched the silver cross hanging around her neck.

"I'm sorry, Mama," she whispered. "I can't... I can't give you what you deserve."

The thought of her mother's body lying alone in their small room sent a fresh wave of grief crashing over her. Emma squeezed her eyes shut, trying to block out the image. She took a deep, shuddering breath, forcing herself to remember her mother's words.

"Keep your faith," Mary had said. Emma clung to those words now, like a lifeline in a storm-tossed sea.

She pushed herself away from the wall, her legs unsteady but holding. As she began the long walk home, Emma's mind raced. She couldn't give her mother a proper burial, but perhaps... perhaps that didn't matter in the grand scheme of things.

"God knows your heart, Mama," Emma murmured, her fingers tracing the outline of the cross. "He'll welcome you home, I know it."

The thought brought a small measure of comfort, easing the crushing weight of her grief. Emma's steps grew more certain as she made her way through the winding streets. She couldn't control what happened to her mother's earthly remains, but she could honour her memory in other ways.

CAST OUT

Clutching at her meagre belongings, Emma hid her mother's silver cross necklace beneath her threadbare dress. The landlord's words echoed in her ears as she stumbled onto the cobblestone street. "No rent, no roof. Out with ye!"

The world spun around her, a dizzying kaleidoscope of indifferent faces and towering buildings. Emma's stomach growled, a painful reminder of her last meal days ago. She shuffled forward, her feet heavy as lead.

"Spare a coin, miss?" Emma's voice cracked as she approached a well-dressed woman. The lady's nose wrinkled in disgust, and she quickened her pace, silk skirts swishing as she hurried away.

Emma tried again and again, her pleas growing more desperate with each rejection. A group of boys jeered at her, tossing pebbles that stung her skin. She ducked into an alley, sinking to the ground and burying her face in her hands.

"Lord," she whispered, "I don't understand."

As the sun dipped low, casting long shadows across the grimy streets, Emma forced herself to her feet. She had to keep moving. Exhaustion clouded her mind, and she barely registered the broad figure that materialised before her until she collided with a wall of blue wool.

"Watch where you're going, girl," a gruff voice barked.

Emma looked up, meeting the stern gaze of a constable. His bushy eyebrows furrowed as he took in her bedraggled appearance.

"I'm sorry, sir," Emma mumbled, her eyes downcast. "I didn't mean—"

"Where are your parents?" the constable demanded, cutting her off.

Emma's lower lip trembled. "Gone, sir. Both of them."

The constable's expression softened a fraction, but his voice remained brusque. "Can't have you wandering the streets, causing trouble. There's a place for the likes of you."

He pointed down the road, towards a looming brick building that seemed to suck the very light from the air around it.

"Grimshaw's Workhouse," the constable said. "They'll take you in there."

GRIMSHAW'S WORKHOUSE

*E*mma stood before Grimshaw's Workhouse, her heart sinking at the sight of the imposing brick edifice. Barred windows glared down at her like accusing eyes, their iron grates a stark warning of the life that awaited within. The very air seemed to thicken around the building, as if hope itself struggled to penetrate its dreary walls.

She clutched her small bag of belongings tighter, feeling the shape of her Bible and the comforting weight of her mother's necklace against her chest. With trembling fingers, Emma pushed open the heavy wooden door and stepped inside.

The interior hit her like a slap -- all cold stone and echoing corridors. The smell of boiled cabbage and despair clung to every surface. Emma's footsteps faltered as a severe-looking woman with pinched features and steel-grey hair approached.

"Name?" The woman's voice cracked like a whip.

"Emma Grace Redbrook, ma'am," Emma whispered.

"I'm Mrs. Grimshaw, matron of this establishment." Her eyes narrowed. "And are you wanting here?"

"I..." Emma faltered. "My parents are both... gone." She

couldn't bring herself to say dead, not yet. "And you see, I have nowhere—"

"You're looking for somewhere to stay then?" Mrs Grimshaw cut in gruffly. "Well, listen closely, girl. You'll work for your keep here, if you are to stay here. No exceptions, no excuses. You'll rise at dawn, complete your assigned tasks, and retire when told. Disobedience means punishment. Is that clear?"

Emma nodded mutely, her throat too tight for words.

Mrs Grimshaw gestured sharply. "This way. Dining hall. You've missed the evening meal, but you can see where you'll take your meals hereafter."

Emma followed, her legs leaden. The dining hall stretched before her, a cavernous space filled with long wooden tables and benches, scrubbed raw by years of use. A few straggling inmates hunched over bowls of thin gruel, not daring to look up as Mrs. Grimshaw passed.

"You'll get three meals a day," the matron continued. "Breakfast, mid-day, and supper. Make them last."

Emma's stomach clenched at the thought. The room seemed to close in around her, unwelcoming and bleak. This was to be her new home, her new life. She blinked back tears.

Emma followed Mrs Grimshaw through the echoing corridors, her footsteps hesitant on the cold stone floor. The matron's keys jangled ominously at her waist, a constant reminder of the authority she wielded.

"This place is run by my husband, Mr Grimshaw," Mrs Grimshaw announced, her voice clipped. "He doesn't allow for any trouble. You'd do well to remember that."

They reached a set of heavy wooden doors. Mrs Grimshaw pushed them open, revealing a cavernous room filled with rows of narrow iron beds. The sight made Emma's heart sink even further.

"This is where you'll sleep tonight. We don't have a bed set up in the girl's dorms, so you'll have to stay in the boys dorm, but we'll get you moved across tomorrow." Mrs Grimshaw said, gesturing to an empty bed. "That there's your blanket. Don't lose it – you won't get another, even though you will be moving."

Emma approached the bed, running her hand over the threadbare blanket. It was thin and rough, nothing like the warm quilts she'd known at home. She swallowed hard, fighting back tears.

"You'll be next to Hawkins." Mrs. Grimshaw continued, nodding towards the adjacent bed. A boy about Emma's age sat there, his face kind but weary. He offered Emma a small, sympathetic smile.

"Get some rest," Mrs Grimshaw ordered. "Work starts at dawn." With that, she turned and left, her keys rattling in her wake.

Emma sank onto her bed, the thin mattress barely cushioning her from the iron frame beneath. All around her, the sounds of the dormitory pressed in - coughing, sniffling, and the muffled sobs of other children.

The enormity of her situation threatened to overwhelm her, but she clung to her mother's final words, her hand instinctively reaching for the silver cross hidden beneath her dress.

The boy in the next bed shifted, catching her attention. He once again offered her a tentative smile, his brown eyes warm despite the weariness etched on his face.

"I'm Thomas," he whispered. "Thomas Hawkins."

Emma swallowed hard, finding her voice. "Emma Grace Redbrook," she replied, her words barely more than a breath.

Thomas leaned closer, his expression softening. "I know it's scary," he murmured, "but everything's going to be okay. I'll look out for you."

His words, simple as they were, pierced through Emma's fog of despair. She felt a flicker of warmth in her chest, a tiny spark of hope in the bleakness of Grimshaw's Workhouse.

"Really?" Emma asked, her voice trembling.

Thomas nodded, his eyes never leaving hers. "Really. We have to stick together in here. It's the only way to survive."

A wave of gratitude washed over Emma. She'd been so alone, so lost since losing her parents. The kindness in Thomas's eyes, the gentle determination in his voice, made her feel like maybe, just maybe, she could endure this place.

"Thank you," Emma whispered, managing a small smile of her own. "I... I don't know what I'm doing here."

"None of us did at first," Thomas replied, his voice low and reassuring. "But we'll get through it. Together."

As the lights dimmed and the dormitory settled into an uneasy quiet, a glimmer of comfort lit in Emma. She wasn't alone anymore. She had a friend in this strange, frightening place. With Thomas watching out for her, perhaps she could face whatever challenges lay ahead.

Emma closed her eyes, her hand still clutched around her mother's necklace. For the first time since entering Grimshaw's Workhouse, she felt a tiny spark of hope flicker to life in her heart.

She lay down, pulling the scratchy blanket over herself. In the darkness, Emma's hand found her mother's silver cross, still hanging around her neck. She clutched it tightly, her last connection to the life she'd lost.

"Please, God," Emma prayed. "Give me strength. Help me make it through this." She thought of her parents, of the love and faith they'd instilled in her. "I'll make you proud," she promised them silently.

As the night wore on, the reality of her situation overwhelmed her. Emma buried her face in her thin pillow, letting her tears fall quietly. She cried for her parents, for her lost home, for the uncertain future that lay ahead. But even as she wept, Emma clung to her faith, determined to keep it alive in this bleak place.

FIRST DAYS

*E*mma awoke with a start, her heart racing as a harsh bell clanged through the dormitory. For a moment, she forgot where she was, the unfamiliar surroundings disorienting her. But then she remembered – Grimshaw's Workhouse.

She sat up, her eyes adjusting to the dim light. All around her, children stirred, their faces etched with weariness even as the day began. The matron strode through the room, barking orders and yanking blankets off those who didn't move quickly enough.

Emma's gaze fell on the pile of clothing at the foot of her bed. A drab grey dress and white apron lay there, stark and uninviting. With trembling hands, she picked them up, the rough fabric scratching her skin. The dress hung loose on her thin frame, the apron barely staying tied. As she smoothed down the fabric, Emma caught sight of her reflection in a dirty window. Her heart-shaped face, usually so bright, looked pale and drawn. But beneath the fear in her eyes, a quiet determination burned.

"Come on," Thomas whispered, appearing at her side. "I'll show you where to go."

They joined the throng of children shuffling towards the workrooms. Emma's stomach churned with anxiety, but Thomas's presence beside her offered a small comfort.

The day passed in a blur of backbreaking labour. Emma's hands, unused to such work, soon became raw and blistered as she scrubbed floors until they gleamed. In the laundry, steam and harsh lye soap left her coughing, her eyes stinging. Through it all, Thomas did his best to guide her, showing her how to avoid the worst of the matrons' scrutiny.

During a brief respite, Emma found herself huddled with a small group of children. A girl with mousy brown hair offered her a sympathetic smile.

"First day's always the worst," she said softly. "I'm Sarah."

Emma managed a weak smile in return. "Emma," she replied.

As they spoke in hushed tones, sharing small kindnesses and warnings about which matrons to avoid, Emma felt a tiny spark of warmth in her chest. These fleeting moments of connection, of shared burden, made the gruelling work a little more bearable. It felt like a small miracle, that the bed Emma was finally assigned in the girl's dormitories was right next to Sarah's.

THE ENFORCER'S SHADOW

Emma followed Thomas down a dimly lit corridor, their footsteps echoing off the grimy stone walls. The acrid stench of lye soap and unwashed bodies gave way to something different—a cloying mix of tobacco and sweat that made her stomach churn.

"That's Mr. Grimshaw's office," Thomas whispered, nodding toward a heavy oak door at the end of the hall. "Best steer clear if you can."

Emma's curiosity got the better of her. She crept closer, peering through a gap where the door stood slightly ajar. The room beyond was a cluttered mess of papers and ledgers, stacked haphazardly on every available surface. Guttering candles cast long shadows across the walls, their feeble light barely penetrating the gloom.

Behind an enormous desk sat Mr. Grimshaw himself. His corpulent frame strained against the confines of his wooden chair, which creaked ominously with each slight movement. Beady eyes, set deep in his fleshy face, darted suspiciously around the room as if searching for unseen threats.

Emma's gaze was drawn to something hanging on the wall

beside him. A leather strap, its surface worn smooth from frequent use, hung there like a silent promise of pain. She shuddered, remembering the welts she'd seen on some of the older children's backs.

"Come on," Thomas tugged at her sleeve. "We don't want to be caught loitering."

As they hurried away, Emma couldn't shake the image of that strap, from her mind. She clutched the silver cross hanging around her neck, silently praying for strength in the face of whatever trials lay ahead.

∽

Brock, "The Brute", Thornhill's hulking figure cast an intimidating shadow that seemed to swallow up half the room, his massive arms crossed over his broad chest. His presence alone was enough to make the air feel thick with tension, each breath a struggle against the oppressive atmosphere he created.

The workhouse's main hall, usually filled with the constant murmur of hushed conversations and the shuffling of weary feet, had fallen into an eerie silence. Children and adults alike kept their eyes fixed on the floor, too afraid to meet the enforcer's gaze directly.

Brock's cold eyes swept the room methodically, ensuring everyone knew they were under his watchful gaze. His face remained impassive, a mask of indifference that somehow made him even more terrifying. It was as if he viewed the people before him not as human beings, but as objects to be controlled and punished at will.

As he surveyed the crowd, Brock's massive hands flexed at his sides. The movement drew attention to the scars crisscrossing his knuckles, each one a testament to the violence he was capable of inflicting. Those hands had broken bones and crushed spirits, and everyone in the room knew it.

With deliberate slowness, Brock brought his hands together and cracked his knuckles. The sound echoed through the still room like a gunshot, causing several of the younger children to flinch visibly. It was a silent threat to any would-be troublemakers, a reminder of the consequences that awaited those who dared to step out of line.

Mr Grimshaw knew that with "The Brute" by his side, his control over the workhouse was absolute.

Emma's eyes darted nervously around the room, her gaze finally settling on a hunched figure in the corner. Silas, "The Snitch", Merriweather crouched there, his bony fingers wrapped around a small notebook as he scribbled furiously. He had been in the employ of Mr Grimshaw about the same amount of time as The Brute, and as sly and slippery as Brock was sturdy and stubborn. Emma's stomach twisted with unease as she watched him, knowing full well the danger he posed to anyone who dared step out of line.

Silas's watery blue eyes flicked back and forth, missing nothing as they swept across the assembled workers. Emma ducked her head, pretending to focus on her mending, but she couldn't shake the feeling of those eyes boring into her. She'd heard whispers about Silas, about how he could ferret out the slightest hint of rebellion or dissent. The thought made her hands tremble slightly as she pushed her rough sponge into the dirty soap water.

A light cough broke the tense silence, and Emma glanced up to see Silas pressing a handkerchief to his mouth. His chronic ailment seemed to accentuate his weaselly demeanour, making him appear even more untrustworthy. As he lowered the cloth, Emma caught sight of his thin lips curling into a smirk. Her heart raced as she realized he must have overheard something – a hushed whisper, perhaps, or a muttered complaint.

Emma's knuckles turned white with the effort of appearing calm. She wanted desperately to warn the others, to tell them to be careful, but she knew that any such action would only draw Silas's attention to herself. Instead, she bowed her head once more, silently praying for strength and protection for herself and her fellow workers.

Emma's muscles ached as she scrubbed the workhouse floor, her knees raw from hours spent on the cold stone. The harsh lye soap stung her cracked hands, but she pressed on, determined to finish her task before the bell signifying dinner rang. As she worked, Emma's mind drifted to the worn Bible hidden beneath her thin mattress, its pages a source of comfort in this bleak place.

When the dinner bell finally rang, Emma hurried to the cramped dormitory. She reached under her mattress, fingers brushing against the familiar leather cover. With practiced stealth, she slipped the Bible into her apron pocket and made her way to the dining hall.

The small portion of watery gruel did little to satisfy her gnawing hunger, but Emma barely noticed. Her attention was focused on the small group huddled around her. As she spooned the bland mixture into her mouth, she whispered verses from memory, her voice barely audible above the clatter of spoons and bowls.

"The Lord is my shepherd, I shall not want," she murmured, her words bringing a dash of hope to the tired eyes around her. Sarah, the timid girl with mousy brown hair, leaned in closer, hanging on every word.

After the meal, Emma noticed an extra piece of bread on her tray – a rare occurrence in the workhouse. Without hesitation, she broke it in half, pressing one portion into Sarah's small hand. The girl's eyes widened in surprise and gratitude.

"But Emma, you need it more than me," Sarah protested weakly.

Emma smiled, her deep hazel eyes warm with kindness. "We all need hope, Sarah. Sometimes it comes in the form of bread."

As they filed out of the dining hall, Thomas fell into step beside her, his taller frame providing a sense of security amidst the chaos of the workhouse.

"You're doing it again," he said, a hint of admiration in his voice.

"Doing what?" Emma asked, though she knew full well what he meant.

Thomas's lips quirked into a half-smile. "Being a light in this dark place. You give people hope, Emma. It's a rare thing here."

Warmth bloomed within Emma, despite the chill that permeated the workhouse.

As they parted ways for their evening tasks, Emma caught sight of her reflection in a grimy window. Her face was thin and pale, marked by the hardships of workhouse life. But her eyes, those deep hazel pools, still shone with an inner fire -- a resilience that no amount of toil could extinguish.

A TEST OF COURAGE

A commotion near the dormitory entrance caught Emma's attention. She looked up to see Mr Grimshaw towering over a small boy, no more than seven years old. The child cowered, his thin frame shaking as Mr Grimshaw's face twisted with anger.

"You dare steal from me, boy?" Mr Grimshaw's voice boomed, echoing off the stone walls. "After all the charity I've shown you?"

Emma's heart raced as she watched the scene unfold. The boy's eyes were wide with terror, his lip quivering as he struggled to form words.

"I... I didn't, sir. I swear it," he stammered.

Mr Grimshaw's hand shot out, grabbing the boy's collar and yanking him forward. "Lying now, are we? That'll earn you extra lashes."

Emma's grip on her scrub brush tightened, her knuckles turning white. She knew the punishment that awaited the boy – she'd seen it before, heard the screams echoing through the night. Her stomach churned at the thought.

As Mr Grimshaw began to drag the boy towards his office,

Emma caught sight of something falling from the workhouse director's pocket. A small, shiny object clattered to the floor, rolling towards her. With a quick glance to ensure no one was watching, Emma scooped it up.

It was a silver sixpence – the very coin Mr Grimshaw accused the boy of stealing.

Emma's mind raced. She knew speaking up could bring Mr Grimshaw's wrath down upon her, but the thought of an innocent child suffering such injustice made her blood boil. Her fingers closed around the silver cross hanging from her neck, her mother's final gift.

"What would God have me do?" The question echoed in her mind, a constant refrain since her arrival at Grimshaw's.

Emma's heart pounded as she stood, her legs shaking beneath her. "Mr Grimshaw, sir," she called out.

The workhouse director turned, his eyes narrowing as they fell upon her. "What is it, girl? Speak up!"

Emma swallowed hard, steeling herself. "I... I found this, sir," she said, holding out the sixpence. "It fell from your pocket just now."

Emma's heart pounded as Mr Grimshaw's gaze bore into her. The silence in the dormitory was deafening, broken only by the soft whimpers of the young boy still in Grimshaw's grasp.

With surprising speed for a man of his bulk, Mr Grimshaw snatched the sixpence from Emma's outstretched hand. He examined the coin as his face flushed a deep shade of red.

"Well, well," he sneered, his voice dripping with barely contained rage. "It seems our little Emma fancies herself a hero."

Emma stood her ground, though her legs felt like jelly beneath her. She silently prayed for strength, her fingers instinctively brushing against the silver cross hidden beneath her dress.

Mr Grimshaw's grip on the boy's collar loosened, and the child stumbled backward, nearly falling in his haste to escape.

Emma's heart ached at the sight of his tear-stained face, but she dared not look away from the workhouse overseer.

"You've got a lot of nerve, girl," Mr Grimshaw growled, leaning in close. His breath was hot and sour. "Don't think for a moment that this act of... charity... will go unpunished."

Emma braced herself for the sting of his leather strap, but it didn't come. Instead, Mr Grimshaw straightened up, his jowls quivering with barely contained fury.

"You may have saved this snivelling brat from a well-deserved thrashing," he spat, "but don't get too comfortable. Your time will come, mark my words."

He jabbed a fat finger in Emma's face, his voice dropping to a menacing whisper. "I'm watching you, Redbrook. One wrong move, and you'll wish you'd never set foot in my workhouse."

With that, Mr Grimshaw turned on his heel and stalked away, his cane thumping angrily against the floor. The tension in the room seemed to dissipate with each echoing step, but Emma knew this was far from over.

THE PRICE OF A SLIP

Emma's hands burned as she scrubbed the rough fabric against the washboard. The icy water sloshed over the sides of the tub, soaking her threadbare apron. She winced as the lye soap found its way into the cracks of her raw, reddened skin.

Eleven now, Emma had spent a year in Grimshaw's Workhouse. The long days of labour had taken their toll. Her fingers, once nimble enough to sew delicate seams, now felt stiff and clumsy. She longed for the gentle touch of her mother's hands, a memory that grew hazier with each passing day.

The clanging of the dinner bell pierced the humid air of the laundry room. Emma's stomach growled in response, a familiar ache that never truly subsided. She dried her hands on her apron and made her way to the dining hall, her steps slow and measured to conserve what little energy she had left.

The sparse room was filled with the shuffling of feet and the scraping of tin bowls against worn tables. Emma took her place in line, her eyes fixed on the floor. When her turn came, she accepted her portion of gruel with a quiet "Thank you," though gratitude was far from what she felt.

Finding an empty spot at one of the long tables, Emma sat down. She stared at the thin, watery gruel in her bowl. Her stomach clenched with hunger, but she hesitated. Glancing to her left, she saw Sarah, the girl she'd befriended on her first day. Sarah's cheeks had grown hollow over the past year, her eyes sunken and dull.

Without a word, Emma carefully divided her portion, sliding half into Sarah's bowl. Sarah's eyes widened in surprise, then softened with gratitude. Emma managed a small smile in return, ignoring the pangs of hunger that gnawed at her insides.

As she ate her reduced portion, Emma felt exhaustion settling over her. Her back ached from hours bent over the washtub, a constant reminder of the toll this place took on her body. She straightened up, fighting against the slight hunch that had begun to form in her spine.

EMMA HAULED the freshly washed laundry across the workhouse yard. The damp clothes seemed to grow heavier with each step, and her back ached from the hours spent bent over the washtubs. She focused on putting one foot in front of the other, willing her weary legs to carry her just a little further.

The cobblestones beneath her feet were slick with mud, a treacherous path that demanded her full attention. But exhaustion clouded her mind, and her concentration wavered. In a moment of distraction, her foot slipped.

Emma felt the world tilt around her as she lost her balance. The basket of laundry flew from her grasp, and she hit the ground hard. Pain shot through her palms and knees as they scraped against the rough stones. The clean clothes she'd spent hours washing lay scattered in the mud, her hard work undone in an instant.

For a moment, Emma could only stare at the mess in dismay.

Then a shadow fell over her, and her heart sank. She knew who it was before she even looked up.

The Brute loomed above her, his massive frame blocking out the weak sunlight. Without a word, he reached down and seized Emma's arm, hauling her to her feet with enough force to make her wince. His grip was like iron, bruising in its intensity.

"Clumsy little rat," Brock growled, his voice a low rumble that sent a chill down Emma's spine. His cruel eyes bore into her. "Think you can laze about in the mud while there's work to be done?"

He gave her a rough shove, nearly sending her stumbling again. "Pick it up," he snarled, gesturing at the scattered laundry. "And if I catch you dawdling again, you'll be scrubbing floors until your fingers bleed."

Emma's hands trembled as she gathered the muddy clothes, her knees stinging from the fall. She could feel Brock's eyes still boring into her back. With shaky fingers, she stuffed the soiled laundry back into the basket, knowing she'd have to wash it all over again.

As she lifted the heavy load, her arms protesting, Emma caught sight of a familiar weaselly figure. Silas stood half-hidden behind a partially open door, his wire-rimmed spectacles glinting in the dim light. His eyes darted back and forth, and he leaned forward, straining to catch every whispered word from the group of workers huddled nearby.

Emma's heart quickened. She knew that look on Silas's face all too well – the hungry gleam of a man who'd just stumbled upon a juicy morsel of information. And there was only one place he'd be taking that tidbit.

She could almost see it playing out in her mind: Silas scurrying into the cramped room, practically salivating as he spilled whatever secrets he'd overheard. And Mr Grimshaw would be there, smiling with cruel satisfaction as he rewarded his loyal snitch with that smug nod of approval.

The thought made Emma's stomach churn. She knew all too well the twisted pleasure Silas took in these moments, how each scrap of information he brought to Grimshaw felt like another brick in the wall of his imagined security. It was a false sense of power, built on the betrayal of his fellow workers, but Silas clung to it like a lifeline.

"Get moving!" Brock ordered, and Emma shook the disconcerting image from her mind as she hurried off.

DREAMS BEYOND THE WALLS

*E*mma sank down onto a worn wooden crate in a shadowy corner of the workhouse yard. She closed her eyes for a moment, savouring this rare respite from the endless drudgery.

A soft shuffling of feet made her look up. Thomas approached, his broad shoulders hunched as if to make himself less noticeable. Emma's heart lifted at the sight of him. Despite the harsh conditions of Grimshaw's, Thomas was growing into a young man of impressive stature. Already the backbreaking work was sculpting his frame, leaving him with the scrawny but muscular build of someone far older than his years.

But it was his eyes that truly captured Emma's attention. Those deep brown orbs seemed to hold all the kindness that the workhouse had stripped from the world. When Thomas looked at her, hope kindled within her, a reminder that not all was lost.

He lowered himself beside her, producing a small chunk of bread from his pocket. Without a word, he broke it in half, offering the larger portion to Emma. She hesitated, knowing how precious every morsel was, but Thomas's gentle nod encouraged her to accept.

"Thank you," Emma whispered, her voice barely audible above the constant din of the workhouse.

Thomas's lips quirked in a half-smile. "We've got to look out for each other," he murmured back.

They ate in companionable silence for a moment, enjoying the stale bread as if it were the finest delicacy. Emma studied Thomas's profile, noting the sharp angle of his jaw and the furrow of concentration that seemed permanently etched between his brows.

"Do you ever think about what's beyond these walls?" Emma asked softly, her words carried on a sigh.

Thomas's eyes met hers, a spark of something – defiance, perhaps, or hope – igniting in their depths. "All the time," he admitted. "I dream of wide-open fields and skies that go on forever."

Emma nodded, a wistful smile tugging at her lips. "And clean clothes that actually fit," she added, plucking at her threadbare sleeve.

"Hot meals," Thomas continued, his voice taking on a dreamy quality. "And a bed that's not full of lumps and bugs."

"Freedom," Emma breathed, the word hanging between them like a fragile soap bubble.

WHISPERS BY THE BACKSTAIRS

The rhythmic sound of brushes against washboards filled the air, punctuated by the occasional bark of an order from one of the overseers. Emma glanced up, her eyes searching the crowded workroom until they locked with Thomas's across the room.

His gaze held hers for a moment. They didn't need words, not anymore; that look alone conveyed volumes. It was a silent promise, a shared resolve to endure whatever Grimshaw's threw at them.

Thomas gave her an almost imperceptible nod before returning to his task, the ghost of a smile playing at the corners of his mouth. Emma bent her head back to her work, but her spirit felt lighter. They would survive this place, together.

Later, as they shuffled through the dinner line, Emma felt Thomas's presence close behind her.

"Meet me by the back stairs after lights out," he breathed, his words tickling her ear.

Emma gave the slightest of nods, her heart racing with a mixture of excitement and fear. She knew the risks of being caught out of bed, but the prospect of a moment alone with Thomas was worth it.

That night, they huddled in the shadows of the creaking staircase, their heads bent close together.

"We can't let them break us," Thomas whispered fiercely. "We've got to find ways to fight back, even if they're small."

Emma nodded, her mind racing with possibilities. "What if we started teaching the younger ones to read?" she suggested. "Mr Grimshaw can't stop us from sharing knowledge."

Thomas's eyes lit up. "That's brilliant, Emma. And maybe we could find a way to sneak extra food to those who need it most."

As if on cue, Emma reached into her pocket and pulled out a small chunk of bread she'd managed to save from dinner. She pressed it into Thomas's hand. "For little Sarah," she explained. "She's looking thinner every day."

Thomas squeezed her hand gratefully. "We'll do it together," he promised. "Tomorrow at breakfast, I'll distract the overseer while you slip it to her."

The floorboards creaked, and Emma's breath caught. She turned to see Silas Merriweather's weaselly face peering at them from around the corner, his eyes gleaming with malicious delight.

"Well, well," Silas sneered, his voice dripping with false concern. "What have we here? Two little birds out of their nests after lights out? Mr Grimshaw will be most interested to hear about this."

Emma's stomach dropped. She reached for Thomas's hand, squeezing it tightly as Silas scurried away, no doubt to report their transgression to the workhouse overseer.

"We need to get back," Thomas whispered urgently, tugging Emma towards the dormitories.

They hurried through the darkened corridors, hearts pounding in their chests. As they reached the threshold of their respective dormitories, Emma met Thomas's gaze one last time.

"Whatever happens," Emma breathed, "we'll face it together."

Thomas nodded, and they parted ways, slipping into their beds just as the sound of heavy footsteps echoed through the halls. Emma pulled her thin blanket up to her chin, squeezing her eyes shut and praying for strength to face whatever punishment morning would bring.

A VOW IN PAIN

The next day dawned grey and foreboding. Emma's stomach churned with dread as she and Thomas were roughly dragged from the breakfast line by Brock Thornhill's meaty hands. The hulking enforcer marched them out to the centre of the workhouse yard, where Mr. Grimshaw stood waiting, a cruel smile twisting his features.

"Let this be a lesson to all of you," Grimshaw's voice boomed across the yard as the other children were herded out to watch. "Disobedience will not be tolerated in my workhouse."

Emma's legs trembled as Brock forced her to her knees beside Thomas. She heard the whisper of leather as the brute drew his strap, and her body tensed in anticipation of the pain to come.

The first lash fell across her back, and Emma bit her lip to keep from crying out. She tasted blood as the strap fell again and again, each stroke sending waves of agony through her small frame. Through the haze of pain, Emma sought Thomas's gaze. Their eyes met, and in that moment, she drew strength from the fire she saw burning within him.

Emma's body throbbed with pain as she stumbled into the

dining hall. The rough fabric of her dress clung to the welts on her back, each movement a fresh agony. After their beating, both she and Thomas had been forced to work the full day. All she could do was grit her teeth through the sharp stabs of pain that tormented her. She collapsed onto one of the uncomfortable benches.

Emma's trembling fingers found the silver cross that hung beneath her dress. She clutched it tightly, feeling the cool metal warm against her palm. The familiar weight of it brought a measure of comfort, and she closed her eyes, lips moving in a silent prayer.

"Lord," she whispered, "give me strength."

As she spooned her gruel into her mouth, Emma made a silent vow. She would endure. She would find a way to make things better, not just for herself and Thomas, but for all the children trapped in this place of misery.

Emma's eyes lifted from her bowl as Thomas entered the dining hall. His gait was stiff, each step carefully measured to minimise the pain from his own beating. Their gazes met across the crowded room.

After obtaining his own gruel, Thomas made his way through the throng of children, his face a mask of determination. As he approached Emma's table, she shifted slightly, wincing at the movement but making space for him on the bench beside her.

Without a word, Thomas eased himself down next to Emma. The bench creaked under his weight. For a moment, they sat in silence, the clamour of the dining hall fading into the background.

Emma's fingers tightened around her spoon. She wanted to speak, to offer some word of comfort or solidarity, but her throat felt tight with unshed tears.

They ate in silence, each spoonful a small act of defiance against the cruelty that surrounded them.

As the meal drew to a close, Emma felt Thomas's hand briefly touch hers under the table. It was a fleeting gesture, barely more than a brush of fingers, but it spoke volumes. In that touch, Emma felt a promise – a vow that they would face whatever came next together.

The pain of her beating served as a reminder of the cruelty that surrounded her, but it also fuelled her determination. Every act of kindness she'd witnessed or participated in – sharing food, offering comfort, standing up for others – strengthened her resolve.

One day, Emma promised herself, she would find a way out of this place. She would create a better life, one where children didn't have to suffer as she had. Until then, she would keep her faith alive, a small flame of hope burning bright in the darkness of Grimshaw's Workhouse.

HOPE BENEATH THE HEAVENS

◈

Emma stood before the cracked mirror in the washroom, barely recognising the girl who stared back at her. Four years had passed since she first stepped through the gates of Grimshaw's Workhouse, and those years had left their mark.

She'd grown taller, though not by much, her frame still slender but wiry from years of hard labour. The workhouse hadn't been kind to her body, but it had failed to break her spirit.

Emma's hazel eyes, deep and expressive, shifted between green and brown as she studied her reflection. They held a wisdom beyond her fourteen years, tempered by hardship. Her face had lost its childish roundness, high cheekbones and a delicate chin giving her a more mature appearance.

As she straightened her threadbare dress, Emma's fingers brushed against the small silver cross hidden beneath the fabric. It was her most treasured possession, a constant reminder of her mother's love and the faith that had sustained her through countless dark days.

A commotion in the hallway drew Emma's attention. She

turned from the mirror, recognising the approaching footsteps. Thomas rounded the corner, filling the narrow corridor.

At fifteen, Thomas had grown into his frame, his body hardened by the relentless toil of workhouse life. His shoulders had broadened, muscles evident even beneath the rough fabric of his shirt. He stood a full head taller than Emma now, but still moved with the same quiet grace she remembered from their first meeting.

Emma's gaze met Thomas's deep brown eyes, and she saw in them the same determination and protectiveness that had been there from the start. Those eyes had been her anchor through countless storms, a silent promise that she wasn't alone in this struggle.

They both headed into the workhouse hall together, ready for the day ahead.

Emma's nimble fingers worked swiftly, sorting through the pile of laundry with practiced efficiency. Her keen eyes darted between the different fabrics, categorising them by type and level of soiling. Beside her, Thomas hefted the heavy baskets of wet linens, his muscles straining beneath his shirt.

"If we sort them first," Emma said, "we can save time on the scrubbing later."

Thomas nodded, allowing a small smile. "Clever as always, Em," he murmured, shifting another basket into place.

They worked in tandem, Emma's quick mind complementing Thomas's raw strength. She devised a system, arranging the laundry in neat piles while Thomas manoeuvred the unwieldy washtubs. Their efficiency didn't go unnoticed; even Brock Thornhill's ever-watchful gaze seemed to pass over them more quickly.

As the morning wore on, a familiar ache settled into Emma's lower back. She straightened, stretching discreetly, and caught Thomas's eye. He jerked his head towards a shadowy corner of the washroom, away from prying eyes.

In their stolen moment, huddled behind a stack of linens, Emma felt some of the tension leave her shoulders. Thomas produced a small crust of bread from his pocket.

"Thomas, you shouldn't—" Emma began, but he pressed it into her hand.

"You need it more than me," he insisted, his voice low. "Can't have that clever mind of yours going hungry."

Emma's protest died on her lips as she saw the earnest look in his eyes. She took a small bite. "Thank you," she whispered.

"Oi! What's going on over there?" Brock's gruff voice cut through their moment of joy.

Emma and Thomas scrambled back to their tasks.

∽

Emma and Thomas crept silently through the darkened corridors of the workhouse. Every creak of the floorboards sent a jolt of fear through her, but the thrill of their secret adventure pushed her forward. Thomas led the way, his larger frame shielding her from view as they navigated the familiar yet treacherous path to the roof.

As they emerged into the cool night air, Emma let out a soft gasp. The sky above London stretched out before them, a vast expanse dotted with twinkling stars. It was a view they rarely got to see, confined as they were to the walls of the workhouse.

Thomas helped Emma settle on a relatively flat section of the roof, their shoulders touching as they sat side by side. For a moment, they simply breathed in the freedom of the moment, enjoying the rare taste of solitude and peace.

"Sometimes," Emma whispered, her eyes fixed on the Heavens, "I think about what life could be like beyond these walls. A place where we could be free, where we could help others like us."

Thomas nodded, his own gaze distant. "A world where

people like us aren't treated like we're nothing. Where we have a chance to make something of ourselves."

Emma turned to him, a small smile playing on her lips. "We will, Thomas. I believe that with all my heart. God has a plan for us, even if we can't see it yet."

She reached for her cross. "There's a verse I love, from Proverbs. 'Strength and dignity are her clothing, and she laughs at the time to come.' It reminds me that no matter what happens, we can face the future with courage."

Thomas's eyes softened as he looked at Emma, marvelling at her unwavering faith. "How do you do it, Em? How do you stay so... hopeful?"

"Because I have to," Emma replied simply. "Without hope, without faith, what do we have left?"

Her words hung in the air between them, filled with quiet determination. Thomas nodded slowly, feeling something stir within him.

"You're right," he said softly. "We deserve better than this. All of us do. Someday, I want to make things right. I want to fight for justice, to make sure no one has to suffer like we have."

Emma reached out, taking Thomas's hand in her own. "We'll do it together," she promised.

GRIMSHAW'S GREED

~~~

The musty office air clung to Emma's skin making her itch beneath the coarse fabric of her workhouse uniform as she sorted through the stack of papers on Mr. Grimshaw's desk She'd been assigned to tidy the cramped room, a task she usually dreaded. But today, as her eyes skimmed over columns of numbers, something caught her attention.

A furrow appeared between her brows as she paused, glancing at the door to ensure she was still alone. She carefully pulled two ledgers closer, comparing the neatly inked figures. Her breath caught in her throat as the discrepancies became clear.

"This can't be right," she whispered to herself, her mind racing to make sense of what she was seeing.

The ledger meant for official inspection showed far less money coming in than the private book hidden beneath a stack of correspondence. Emma's hands shook as she flipped through more pages, her suspicions growing with each passing moment. The numbers didn't lie – Mr. Grimshaw had been pocketing funds meant for the orphans' care.

Emma's initial shock gave way to a simmering rage. She

thought of Sarah's gaunt face, of Thomas's calloused hands, of the constant gnawing hunger that plagued them all. How many meals had been denied them? How many warm blankets or pairs of shoes had been sacrificed to line Grimshaw's pockets?

Her fingers clenched around the edge of the desk as righteous fury burned through her veins. Emma's mind raced with the implications of her discovery.

Emma did her best to slip out of Mr. Grimshaw's office quietly, but her mind was racing. She scanned the dreary workhouse yard, searching for Thomas's familiar figure. There, by the crumbling brick wall, she spotted him hauling a heavy sack of coal.

She hurried over, her shoes scuffing against the uneven ground. "Thomas," she hissed, grabbing his arm. "I need to talk to you. Now."

Thomas's frowned at the urgency in her voice. He glanced around, making sure no one was watching, then followed Emma to a secluded corner of the yard.

"What is it, Em?" he asked, wiping coal dust from his hands.

Emma leaned in close. "I found something in Grimshaw's office. Ledgers. Two sets of them." Her words tumbled out in a rush. "He's been stealing from us, Thomas. Taking money meant for our food, our clothes, everything."

Thomas's eyes widened, disbelief etched across his features. Then, as Emma's words sank in, his expression hardened. His jaw clenched, and his hands balled into fists at his sides.

"That bloated pig," he spat, his voice dangerous. "I always knew he was rotten, but this..." Thomas shook his head, struggling to contain his anger.

Emma nodded, her own fury burning bright in her eyes. "We have to do something, Thomas. We can't let him keep hurting us, hurting everyone here." Her voice quivered with emotion, but her gaze remained steady. "We need to expose him."

Thomas studied Emma's face, seeing the determination

blazing there. "You're right," he said, his voice growing stronger. "We can't let this stand. But Em, it's dangerous. If Grimshaw finds out we know..."

Emma reached out, gripping Thomas's hand. "I know the risks. But we have to try. For Sarah, for all the little ones who don't have enough to eat. For everyone here who deserves better."

Thomas didn't have to say a word. Emma could tell from his resolute expression that he would do whatever was necessary to expose their tyrannical overseer and bring him to justice.

A DANGEROUS DANCE

The air hung heavy with the acrid smell of coal smoke, but here, hidden from prying eyes, Emma and Thomas could breathe a little easier. They had found a crumbling wall at the far end of the workhouse yard that they could slip behind whenever they got a chance, to confer privately.

"We need a plan," Emma whispered. "We can't just accuse Mr. Grimshaw without proof. We need more evidence."

Thomas nodded. "You're right. We'll have to be careful, though. If he catches us snooping..."

Emma shuddered, remembering the sting of Brock's leather strap. She pushed the thought aside, focusing on the task at hand. "I can try to get back into his office, maybe during meal times when everyone's distracted. There must be more ledgers, more proof of what he's doing."

"Good idea," Thomas agreed. He ran a hand through his unruly dark hair, thinking. "We should write everything down, keep a record of what we find. But where could we hide it?"

Emma's fingers unconsciously went to her silver cross. "There's a loose floorboard under my bed. I've been keeping my Bible there. We could use that spot."

Thomas's eyes lit up. "Perfect. And I think I know where we can get some paper and a pencil stub. Old Silas is always scribbling in that notebook of his. Bet he's got a stash somewhere."

Emma nodded, a grin tugging at her lips despite the gravity of their situation. "We'll need help, though. Someone on the outside who can take our evidence to the proper authorities."

"What about the Reverend who comes to preach sometimes?" Thomas suggested. "He seems decent enough. Might be willing to listen."

"Reverend Davies," Emma said, remembering the kind-faced man who occasionally visited the workhouse. "Yes, that could work. We'll have to find a way to get a message to him."

As they continued to whisper, formulating their plan, Emma felt a glimmer of hope. It was dangerous, yes, but for the first time in years, she felt like they might actually have a chance to change things. To bring a little justice into their bleak world.

∼

OVER THE NEXT FEW WEEKS, Emma repeated her dangerous dance of slipping into Mr Grimshaw's office and stealing various ledgers or reports, each time returning with another damning piece of evidence. She'd wait until meal times, when the clatter of tin plates and the rumble of hungry voices provided cover for her absence. Every creak of a floorboard, every distant shout made her jump, certain she'd be caught.

Thomas, meanwhile, put his strength to good use. In the dead of night, when even Silas's prying eyes were closed in sleep, he'd slip out of bed. With careful hands, he pried loose floorboards and hollowed out spaces behind crumbling bricks. Each hiding spot was a small triumph, a secret refuge for their growing collection of evidence.

One particularly tense afternoon found Emma and Thomas huddled in a dusty corner of the laundry room. They'd managed to pilfer some scraps of paper and a stub of pencil, likely dropped by one of Grimshaw's cronies.

Together, they bent over the stolen ledger, painstakingly copying each damning figure onto their scraps of paper. Emma's hand cramped from the unfamiliar task, but she pressed on, knowing the importance of what they were doing.

CODES AND CAUTION

~~~

*E*mma caught Silas's beady eyes following her across the workhouse yard. The weaselly informant seemed to materialise around every corner, his gaze narrowed with suspicion. She ducked her head, quickening her pace towards the laundry room where Thomas waited.

"Did you see the new linens?" Emma asked loudly as she entered, her eyes darting meaningfully to Thomas. It was their code, warning of Silas's increased attention.

Thomas nodded imperceptibly, his jaw tightening. "Aye, quite a sight. We'll need to be extra careful with the washing today."

Emma understood his meaning. They'd have to be more cautious than ever in their efforts to expose Mr. Grimshaw's corruption. As they worked side by side, scrubbing sheets raw, Emma and Thomas communicated through the subtlest of gestures – a brush of fingers passing soap, a quick squeeze of the arm, a shared glance heavy with unspoken words.

That evening in the dining hall, Emma's spoon clinked against her bowl in a seemingly random pattern. To most, it was merely the noise of a hungry child eating. But Thomas, seated across the room, recognised it as a warning. Silas had positioned himself unusually close, his ever-present notebook at the ready.

When darkness fell and the other children's breathing evened out in sleep, Emma clutched her hidden silver cross. Its cool metal pressed against her skin, a tangible reminder of her mother's love and the faith that sustained her. She closed her eyes, her lips moving in silent prayer.

"Lord," she prayed to herself, "guide our steps and protect us from harm. Give us the strength to do what's right, even when the path is dangerous."

Her fingers tightened around the cross as she thought of Thomas, hoping he too found comfort in the quiet of the night. Together, they would weather this storm of suspicion, their bond growing stronger with each shared risk and silent exchange.

∼

IN THE DEAD of night no light crept through the grimy windows of Grimshaw's Workhouse, casting no shadows across the worn floorboards. Emma silently made her way through the quiet corridors. The air felt thick with tension, every creak and groan of the old building making her flinch.

She found Thomas waiting in their agreed-upon spot, his face a mask of determination tinged with fear. Emma's hands trembled slightly as she reached into her pocket, feeling the documents they'd painstakingly gathered over the past weeks.

"Are you ready?" Thomas whispered, his eyes darting nervously down the hall.

Emma nodded, unable to find her voice. She pulled out the carefully folded papers, evidence of Mr Grimshaw's corruption that could change everything for the children trapped within these walls. As she began to tuck them into the hidden pocket they'd sewn into Thomas's coat, Emma's fingers brushed against the cool metal of her silver cross necklace.

A wave of emotion washed over her, memories of her mother's last words echoing in her mind. Emma closed her eyes, clutching the cross tightly.

"Lord," she prayed, her voice only just audible to Thomas standing beside her, "please watch over us. Guide Reverend Davies to see the truth and give us the strength to see this through."

Thomas placed a comforting hand on her shoulder, and hope ignited within her. Whatever challenges lay ahead, they would face them together.

THE GATE TO FREEDOM

*E*mma glanced at Thomas, his face a mask of concentration as he led the way. The familiar smell of damp and despair clung to the air, but today it felt different. Today, they had a chance to change everything.

As they rounded a corner, Emma took in a short breath. She grabbed Thomas's arm, pulling him back into the shadows. They pressed themselves against the wall, hardly daring to breathe as the heavy footsteps of Brock "The Brute" Thornhill passed by.

Once the coast was clear, they continued their careful journey towards the workhouse gates. Would Reverend Davies believe them? Would their evidence be enough to bring down Grimshaw's cruel regime?

Just as they reached the main entrance hall, a floorboard creaked behind them. Emma whirled around. There, in the shadows of a nearby doorway. Was Silas's gleaming eyes in the darkness? Was that his silhouette that quickly disappeared behind the corner, or was it just a trick of the light?

Emma tugged on Thomas's sleeve. They couldn't let Silas ruin everything now, not when they were so close. As they slipped out into the misty night air, Emma could almost feel Silas's gaze boring into her back. If he was in fact there, she knew he would follow, knew he wouldn't be able to resist the temptation of uncovering their secret.

"Thomas, wait," she whispered urgently, her eyes darting back to the shadows where she thought she had glimpsed Silas. "I think we've been spotted. We should turn back, try again another night."

Thomas shook his head, his jaw set with determination. "No, Emma. We've come too far to give up now. This might be our only chance." Without waiting for her response, he strode towards the gate, the precious documents hidden in his secret pouch.

Emma watched him go, torn between following and retreating to safety. She bit her lip, indecision rooting her to the spot.

From the corner of her eye, she caught a flicker of movement. Silas slunk from shadow to shadow, his weaselly face alight with malicious glee. Emma's blood ran cold as she watched him scurry towards the dormitories where Brock slept.

"Thomas," she hissed, but he was too far ahead to hear her.

Moments later, Brock's hulking form emerged from the workhouse, his face twisted in a cruel grin. Emma held in a shout as she watched the brute lumber towards the unsuspecting Thomas.

Thomas had just reached the workhouse boundary when Brock's meaty hand clamped down on his shoulder. Emma clapped a hand over her mouth to stifle a scream as Thomas was yanked backwards, the documents scattering across the muddy ground as they fell out of his coat.

"Well, well, what do we have here?" Brock's gravelly voice carried through the still night air. "Looks like we've caught ourselves a little rat."

Emma pressed herself against the cold stone wall, her heart

breaking as she watched Brock drag a struggling Thomas back towards the workhouse. She caught a glimpse of Silas's face in an upstairs window, his thin lips curled in a triumphant smirk before he disappeared, no doubt hurrying to report to Mr Grimshaw.

THE PRICE OF DEFIANCE

*E*mma stood helpless among the other children in the workhouse yard. The morning air was dripping with dread, and she could barely breathe as she watched Brock drag Thomas to the centre of the yard. Mr Grimshaw stood there, a cruel smile twisting his features, the infamous leather strap dangling from his meaty hand.

Emma's fingers clutched at her hidden silver cross, her knuckles white with the effort of not crying out. She wanted to run to Thomas, to shield him from what was to come, but her feet remained rooted to the spot.

Brock's muscles bulged as he roughly tied Thomas to the post. Emma could see the determination in Thomas's eyes, even as fear flickered across his face. The other children huddled together, their faces pale and drawn, some averting their eyes while others stared in horrified fascination.

Mr Grimshaw circled Thomas like a vulture, his pig-like eyes gleaming with malicious anticipation. He cleared his throat, his voice booming across the yard. The other children fell silent, their eyes wide with fear and anticipation.

"Children of Grimshaw's Workhouse," he began, his jowls

quivering with each word, "we are gathered here today to witness the consequences of treachery and ingratitude." He gestured dramatically towards Thomas, who stood defiant despite his bindings. "This boy, Thomas Hawkins, whom we have clothed, fed, and sheltered, has repaid our kindness with malice and deceit."

Emma's fingers tightened around her hidden cross as Mr. Grimshaw continued, his voice dripping with false sincerity. "He has attempted to frame me, your benevolent caretaker, with false accusations of embezzlement and mistreatment. Can you imagine such wickedness?"

A murmur rippled through the crowd of children. Emma glanced around, seeing confusion and fear on their faces. She wanted to shout out the truth, but terror kept her silent.

Mr Grimshaw's voice rose. "This workhouse provides for you all, gives you purpose and direction. And yet, this ungrateful wretch sought to destroy it with his lies!"

From the edge of the yard, Mrs Grimshaw's shrill voice rang out. "It's true! I've seen the forged documents myself!" She bustled forward, her keys jangling ominously. "My husband works tirelessly for your benefit, and this is how he's repaid? Shameful!"

Mrs Grimshaw's eyes swept over the assembled children, daring any of them to object. "We give you everything," she added, her thin lips pressed into a severe line, "and this is the thanks we get? Thomas Hawkins is a liar and a thief, and he'll be punished accordingly!"

Mr Grimshaw nodded solemnly, his expression a mask of false regret. "Indeed, my dear. It pains me to do this, but for the good of all, young Thomas must learn the error of his ways."

Emma felt sick to her stomach as she watched Mr. Grimshaw raise the leather strap. She knew the truth, but in that moment, surrounded by the Grimshaws's lies and the fearful silence of her fellow orphans, she had never felt more helpless.

"Let this be a lesson to all of you," he bellowed, his voice echoing off the workhouse walls. "This is what happens to thieves and troublemakers!"

The first crack of the leather strap against Thomas's back made Emma flinch. Thomas's body jerked, but he didn't make a sound. The second blow fell, then the third, each one leaving angry red welts on Thomas's skin.

It was the fourth lash that broke Thomas's resolve. His scream, raw and agonised, tore through the air. Emma's legs trembled as the sound reverberated through the workhouse courtyard, seeming to go on forever. Tears streamed down her face as Thomas's cries continued, each one feeling like a physical blow to her own body.

Emma watched in horror as Mr Grimshaw continued to rain blows upon Thomas's back. Each crack of the leather strap made her flinch, and she could see Thomas's body trembling with pain. His cries had turned to whimpers, almost inaudible over the sound of the punishment.

As the beating went on, Mr Grimshaw's face grew red with exertion, his breath coming in heavy pants. Sweat beaded on his forehead, and his movements became slower, less precise. Emma noticed Mrs Grimshaw watching her husband with a mixture of concern and impatience.

Finally, Mrs Grimshaw stepped forward. "My dear," she said, her voice cutting through the air, "perhaps it's time to let Brock take over. We wouldn't want you to overexert yourself."

Mr Grimshaw paused, his chest heaving as he caught his breath. He nodded, a cruel smile twisting his features. "An excellent suggestion, my dear. Brock!"

Mr Grimshaw handed the blood-stained strap to Brock. The hulking man took it with a grim nod, his muscles flexing as he prepared to continue the punishment.

Brock's first blow was even more brutal than Mr Grimshaw's had been. Thomas's body jerked violently against his bindings, a hoarse cry escaping his lips. Emma wanted to look away, but found herself unable to tear her eyes from the horrific scene.

Blow after blow fell, each one accompanied by a sickening crack. Emma could see Thomas's strength fading, his reactions becoming weaker with each lash. Finally, his body went limp, his head lolling forward as consciousness fled.

Mrs Grimshaw's voice rang out, sharp and cold. "That's enough. Children, back to work! There's nothing more to see here."

Emma felt herself being pushed along with the crowd of stunned, silent children. As they filed out of the yard, she caught one last glimpse of Thomas, still tied to the post, his back a mess of angry welts and blood. The sight burned itself into her memory, an immortal memory of the cruelty they faced and the price of defiance.

∼

REVEREND ARTHUR DAVIES knelt before the altar, his hands clasped in prayer. The early morning light filtered through the stained glass windows, casting a kaleidoscope of colours across the worn stone floor. The scent of incense lingered in the air, a remnant from last night's vespers.

"Lord, guide my hands to do Your work," he murmured, his Welsh lilt soft in the quiet sanctuary. "Grant me the strength to be a beacon of hope for those in need."

As he rose, his knee protested with a familiar twinge. Arthur smiled ruefully, remembering the rugby match that had given him that particular souvenir. He made his way down the aisle, each step echoing in the empty church.

Pausing at the back pew, Arthur ran his hand along the

smooth wood, polished by years of faithful congregants. His eyes drifted to the small side chapel where he and Mary had exchanged their vows. The memory of her smile, radiant even in the face of illness, warmed his heart.

"I'm trying my best to carry on your work, my love," he whispered.

Arthur's gaze fell upon the collection box near the door. It was nearly empty, save for a few copper pennies. Times were hard for everyone, but especially for those in his parish. He sighed, thinking of all the good that could be done with just a little more.

Shaking off the melancholy, Arthur straightened his collar and stepped out into the churchyard. The morning air was crisp, carrying the promise of spring. He breathed deeply, savouring the moment of peace before the day's work began.

A PROMISE SEALED

*E*mma waited impatiently, counting down the seconds for the lunch bell to ring. The morning had dragged on endlessly, her mind consumed with worry for Thomas. When the shrill sound finally pierced the air, she bolted from her workstation, ignoring the curious glances of the other children.

She snatched a cup of water from the dining hall and hurried to the small alcove where Thomas lay. The sight of him made her heart skip a beat. His face was pale and drawn, his body curled into itself as if to ward off further blows.

"Thomas," she whispered, kneeling beside him. Her hands trembled as she gently cradled his head, lifting it slightly. "Here, drink this."

Thomas's eyes fluttered open, unfocused at first. A low groan escaped his lips as he tried to move.

"Shh, don't try to speak," Emma soothed. She pressed the cup to his cracked lips, tilting it carefully. "Small sips, that's it."

As Thomas drank, Emma's eyes darted nervously around the yard. She knew they had precious little time before Brock or Silas might spot them. Her fingers ghosted over the angry welts on Thomas's back, and she bit back a sob.

"I'm so sorry," she murmured, her words thick with unshed tears. "This is all my fault. If I hadn't—"

Thomas's hand weakly grasped hers, silencing her. His eyes, though clouded with pain, held a fierce determination that made Emma's breath catch.

"Not... your fault," he managed to rasp. "We did... right thing."

Emma squeezed his hand, drawing strength from his unwavering spirit. "We'll find a way, Thomas. We'll make things better, I promise."

Emma heard heavy footsteps approaching, and flinched as she saw who they belonged to. She instinctively tightened her grip on Thomas's hand, her eyes raising to meet the workhouse master's cruel gaze.

Mr Grimshaw loomed over them, his corpulent form blocking out the weak sunlight. A malicious smile played across his face, making his eyes glitter with sadistic pleasure.

"Well, well," he sneered. "What a touching scene. Our little troublemakers, thick as thieves."

Emma fought the urge to shrink away, forcing herself to meet Mr Grimshaw's gaze. She wouldn't give him the satisfaction of seeing her cower.

"I've had a most illuminating discussion with Mrs Grimshaw," he continued, puffing out his chest. "We've decided on a fitting punishment for young Thomas here."

Emma's breath caught in her throat. She glanced down at Thomas, seeing the pain etched across his features. But beneath the bruises and blood, she saw a shade of the same defiance that burned in her own heart.

"Is this not enough?" Emma was surprised at herself. Her voice was strong. "Have you not made your point? Have we not suffered enough already?"

Mr Grimshaw's voice cut through her defiance like a whip. "You'll be leaving us, boy. We've arranged an apprenticeship for you – with a blacksmith in a town far from here." His lips curled into a cruel smile. "I hear he has quite the reputation for... disciplining his charges."

Emma's blood ran cold. She knew what this meant – separation, more abuse, perhaps even death for Thomas. She opened her mouth to protest again, but Thomas's grip on her hand tightened, silencing her.

With a herculean effort, Thomas lifted his head. His deep brown eyes, filled with a mix of determination and barely contained fury, locked onto Mr Grimshaw's. The workhouse master's smile faltered for a moment, taken aback by the intensity of Thomas's glare.

For a moment, the air crackled with tension, a silent battle of wills between the battered boy and the corpulent tyrant. Then, with a huff and a scowl, Mr Grimshaw turned on his heel and stalked away, his gait betraying his frustration at not eliciting the tears he'd hoped for.

"You'll be off in the morning, boy." Mr Grimshaw almost spat as he stalked away.

As the workhouse master's footsteps faded, Emma felt Thomas's grip on her hand tighten. She looked down, her heart clenching at the sight of his battered face, now etched with grim determination.

"Emma," Thomas whispered, his voice weak but steady. "Listen to me. This isn't the end. We'll see each other again, I swear it."

Emma's eyes stung with unshed tears, but she blinked them back fiercely. "Thomas, I—"

"No," he interrupted, a fire burning in his eyes despite his pain. "You have to promise me something. Promise you'll continue our fight. For justice, for all of us here. Don't let them break you, Emma. Don't let them win."

Emma's free hand went to her throat, her fingers closing around the small silver cross that hung there. Without hesitation, she pulled the chain over her head and pressed the necklace into Thomas's palm.

"I promise," she whispered, her eyes meeting his, reflecting both her fear and her fierce determination. "Take this. To remember our promise, our faith. To remember me."

Thomas's fingers curled around the cross, a ghost of a smile touching his lips. "I could never forget you, Emma Redbrook."

THE WAGON AWAITS

※

The early morning air bit at Emma's skin, but she barely noticed, her eyes fixed on the scene unfolding before her.

Brock Thornhill's hulking form emerged from the dormitory, dragging a battered Thomas behind him. Two other workers flanked them, their faces grim and purposeful. Thomas stumbled, his legs barely able to support him, but Brock showed no mercy. He yanked Thomas forward, eliciting a muffled groan of pain.

Emma's fingers dug into the rough wood of the crates she was hiding behind, splinters piercing her skin. She wanted to cry out, to run to Thomas, but she knew it would only make things worse. She had made a promise, and she intended to keep it.

A rickety wagon waited at the workhouse gates, its driver a hunched figure wrapped in a threadbare cloak. Brock roughly shoved Thomas towards it, his massive hands gripping the boy's shoulders.

"Get in," Brock growled, his voice carrying across the yard. "And don't think about trying anything stupid."

Thomas didn't resist. He couldn't. His body was a patchwork of bruises and cuts, each movement clearly causing him pain. Yet, as he was roughly pushed into the wagon, he managed to turn his head.

Emma let out a small gasp as Thomas's eyes found hers. Even from this distance, she could see the depth of emotion in his gaze – pain, fear, but also a fierce determination.

Tears blurred Emma's vision, hot and stinging. She blinked rapidly, desperate not to lose sight of Thomas in these final moments. The wagon creaked as the driver flicked the reins, urging the horse forward.

As the wagon began to move, Thomas's gaze remained locked on Emma's hiding spot. His lips moved, forming words she couldn't hear but understood in her heart. "I'll come back," they seemed to say. "I promise."

Then, with a lurch, the wagon passed through the gates and out of sight, taking Thomas with it.

FLICKERING HOPE

Emma's world had dimmed without Thomas, but she refused to let the darkness consume her. Each morning, she rose from her thin mattress with renewed vigour. Their shared mission pressed upon her shoulders, a constant reminder of the promise they'd made.

In the laundry room, Emma attacked her work with fierce concentration. Her raw hands plunged into the scalding water, scrubbing until her knuckles bled. But the pain was a welcome distraction from the ache in her heart.

"You're going to work yourself to the bone," Sarah whispered, her small face creased with concern.

Emma managed a wan smile. "Just doing my part," she murmured.

As the days passed, Emma found solace in the quiet moments with Sarah and Lucy. The three girls huddled together during meal times, sharing scraps of bread and whispered words of encouragement. Lucy, older and street-smart, became a protective presence, her sharp eyes always on the lookout for Brock or Silas.

"We've got to stick together," Lucy would say, her voice low and fierce. "It's the only way to survive this place."

Emma nodded, grateful for their companionship. But even as she drew strength from her friends, her mind never strayed far from her goal. She watched Mr Grimshaw with careful eyes, noting his comings and goings, the ledgers he carried, the hushed conversations in corners.

During her cleaning duties, Emma lingered near Mr Grimshaw's office, straining her ears for any useful information. She memorised the names of visitors, the dates of important meetings, piecing together a mental map of the workhouse's inner workings.

One evening, as Emma folded laundry, she overheard Silas muttering to himself nearby. His reedy voice carried just far enough for her to catch fragments: "...shipment coming... extra mouths to feed..."

Emma's hands stilled, her mind racing. A new shipment of children? Or something else entirely? She filed the information away, determined to uncover its meaning.

~

"Good afternoon, Miss Redbrook. How are you faring today?"

Emma's head snapped up, her eyes meeting the kind gaze of Reverend Davies. She hadn't seen him enter the laundry room, his visits to the workhouse becoming less frequent as of late. The sight of his weathered face, creased with concern, stirred something within her – a hope she'd thought long extinguished.

"I'm well enough, Reverend," Emma replied. She cast a furtive glance around the room, wary of Silas's prying eyes or Brock's looming presence.

Reverend Davies stepped closer, his brow furrowing as he studied her face. "You seem... different, my dear. There's a weight upon you that wasn't there before. Is everything all right?"

Emma's fingers tightened around the fabric in her hands. She longed to unburden herself, to share the terrible secrets she'd uncovered. But Thomas's fate loomed large in her mind, a stark warning of the consequences of speaking out.

"Life here is... challenging, Reverend," Emma said carefully, choosing each word with deliberation. "But we endure as best we can."

The Reverend's eyes softened with understanding. "I see," he murmured. "And how do you find strength in such trying times?"

Faith," she answered simply. "And the hope that one day, things might change for the better."

Reverend Davies nodded, a flicker of something – admiration, perhaps? – crossing his features. "Your spirit is truly remarkable, Miss Redbrook. I pray it never wavers."

Emma managed a small smile, genuine despite her caution. "Thank you, Reverend. Your kindness... it means more than you know."

Emma watched as Reverend Davies departed, his kind words echoing in her mind. The laundry room felt emptier without his presence, the constant hum of work and chatter fading into the background. She turned back to her task, her hands moving mechanically as her thoughts drifted to Thomas.

The ache of his absence was a constant dull throb in her chest that never truly subsided. Emma closed her eyes for a moment, remembering the warmth of his smile, the strength in his voice when he spoke of justice and a better future. Though he was gone, his spirit lingered in every corner of the workhouse, in every act of kindness she witnessed or performed.

As she worked, Emma's fingers brushed against the spot where her mother's silver cross had once rested. Though the necklace now resided with Thomas, she could still feel its weight, a phantom reminder of her faith and the love that had shaped her. She took a deep breath, drawing strength from the memory of her mother's words and Thomas's unwavering belief in her.

The day wore on, each hour blending into the next in a haze of endless toil. Yet even as her body ached and her spirit wavered, Emma refused to let the flame of hope within her die. She clung to it fiercely, nurturing it with every stolen moment of kindness, every whispered prayer, every memory of better days.

As night fell and the workhouse settled into its uneasy slumber, Emma lay awake in her narrow bed. The dormitory was dark, filled with the soft sounds of breathing and the occasional whimper of a child caught in a nightmare. Emma's hand slipped beneath her thin pillow, retrieving a small stub of candle and a carefully hoarded match.

With trembling fingers, she struck the match against the rough stone wall, cupping her hand around the tiny flame. The warm glow illuminated her face, casting flickering shadows across the room. Emma placed it carefully in a hidden corner where its light would not disturb the others.

She watched the small flame dance, steady and unwavering despite the drafts that whispered through the dormitory. In its gentle light, Emma saw a reflection of the hope she and Thomas had kindled together -- a beacon in the darkness, a promise of better days to come.

WHISPERS OF REBELLION

※

*E*mma's eyes scanned the workhouse yard, searching for a moment of relative calm amidst the constant bustle and noise. Her gaze settled on Sarah and Lucy, huddled together near the far wall. With a quick glance to ensure no watchful eyes were upon them, Emma made her way across the yard, her steps purposeful yet unhurried.

Sarah looked up as Emma approached, her large brown eyes widening with a mixture of fear and hope. Lucy's dark, guarded gaze flicked between Emma and the yard, ever watchful for danger.

"Sarah, Lucy," Emma whispered, her voice low but filled with quiet determination. "I need to speak with you both."

The two girls shifted, making space for Emma in their small circle. Emma knelt beside them, her grey dress pooling around her on the dusty ground.

"I've been thinking," Emma began, her words carefully measured. "About how we might make things better here, even in small ways."

Lucy's eyebrow arched skeptically, but she remained silent,

listening. Sarah leaned in closer, her thin frame trembling slightly with nervous energy.

"What if," Emma continued, "we could teach the younger children to read?"

Sarah's gasp was almost inaudible, but her eyes shone with sudden understanding. Lucy's guarded expression softened, interest crossing her features.

"It would be dangerous," Emma acknowledged, her fingers absently tracing the spot where her mother's cross had once rested. "But think of the difference it could make. Knowledge is power, and if we can give these children even a taste of that..."

Lucy nodded slowly, her usual cynicism giving way to a cautious hope. "It could change everything for them," she murmured.

Sarah's voice quavered as she spoke. "But how? When? Where would we even start?"

Emma's smile was small but determined. "I have a plan. But I can't do it alone. Will you help me?"

The silence that followed seemed to stretch for an eternity. Emma held her breath, watching the emotions play across her friends' faces. Finally, Lucy spoke low and firm.

"I'm in," she said simply.

Sarah nodded vigorously, her fear overshadowed by a newfound resolve. "Me too," she whispered.

Warmth bloomed in her chest, a feeling of purpose and hope that she hadn't experienced since Thomas's departure. "Thank you," she breathed, reaching out to squeeze both girls' hands. "Together, we can make a difference. I know we can."

LESSONS BY CANDLELIGHT

The night air hung heavy with the soft snores and restless murmurs of sleeping children. Emma paused, listening intently for any sign of Silas's tell-tale shuffling gait or the heavy tread of Brock's boots.

Satisfied that the coast was clear, Emma made her way to Sarah's bed, gently shaking her awake. Sarah's eyes flew open, fear quickly replaced by determination. Without a word, the two girls moved to Lucy's cot, rousing her with a gentle touch.

The three conspirators exchanged silent nods, their faces ghostly in the dim moonlight filtering through the grimy windows. Emma's fingers found the loose floorboard beneath her bed, carefully prying it up to reveal the hidden treasure within – her mother's tattered Bible.

With practiced stealth, Emma, Sarah, and Lucy began to wake a select few of the younger children. Tiny hands were grasped, reassuring smiles offered, as they guided their bleary-eyed charges to a secluded corner of the dormitory.

Emma's heart swelled with pride as she looked at the small group gathered before her. Their faces, so often etched with hunger and fear, now shone with curiosity and excitement. She couldn't help but think of Thomas, wondering if he would approve of their clandestine classroom.

Lucy produced a stubby candle, shielding its feeble flame with cupped hands. The warm glow cast dancing shadows on the wall, transforming their drab surroundings into something almost magical.

Emma opened the Bible with reverent care, its pages whispering promises of hope and redemption. She found a simple verse, one her mother had often read to her in happier times. Taking a deep breath, she began to speak.

"In the beginning," Emma read softly, her finger tracing each word, "God created the heavens and the earth."

The children leaned in close, their eyes wide with wonder. Sarah and Lucy flanked Emma, ready to offer assistance or keep watch for any approaching danger.

"Now, let's sound out these words together," Emma encouraged, her heart swelling with purpose. "In... the... be-gin-ning..."

A chorus of tiny voices echoed her words, stumbling over unfamiliar syllables but pressing on with determination. Emma felt a surge of hope as she watched their eager faces, illuminated by the flickering candlelight.

Emma's fingers traced invisible letters in the air, her movements fluid and graceful. The children's eyes followed her hand, their faces scrunched in concentration as they tried to mimic the shapes with their own small digits.

"See how the 'S' curves like a snake?" Emma whispered. She reached into her pocket, pulling out a handful of buttons she'd collected from the laundry floor. With nimble fingers, she arranged them on the floor to form the letter.

"Now you try," she encouraged, watching as tiny hands reached out to rearrange the buttons. A young girl with a mop of unruly hair bit her lip in concentration, her brow furrowed as she carefully formed an 'S' of her own.

Emma's heart swelled. She glanced at Sarah, who sat with

her arm around a trembling girl no more than six years old. Sarah's soft voice carried to Emma's ears as she whispered words of encouragement.

"You're doing so well, Annie," Sarah murmured, her own eyes bright with unshed tears. "Just imagine all the stories you'll be able to read soon."

Lucy stood sentinel by the dormitory entrance, her sharp eyes scanning the darkness beyond. Every few moments, she would turn back to the group, giving Emma a quick nod before resuming her watch.

Emma reached into her apron pocket, pulling out scraps of paper she'd salvaged from the rubbish bin in Mr Grimshaw's office. On each, she'd painstakingly written a single letter or simple word. She held them up one by one, her voice a gentle whisper as she sounded out each one.

"Cat," she said, showing the scrap to the eager faces before her. "Can anyone tell me what sound 'C' makes?"

A chorus of hushed "Kuh" sounds filled the air, bringing a smile to Emma's face. She felt a warmth in her chest, a sense of purpose that burned brighter than any candle. For a moment, the grim walls of the workhouse faded away, replaced by the hope shining in the children's eyes.

THE UNDERGROUND CLASSROOM

Over the next few weeks, Emma, Sarah, and Lucy fell into a rhythm as natural as breathing. Every few nights, they'd gather their small flock of eager learners in the shadowy corners of the dormitory. Emma's heart filled with pride as she watched the children's eyes light up, hungry for knowledge in a place that sought to starve their spirits.

Emma's clever mind worked overtime, conjuring up simple games and quizzes to reinforce their lessons. She'd arrange buttons into shapes, challenging the children to guess the letter or word they formed. Sarah's gentle voice would guide them through the sounds, while Lucy kept watch with the vigilance of a mother hen.

"What does this spell?" Emma would whisper, her finger tracing invisible letters in the air.

Tiny voices would chorus back, stumbling over syllables but growing more confident with each passing night. Emma savoured these moments, storing them away like precious jewels to be examined in darker times.

As the candle burned low, Emma would always end their

clandestine lessons the same way. She'd gather the children close, their faces aglow with newfound knowledge and hope.

"Let us pray," she'd murmur. "Lord, grant us strength to face each day with courage. Help us to see the light in the darkness, and to be that light for others."

Then, she'd open her mother's Bible to a carefully chosen verse. "Remember," Emma would say, her eyes meeting each child's gaze, "No matter how hard things seem, there is always hope."

When dawn broke, Emma, Sarah, and Lucy threw themselves into their workhouse duties with renewed vigour. The secret they shared burned within them, fuelling their strength as they scrubbed floors and laundered endless piles of linens. Emma's hands might blister and crack from the harsh soap, but her spirit remained unbroken.

As she worked, Emma would catch Sarah's eye across the laundry room, exchanging a small smile. Lucy, ever watchful, would give them a subtle nod as she passed, carrying heavy baskets of wet clothes.

Their shared purpose gave them strength, transforming the gruelling labour into a test of endurance they were determined to pass. With each task completed, they were one step closer to their next lesson, one day closer to a future where knowledge could bloom even in the harshest of soils.

Emma couldn't help but smile as she watched the younger children during their daily chores. What had once been a monotonous drone of scrubbing and sweeping now held a secret melody. Whispered letters floated on the air, barely audible but unmistakable to her trained ear.

"P-s-s-t," a small voice hissed. "What letter comes after 'M'?"

"N!" came the hushed reply, followed by a giggle quickly stifled.

These stolen moments of learning were like rays of sunshine breaking through the perpetual gloom of Grimshaw's Workhouse. She caught Sarah's eye across the room, sharing a look of quiet triumph.

But it was Hannah who truly astounded Emma. The girl with eyes as bright as summer skies had taken to their lessons like a fish to water. Emma often found Hannah tracing letters in the dust or arranging pebbles into words during their brief moments of rest in the yard.

"Miss Emma," Hannah whispered one evening as they huddled in their hidden corner of the dormitory. "Can I help teach today? I've been practicing."

Emma nodded, her throat tight with emotion. "Of course, Hannah. Show us what you've learned."

Hannah's face lit up like a candle flame. She turned to the younger children, her voice soft but steady. "Let's spell 'hope' together. H-O-P-E. What does each letter sound like?"

As the children sounded out each letter, Emma watched in awe. Hannah's enthusiasm was contagious, spreading through the group like wildfire. Even the most timid among them found their voices, eager to join in the quiet chorus of learning.

Emma felt a tug on her sleeve and looked down to see Lucy's worried face. "Silas is coming," Lucy breathed. "We need to wrap up."

With a quick nod, Emma gathered the children close. "Remember," she whispered, "carry these letters in your heart. They're yours now, and no one can take them away."

As they scattered back to their beds, Emma caught Hannah's eye. The girl's face shone with a mixture of pride and determination that made Emma's chest ache with a bittersweet hope.

UNEXPECTED ALLY

◈

*E*mma's heart skipped a beat as she saw Reverend Davies enter the workhouse yard. His visits had become more frequent of late, and she couldn't help but wonder if he'd noticed the subtle changes in the children. As she scrubbed linens, she watched him from the corner of her eye, noting how he paused to speak with little Hannah.

The girl's eyes sparkled as she answered the Reverend's questions, her back straighter than Emma had ever seen it. Fulfilment swelled in Emma's chest, mingling with a hint of anxiety. They'd been so careful, but children's joy was a difficult thing to hide entirely.

When Reverend Davies approached her, Emma schooled her features into a mask of polite deference. "Good day, Reverend," she said, wringing out a sheet with practiced efficiency.

"Good day, Emma," he replied, his kind eyes searching her face. "I couldn't help but notice a change in the air here. The children seem... different. Brighter, somehow."

Emma's hands stilled for a moment before she resumed her work. "Perhaps it's the spring weather, sir. It does lift the spirits."

The Reverend nodded slowly. "Indeed it does. But I sense

there's more to it than that. Almost as if..." he paused, choosing his words carefully, "as if they've found a new source of hope."

Emma met his gaze, her heart pounding. "Hope is a powerful thing, Reverend. It can flourish even in the darkest places, if one knows where to look."

"And where might one look for such hope, I wonder?" Reverend Davies asked, his tone gentle but probing.

"In the words of the Lord, of course," Emma replied. "His teachings can illuminate even the gloomiest corners."

The Reverend's eyes narrowed slightly, a hint of a smile playing at the corners of his mouth. "How fortunate these children are, to have such... guidance."

Emma nodded, her expression carefully neutral. "We all do our best to support one another, sir. It's what keeps us going in times of hardship."

As they continued their conversation, Emma felt as though they were engaged in an intricate dance, each step measured and deliberate. The air between them crackled with unspoken understanding, a shared secret hovering just beyond reach.

She glanced around, ensuring no prying eyes or ears were nearby. With trembling hands, she reached into the folds of her dress and withdrew the tattered Bible, its pages worn and soft from countless secret readings.

"Reverend," she began, "I have something to show you."

Emma carefully opened the Bible, revealing the faint pencil marks and smudged fingerprints that betrayed its clandestine use. She watched the Reverend's face, searching for any sign of disapproval or alarm.

"I've been teaching the children to read," she confessed, her words tumbling out in a rush. "Using this Bible, and any scraps of paper we can find. It's not much, but... I couldn't bear to see them grow up without knowledge, without hope."

Reverend Davies's eyes widened, a mix of surprise and admiration flickering across his features. He gently took the

Bible from Emma's hands, thumbing through its pages with reverence.

"Emma," he said softly, "what you're doing is incredibly brave. And incredibly dangerous."

Emma nodded, swallowing hard. "I know, sir. But I couldn't stand by and do nothing. These children, they deserve a chance at a better life. Even if it's just the ability to read a few words..."

The Reverend's gaze met hers, and Emma saw something there that made her breath catch – understanding, compassion, and a fierce pride that brought unexpected tears to her eyes.

"You're right," he said, his voice thick with emotion. "They do deserve better. And I want to help."

Emma blinked, scarcely daring to believe what she was hearing. "You... you do?"

Reverend Davies nodded, a conspiratorial smile spreading across his face. "I can't do much without raising suspicion, but I can bring you supplies. Paper, ink... I'll hide them among the other donations I bring. It's not much, but it's a start."

Emma felt a weight lift from her shoulders, a burden she hadn't realised she'd been carrying alone for so long. "Thank you, Reverend," her voice choked with gratitude. "You don't know what this means."

A CLOSE CALL

Emma's quiet strength grew like a steady flame, warming those around her in the cold confines of Grimshaw's Workhouse. The years etched lines of determination on her young face, but they couldn't dim the light in her hazel eyes. As she moved through the daily routines of laundry and chores, Emma felt countless gazes upon her – children seeking guidance, hope, and the courage to endure.

She never asked for leadership, but it found her nonetheless. A gentle touch here, a whispered word of encouragement there – Emma's presence became a balm for weary souls. The younger children gravitated towards her, their eyes wide with a mixture of admiration and need. Even some of the older inmates found themselves drawn to her unwavering faith, like moths to a candle in the darkest night.

Sarah and Lucy, once timid shadows in the workhouse halls, blossomed under Emma's influence. Sarah's stutter faded when she helped the little ones sound out words, her voice growing stronger with each lesson. Lucy's sharp wit, once turned inward as a shield, now found purpose in devising clever ways to keep their secret classes hidden.

"We need a signal," Lucy whispered one day, her dark eyes darting around the laundry room. "In case Silas or Brock comes sniffing about during lessons."

Emma nodded, wringing out a sheet with practiced hands. "What did you have in mind?"

Sarah piped up, her voice steady. "I could hum a tune. Something simple, like 'God Save the Queen.' It wouldn't raise suspicion if anyone heard."

"Brilliant," Emma said, a rare smile lighting up her face. "Lucy, you're our best lookout. You'll give Sarah the nod if danger's near."

Lucy's chest puffed up with pride. "Leave it to me. I've got eyes like a hawk and ears like a... well, something with really good hearing."

The three girls shared a quiet laugh, the sound a precious rarity in the grim workhouse, before returning to their tasks. She might not have chosen this path, but with Sarah and Lucy by her side, she knew they could face whatever challenges lay ahead.

∽

EMMA GUIDED Hannah's small hand across the tattered page, tracing the letters of a Bible verse. The dormitory's dim light cast long shadows, but the children's eyes shone with eagerness. Sarah's soft voice murmured encouragement to a group sounding out words, while Lucy kept watch by the door, her keen ears attuned to any approaching footsteps.

A sudden hush fell over the room. Lucy's hand shot up, her face pale in the moonlight. "Someone's coming," she whispered urgently. "And it ain't Brock's heavy tread."

Emma's blood ran cold. "Mr Grimshaw," she breathed. In an instant, the peaceful scene erupted into silent chaos. Emma snatched up the Bible, her fingers fumbling with the loose floorboard where she kept it hidden. Sarah herded the younger children back to their beds, her movements quick but gentle. Lucy darted between the rows, scooping up stray bits of paper and smuggled pencil stubs.

"Under your pillows," Emma hissed, passing out the evidence to trusted hands. "Remember, not a sound."

The floorboards outside creaked ominously. Emma had just slipped under her own thin blanket when the door swung open with a groan. Mr Grimshaw's bulk filled the frame, his beady eyes glinting in the darkness. Emma forced her breathing to slow, willing her hammering heart to quiet.

Mr Grimshaw shuffled into the room, his gaze sweeping over the rows of seemingly sleeping children. Emma could smell the sour stench of cheap gin on his breath as he passed. She kept her eyes shut, every muscle tense as she feigned sleep.

"What's this, then?" Grimshaw's voice cut through the silence. Emma's eyes flew open to see him bending over Hannah's bed. The little girl clutched her blanket, eyes wide with fear. Emma's stomach twisted as she realized a corner of paper peeked out from beneath Hannah's pillow.

Mr Grimshaw swayed slightly, his bulk casting a menacing shadow. He leaned closer to Hannah, his pig-like eyes narrowing. Emma held her breath, certain he'd spot the tell-tale corner of paper.

But then, Grimshaw's foot caught on the uneven floorboard. He stumbled, barely catching himself on the edge of Hannah's bed. The sudden movement sent a wave of gin-scented breath wafting through the room.

"Blasted floorboards," he muttered, his words slurring. He straightened up, tugging at his rumpled waistcoat. His gaze swept unfocused across the room once more.

Emma watched through half-closed lids as Grimshaw shuffled towards the door, his gait unsteady. He paused at the threshold, as if trying to remember why he'd come in the first place. Then, with a grunt of frustration, he lumbered out into the hallway.

The door creaked shut behind him. Emma counted her heartbeats, listening to Grimshaw's heavy footsteps fade away. Only when silence fell did she dare to exhale.

She sat up slowly, meeting Sarah's wide-eyed gaze across the room. Lucy crept back from her post by the door, her face pale in the moonlight.

"That were too close," Lucy rasped.

Emma nodded, her hands still shaking. She slipped out of bed, padding silently to Hannah's side. The little girl's eyes glistened with unshed tears.

"It's all right now," Emma murmured, gently smoothing Hannah's hair. "You were very brave."

Hannah's small hand found Emma's, squeezing tight. "Will we still learn tomorrow?" she asked.

Emma hesitated, weighing the risks against the hunger for knowledge she saw in Hannah's eyes. It was the same hunger she'd seen in Thomas, all those years ago. The memory of him, of his unwavering belief in their shared dream, settled like a warm weight.

"Yes," Emma decided, her voice stronger now. "We'll be more careful, but we won't stop."

Relief washed over Hannah's face, and she nestled deeper into her thin pillow. Emma stayed by her side until the child's breathing evened out in sleep.

Rising slowly, Emma made her way to the small window. The glass was grimy, distorting the view of the London night beyond. But even through the dirt and darkness, she could make out the faint glow of distant lights. Each pinprick of brightness seemed to whisper of a world beyond these walls, of the life she and Thomas had once dreamed of.

She thought of her mother's words, of Thomas's unwavering spirit, of the children who looked to her with such trust. In that moment, standing in the hushed darkness of the dormitory, a renewed sense of purpose settled over her.

FORGED IN FIRE

༄

Thomas Hawkins wiped the sweat from his brow, his calloused hand leaving a streak of soot across his forehead. The once-soft features of his face had hardened over the past year, chiselled by the unforgiving heat of the forge and the weight of crushed dreams. His eyes, once bright with hope, now held a dull sheen of resignation.

The workshop around him pulsed with oppressive heat, the air thick with the acrid scent of burning coal and hot metal. Thomas's shirt clung to his back, damp with sweat and grime. The walls were lined with an array of tools, each one a potential instrument of creation or torment, depending on Master Grimm's mood. Half-finished projects cluttered the workbench, a testament to the relentless pace of their labour.

Thomas felt Master Jerome Grimm's gaze upon him. He didn't need to look up to know that those cold, steel-grey eyes were scrutinising his every move. Grimm's powerful frame cast a long shadow across the workshop, his very presence a constant reminder of the harsh reality Thomas now lived in.

As Thomas hammered away at a piece of glowing metal, he caught a glimpse of his reflection in a polished shield hanging nearby. The face that stared back at him was barely recognisable – gaunt, with a perpetual shadow of stubble and exhaustion etched into every line. He quickly averted his eyes, focusing instead on the task at hand.

"Put your back into it, boy!" Grimm's gravelly voice boomed across the workshop. "That metal won't shape itself!"

Thomas gritted his teeth, his muscles straining as he brought the hammer down with renewed force. The rhythmic clanging filled the air, drowning out the echoes of his past and the whispers of a future that seemed increasingly out of reach.

Thomas's arms ached as he brought the hammer down again and again, each strike sending shockwaves through his exhausted muscles. The piece of metal before him slowly took shape, but not fast enough to satisfy Master Grimm's exacting standards.

"Is that what you call craftsmanship, boy?" Grimm's voice cut through the air like a scythe. He glanced up to see Grimm's face twisted in a sneer, his craggy features accentuated by the harsh shadows cast by the forge.

"I've seen better work from a blind cripple," Grimm spat, his words dripping with disdain. "No food for you until you get it right. Maybe an empty belly will teach you to use that empty head of yours."

Thomas's stomach clenched at the thought of another missed meal, but he forced himself to focus on the task at hand. The heat of the forge seemed to intensify, sweat pouring down his back as he worked tirelessly to meet Grimm's impossible expectations.

Hours passed, and Thomas felt his strength ebbing away. His vision blurred, the metal before him swimming in and out of focus. Suddenly, a loud crack split the air. Grimm's iron rod slammed into the ground mere inches from Thomas's foot, sending sparks flying.

"Did I say you could rest?" Grimm's gravelly voice boomed,

filling the workshop. "Get back to work, or the next strike won't miss."

Thomas's hands shook as he lifted the hammer once more, his body screaming in protest. As he worked, his gaze drifted to the small table in the corner where a meagre portion of bread and cheese sat tantalisingly out of reach. His mouth watered at the sight, his empty stomach twisting painfully.

The hunger gnawing at his insides seemed to mirror the hollowness he felt in his soul. Thomas couldn't remember the last time he'd felt truly full – of food, of hope, of anything but exhaustion and despair.

Thomas's hand drifted to the silver cross hanging around his neck, its weight seeming to increase with each passing day. The metal felt cold against his skin, a stark contrast to the oppressive heat of the forge. He'd once cherished this gift from Emma, a symbol of hope and faith. Now, it felt more like a shackle, tethering him to a past that grew dimmer with each swing of his hammer.

As he worked, Thomas's mind wandered, grappling with questions that had plagued him since his arrival at Master Grimm's workshop. Where was God in this hellish place? How could a loving deity allow such suffering to exist? The rhythmic clanging of metal on metal became a mocking chorus, echoing his doubts.

"If You're really there," Thomas thought bitterly, "why have You abandoned me? Why have You abandoned all of us?" The unanswered prayers of countless nights rose up in his memory, each one another crack in the foundation of his once-unshakeable faith.

Thomas tried to conjure Emma's face in his mind, seeking solace in the memory of her kindness. But to his dismay, the image that formed was hazy and indistinct. Her deep hazel eyes, once so vivid in his recollection, now seemed to blur into the smoky air of the workshop. The hopeful smile that had given him strength through countless hardships at the workhouse was fading, like a painting left too long in the sun.

He squeezed his eyes shut, desperately trying to hold onto the memory. But Emma's features slipped away like water through his fingers, leaving behind only a vague impression of warmth and compassion. The realisation sent a pang through Thomas's heart, sharper than any physical pain Master Grimm could inflict.

PART II
THE CRUCIBLE OF FAITH

That the trial of your faith, being much more precious than of gold that perisheth, though it be tried with fire, might be found unto praise and honour and glory at the appearing of Jesus Christ:
   – I Peter 1:7

ESCAPE THROUGH SMOKE

The air hung heavy in Grimshaw's Workhouse, thick with the stench of unwashed bodies and despair. Emma Grace Redbrook's shoulders ached as she scrubbed the floor. Around her, children shuffled about their tasks, eyes downcast, movements mechanical. The usual din of clanking pots and barked orders seemed muffled, as if the very walls held their breath.

Emma's gaze darted to Sarah, hunched over a pile of laundry. Their eyes met for a fleeting moment, a silent conversation passing between them. Sarah gave an almost imperceptible nod before returning to her work.

In the far corner, little Hannah sorted buttons with trembling fingers. Emma's heart clenched at the sight. Hannah had grown so much in the past few years, yet remained painfully small for her age, her frame stunted by years of meagre rations.

As Brock's heavy footsteps echoed down the corridor, Emma inched closer to Sarah and Hannah. "Something is going to happen soon. I can feel it," she whispered. "We must be ready."

Sarah's eyes widened, worry quickly replaced by determination. Hannah's small hand found Emma's, squeezing it tight.

Emma's thoughts drifted to Lucy, sent away over a year ago when she'd grown too old for the workhouse. The ache of her absence still gnawed at Emma's heart. At eighteen, Emma knew her own time was running short. Soon, she too would be cast out into the unforgiving streets of London.

But not before she'd done all she could for those left behind.

As darkness fell and the workhouse settled into its nightly routines, Emma felt a strange electricity in the air. Something was different tonight. Whether it was a blessing or a curse, she couldn't say. But as she watched Sarah and Hannah exchange meaningful glances across the dormitory, Emma knew that whatever came, they would face it together.

Emma's nostrils flared as an acrid smell tickled her senses. She glanced up and her eyes widened as she saw tendrils of smoke seeping under the laundry room door. Heart pounding, she rushed forward, flinging the door open. The sight that greeted her stole her breath away.

Flames danced across piles of dry rags, licking up the walls with terrifying speed. A toppled lamp lay shattered on the floor, its spilled oil feeding the inferno. The heat hit Emma like a physical blow, forcing her back a step.

For a moment, time seemed to stand still. Emma's mind raced, memories of her parents' deaths and years of hardship flashing before her eyes. Then, with startling clarity, she knew what she had to do.

"Sarah! Hannah!" Emma's voice cut through the crackling flames. She spun around, her eyes reflecting the fire as they locked onto her friends. "This is it! We have to go now!"

Sarah's face paled, but she nodded resolutely, grabbing Hannah's hand. The younger girl trembled, her eyes wide with fear.

As if on cue, alarms began to blare throughout the workhouse. Shouts and screams filled the air, a cacophony of panic that seemed to shake the very foundations of the building. Emma seized Sarah's free hand, forming a human chain.

"Stay close!" Emma yelled over the din. "We'll use the noise as cover!"

They plunged into the smoky corridor, the chaos around them both terrifying and oddly liberating. Years of pent-up desperation fuelled their steps as they raced towards freedom, the roar of the flames nipping at their heels.

Emma's heart raced as she led Sarah and Hannah through the smoke-filled corridors. Her grip on Sarah's hand tightened, while Hannah clung desperately to Emma's shawl. The acrid smoke stung their eyes and burned their lungs, but Emma pressed on, her mind focused solely on escape.

"This way," Emma whispered hoarsely, ducking under a beam that had partially collapsed. The roar of the flames seemed to grow louder with each passing moment, spurring them to move faster.

As they rounded a corner, Emma spotted a group of younger children huddled together, eyes wide with terror. Without hesitation, she veered towards them. "Come on," she urged, her voice gentle but firm. "Follow us. We'll get you out."

The children fell in line behind them, forming a ragged procession through the chaos. Emma's eyes darted from side to side, searching for the safest path through the inferno. She could hear Sarah's laboured breathing behind her and felt Hannah's trembling hand on her shawl.

Suddenly, a familiar bellow cut through the crackling of flames and screams of panic. "You there! Stop!" Brock's voice boomed, sending a chill down Emma's spine despite the oppressive heat.

Emma froze for a split second, her mind racing. She knew every nook and cranny of this wretched place, every hidden corner and forgotten passageway. In that moment, she remembered a service entrance rarely used, tucked away near the kitchen.

"This way," Emma hissed, tugging Sarah and the others down a narrow side corridor. The smoke was thinner here, allowing them a brief respite to catch their breath. Emma could hear Brock's heavy footsteps and angry shouts growing fainter as they put distance between themselves and the main corridors.

As they neared the secret exit, Emma's pace slowed. She pressed a finger to her lips, signalling for silence. The group crept forward, the children's eyes wide with a mixture of fear and hope. Emma's hand found the handle of the service door, cool metal against her palm.

As she pushed open the service door, the cool night air a stark contrast to the inferno behind them. But her relief was short-lived. There, blocking their path, stood Silas Merriweather, his watery eyes widening in shock as he took in the scene before him.

For a heartbeat, time seemed to stand still. Emma could hear Sarah's sharp intake of breath, feel Hannah's small hand tighten on her shawl. Silas's mouth opened, no doubt to raise the alarm.

Emma didn't hesitate. "Run!" she shouted to Sarah and Hannah, her voice hoarse from the smoke. In one fluid motion, she lunged forward, throwing her weight against a stack of empty crates near the door. The wooden boxes toppled with a thunderous crash, forcing Silas to stumble backward.

"Go! Now!" Emma urged, pushing Sarah and Hannah towards the narrow alley beyond. The other children followed, their feet pounding on the cobblestones as they fled into the night.

Emma spared one last glance at Silas, who was struggling to regain his footing amidst the fallen crates. His face contorted with rage as he shouted, "Brock! They're escaping!"

The sound of heavy footsteps and angry bellows echoed from within the burning workhouse. Emma's heart leapt to her throat as she recognised Brock's furious roar. She turned and ran, her legs pumping furiously as she followed Sarah and Hannah into the labyrinthine streets of London.

Behind her, she could hear Brock and Silas giving chase, their shouts carrying over the crackling flames and general chaos of the fire. Emma's lungs burned as she ran, but she pushed herself harder, determined to put as much distance as possible between them and their pursuers.

Emma's lungs burned as she followed after Sarah and Hannah. The gas lamps cast eerie shadows, transforming familiar corners into menacing shapes. Her eyes darted frantically, searching for any sign of pursuit.

As she emerged from the alley, she practically ran over the two girls. A wall of noise and scents assaulted them. They had stumbled into one of London's night markets, a chaotic mess of humanity even at this late hour. Emma felt a flicker of hope – here, they might lose themselves in the crowd.

"Oysters! Fresh oysters!" a vendor bellowed, his rough voice cutting through the general din. The pungent smell of fish hung heavy in the air, mingling with the earthy scent of vegetables and the sickly-sweet aroma of overripe fruit.

Emma pushed forward, weaving between stalls and carts. Sarah clung to her hand, Hannah trailing close behind. The clamour of the market enveloped them – the shouts of haggling customers, the clatter of coins changing hands, the squawk of caged chickens.

"Watch it!" a burly man growled as Emma bumped into him. She mumbled an apology, her eyes never stopping their frantic scan of the crowd. Had they lost Brock and Silas? Or were their pursuers still hot on their trail, hidden somewhere in this sea of faces?

A child's cry pierced the air, making Emma flinch. For a moment, she was back in the burning workhouse, surrounded by terrified children. She shook her head, forcing herself to focus on the present. They weren't safe yet.

Emma's grip on Sarah's hand tightened. The cacophony of voices and the press of bodies threatened to overwhelm her senses. Hannah clung to her shawl, a small anchor in the sea of humanity.

"Stay close," Emma shouted over her shoulder, her voice only just cutting above the din. She could feel Sarah's fingers trembling in her own, the girl's fear palpable.

A burly man with a cart of cabbages pushed his way through the crowd, forcing Emma to sidestep. She stumbled, her shoulder colliding with a fishmonger's stall. The smell of rotting fish assaulted her nostrils, making her gag.

"Oi!" the fishmonger bellowed, his face red with anger.

Emma tried to regain her footing. The crowd surged around her, a living, breathing entity with no regard for the three frightened girls in its midst. Emma felt Sarah's hand begin to slip from her grasp.

"Sarah!" she cried, desperately trying to maintain her hold. But the press of bodies was too much. A woman with a squawking chicken under her arm shoved past, breaking Emma's grip on Sarah's hand.

Emma spun around, her eyes wide with panic. "Sarah! Hannah!" she called out, her voice lost in the cacophony of the market. She caught a glimpse of Sarah's terrified face, saw Hannah's small form being swept away by the crowd. Then, in an instant, they were gone, swallowed up by the sea of people.

Emma stood frozen, her heart pounding. The noise of the market faded to a dull roar in her ears as the reality of the situation sank in. She was alone, separated from her friends in a part of London she barely knew.

"Sarah! Hannah!" Her voice cracked.

A burly man shoved past her, nearly knocking Emma off her feet. She stumbled, catching herself on a nearby stall. The vendor barked at her to move along, but Emma barely heard him. Her focus remained on the sea of unfamiliar faces surrounding her.

Panic clawed at her throat as she realised she could no longer see Sarah or Hannah. The crowd seemed to close in, bodies pressing against her from all sides. Emma's breath came in short gasps, the smell of unwashed bodies and rotting vegetables threatening to overwhelm her.

"Please, have you seen two girls?" she pleaded with a woman carrying a basket of fish. The woman merely shook her head and hurried on.

Emma spun around, searching for any familiar landmark. But the market stalls all blurred together, a dizzying maze of canvas and wood. She had no idea which direction they'd come from or where Sarah and Hannah might have gone.

A child's cry pierced the air, and Emma's heart leapt. "Hannah?" she called, pushing towards the sound. But it was just another market urchin, wailing for its mother.

The crowd seemed to carry Emma along like a leaf in a stream. She found herself being pushed down unfamiliar streets, the gas lamps casting long shadows across cobblestones she'd never seen before. The market's noise faded behind her, replaced by the eerie quiet of sleeping houses.

Emma's steps slowed as she realised she was utterly lost. The narrow streets loomed over her, dark and forbidding. She hugged herself tightly, her thin shawl offering little comfort against the chill night air.

"Oh Lord," her voice trembled, "please help me find them."

MAZE OF SHADOWS

As her breathing slowed, Emma took in her surroundings. Narrow, winding alleys stretched out before her, their cobblestones slick with something she didn't want to contemplate. Tall buildings loomed on either side, their upper stories jutting out over the street as if reaching for one another. The overhanging structures blocked out most of the night sky, leaving only slivers of starlight visible between the crooked rooflines.

The distant sounds of the market grew fainter with each passing moment. Emma strained her ears, hoping to catch a familiar voice or the echo of footsteps, but all she heard was the occasional scurrying of rats and the muffled voices of unseen residents behind shuttered windows.

A chill wind whispered through the alley, carrying with it the stench of rotting garbage and human waste. Emma wrapped her thin shawl tighter around her shoulders, shivering despite the lingering warmth of the summer night. She took a tentative step forward, then another, her eyes darting from shadow to shadow.

The labyrinth of streets seemed to shift and change with

each turn. Emma found herself passing the same crooked doorway twice, then thrice, panic rising in her as she realised she was walking in circles. Every alley looked the same in the dim light – a maze of crumbling brick and peeling paint, with no sign of which way might lead back to the familiar parts of the city.

Emma closed her eyes. "Lord," she prayed, her voice barely audible above the distant sounds of the city, "guide my steps and grant me courage. I am lost, but I know You are with me."

As the words left her lips, a sense of calm washed over her. The panic that had threatened to overwhelm her moments ago receded like the tide, leaving behind a quiet resolve. Emma took a deep breath, inhaling the pungent air of the unfamiliar streets, and opened her eyes.

In the darkness, her mother's face swam before her – kind eyes crinkling at the corners, weathered hands clasping her own as they knelt in prayer together. "Emma, my little dear," her mother's voice echoed in her memory, "faith is a light that shines brightest in the darkest places."

A ghost of a smile tugged at Emma's lips as she remembered Thomas, his eyes bright with determination even in the gloom of the workhouse. How many times had they huddled together, whispering dreams of a better life beyond those oppressive walls? His unwavering belief in their shared vision had been a constant source of strength, pushing her forward when despair threatened to drag her under.

Drawing upon these memories, Emma squared her shoulders and took a tentative step forward. The fear still lingered, a cold knot in the pit of her stomach, but it no longer paralysed her. She may not know where she was or what dangers lurked in the shadows, but she knew who she was – Emma Grace Redbrook, a child of God, forged in the fires of adversity.

With each step, her confidence grew. The maze-like alleys were still confusing, but Emma approached each turn with renewed purpose. She would find her way out of this labyrinth, just as she had found her way through every other challenge life had thrown at her.

Emma's eyes darted from shadow to shadow, her mind cataloguing every detail of the unfamiliar streets. A crooked lamppost caught her attention, its flickering light casting eerie shadows across the cobblestones. She committed its unique silhouette to memory, using it as a beacon to orient herself in the maze-like alleys.

As she crept forward, a door painted a vibrant shade of blue stood out against the drab facades. Emma noted its position, creating a mental map of her surroundings. Each landmark became a breadcrumb, guiding her through the labyrinth of London's underbelly.

Her feet found a patch of cobblestones that felt different underfoot – smoother, less worn than the others. Emma paused, committing the sensation to memory. This subtle change in texture could be her lifeline if she needed to retrace her steps.

The oppressive darkness pressed in on all sides, threatening to swallow her whole. But Emma's inner resolve burned bright, a flame kindled by years of hardship and faith.

Side streets branched off like spindly fingers, each one a potential haven or trap. Emma weighed her options carefully, choosing paths that offered the most cover. She hugged the walls, her slight frame melting into the shadows as she explored each new alley.

Every sound – a distant shout, the scrabbling of rats, the creak of a shutter – sent Emma's heart racing. But she forced herself to breathe slowly, to think clearly. She couldn't afford to panic, not when Sarah and Hannah might still be out there, lost and alone.

A flash of movement caught her attention. Emma pressed herself against a grimy wall, barely daring to breathe as Brock's hulking figure lumbered past the mouth of the alley. His massive frame blocked out what little light filtered down from the narrow strip of sky above. Emma's fingers dug into the rough brickwork behind her, willing herself to become one with the shadows.

As Brock's heavy footsteps faded, Emma allowed herself a shaky exhale. But her relief was short-lived. A familiar, weaselly figure slipped into view, his eyes scanning the alleyway with unsettling intensity. Silas. Emma's stomach churned at the sight of him, remembering all the times she'd caught him spying on the children, his quill scratching furiously in that ever-present notebook.

Emma inched along the wall, her movements slow and deliberate. Every muscle in her body screamed for her to run, but she forced herself to remain calm. Panic would only lead to mistakes, and she couldn't afford any now.

A stack of wooden crates loomed ahead, offering a moment's refuge. Emma darted behind them, her heart in her throat as she heard Brock's voice booming nearby.

"Where are you, you little rats?" His words were punctuated by the sound of something – or someone – being shoved roughly against a wall. "Nobody gets away from us." He spat. "No one." The pride in his voice was terrifying. This was no longer for Mr Grimshaw and the workhouse. This was personal.

Emma curled into herself, making her already small frame even tinier. She held her breath as Brock's heavy footsteps drew nearer. Through a gap in the crates, she caught a glimpse of his face, those cold steel-grey eyes scanning the alley with predatory intensity.

Brock's massive form lumbered past her hiding spot.

Emma held her breath, willing herself to become one with the shadows that cloaked her. As soon as the hulking enforcer moved out of sight, Emma seized her chance.

With nimble steps honed by years of avoiding trouble in the

workhouse, she slipped from behind the crates. Her eyes darted left and right, searching for any sign of Silas's weaselly figure. The coast seemed clear, but Emma knew better than to trust appearances.

She moved swiftly, her bare feet barely making a sound on the damp cobblestones. The hem of her tattered dress whispered against her ankles as she ducked into a narrow alley, barely wide enough for her slender frame. The brick walls on either side seemed to close in, but Emma pushed forward, ignoring the claustrophobic feeling that threatened to overwhelm her.

A rat scurried across her path, its beady eyes glinting in the dim light. Emma bit back a startled gasp, pressing a hand to her mouth to stifle any sound. She paused, listening intently for any sign that her pursuers had heard her momentary lapse.

Silence reigned for a heartbeat, then two. Just as Emma began to relax, a distant voice reached her ears. Silas, his nasal tones carrying through the twisting alleys. "I swear I heard something, Mr. Thornhill. This way!"

Emma's blood ran cold. Without a second thought, she bolted down the alley, her feet carrying her swiftly away from the approaching danger. She turned one corner, then another, her mind racing to keep track of her path through this urban maze.

Emma's weary feet carried her through the winding alleys, her heart pounding with each distant shout or sudden movement in the shadows. The unfamiliar streets seemed to shift and change with every turn, leaving her disoriented again and increasingly desperate. As she rounded yet another corner, a flicker of hope ignited in her chest.

There, nestled between two looming tenements, stood a small church. Its weathered stone facade bore the marks of years of neglect, ivy creeping up the walls and obscuring faded carvings. The wooden door hung slightly ajar, as if inviting her in.

Emma hesitated, her body tensed to flee at the slightest sign of danger. She edged closer to the entrance, her fingers brushing against the rough wood of the door frame. Peering inside, she saw rows of dusty pews bathed in the soft glow of a few guttering candles. The air was heavy with the scent of old incense and damp stone.

For a moment, Emma stood frozen on the threshold. The empty church offered a promise of sanctuary, a brief respite from the dangers lurking in the streets behind her. Yet the shadows that cloaked the corners of the nave whispered of potential hiding places for unseen threats.

Emma's gaze darted back to the alley, straining to catch any sign of pursuit. The distant echo of Brock's gruff voice sent a shiver down her spine. With a silent prayer on her lips, she slipped inside the church, easing the door closed behind her.

REST AMONG THE PEWS

Emma crept through the dimly lit church, her footsteps echoing softly in the cavernous space. The flickering candlelight cast long shadows across the worn stone floor, and the musty scent of old hymnals filled her nostrils. She made her way to the altar, her legs trembling with exhaustion and fear.

She knelt before the weathered wooden cross. "Lord," she whispered in the silence of the empty church, "please watch over Sarah and Hannah. Keep them safe from harm." Emma's thoughts turned to the chaos of their escape, the acrid smell of smoke still clinging to her clothes. "Guide them to shelter, and... and guide me to them."

Emma's prayer faltered as she struggled to find the right words. How could she ask for more when she'd already been granted the miracle of escape? Still, she pressed on, her faith a flickering flame in the darkness. "Give me strength, Lord. The strength to keep going, to find my friends, to..."

She trailed off, overwhelmed by the enormity of the task before her. Emma took a deep breath, steadying herself. In the quiet of the church, she allowed her racing thoughts to slow, considering her next move.

She couldn't stay here long – Brock and Silas were still out there, hunting for her and the others. But she needed a plan, a destination. The streets of London stretched out in her mind, a confusing maze of possibilities and dangers.

Emma's body ached for rest, her eyelids heavy with fatigue. She knew she couldn't keep running forever. Just a few moments of respite, she decided, to gather her strength and her wits. Then she would venture out again, continuing her search for Sarah and Hannah.

With a final, silent prayer, Emma rose from her knees. She scanned the church for a safe place to rest, her eyes settling on a shadowy alcove behind a statue of the Virgin Mary. It would offer some protection if anyone entered the church, while still allowing her a clear view of the door.

∼

EMMA'S EYES FLUTTERED OPEN, the brief respite having done little to ease her bone-deep weariness. Still, a flicker of renewed determination sparked within her. She pushed herself up from the cold stone floor, her muscles protesting the movement.

In the minimal light, Emma's gaze fell upon a discarded prayer book. She gently pried it open, finding a scrap of paper and a stubby pencil tucked inside. With trembling fingers, she scrawled a hasty note:

"Sarah, Hannah - If you find this, I'm searching for you. Stay safe. Trust in God. I'll return here when I can. - Emma"

She tucked the note beneath the Virgin Mary statue, praying it would reach her friends if they stumbled upon this sanctuary.

Emma crept towards the church's heavy wooden door, her heart thundering. She pressed her ear against the rough grain, listening intently for any sign of pursuit. Hearing nothing but the distant rumble of carriages, she took a quick breath and eased the door open.

The chill night air nipped at her face as Emma slipped out onto the cobblestone street. London sprawled before her, a labyrinth of shadows and flickering gaslights. The vastness of the city threatened to overwhelm her, but Emma squared her shoulders.

"Lord, guide my steps," she whispered, her words barely audible above the city's nocturnal chorus.

With one last glance at the church's spire, silhouetted against the starry sky, Emma set off into the night. Her feet carried her swiftly down the winding streets, eyes darting from shadow to shadow, searching for any sign of her friends or their pursuers.

AMONG THE LOST

                                                                                ❦

*E*mma hunched her slender frame against the biting cold, her tattered shawl offering scant protection from the chill that seemed to seep into her very bones. The foggy, gas-lit streets of London stretched before her, a maze of shadows and flickering light that both concealed and revealed.

She moved with cautious steps. The cacophony of the city assaulted her senses. Horse-drawn carriages clattered past, their wheels sending up sprays of muddy water. Street vendors called out their wares in raucous voices, hawking everything from hot chestnuts to yesterday's newspapers. The smell of coal smoke hung heavy in the air, mingling with the less savory odors of the crowded streets.

Emma wove her way through the throng, her body tense and ready to bolt at the first sign of danger. The fear of capture was a constant companion, as ever-present as the fog that clung to her damp clothes. In her mind's eye, she saw The Brute's hulking form, his meaty fists clenched and ready to strike. And lurking in the shadows, she imagined "The Snitch", his watery eyes gleaming with malice as he waited to betray her whereabouts.

A group of rowdy men stumbled out of a nearby pub, their laughter harsh and grating. Emma pressed herself against a wall, willing herself to become invisible. As they passed, she caught a whiff of cheap gin and unwashed bodies. She held her breath, not daring to move until their footsteps faded into the distance.

Her stomach growled, a painful reminder of the meals she'd missed since fleeing the workhouse.

A deep sigh escaped her chapped lips as her mind wandered to the chaos of their escape. Sarah's face swam before her eyes, those large brown eyes wide with fear as they'd been separated in the crowd. Emma could almost hear Sarah's soft voice, usually so full of quiet determination, calling out her name before being swallowed by the din of the market.

Then there was Hannah, sweet little Hannah with her bright blue eyes and quick mind. Emma's heart clenched as she recalled the panic on the young girl's face as they'd lost sight of each other. She prayed fervently that Hannah's cleverness would keep her safe in these dangerous streets.

Emma's thoughts drifted to Lucy, sent away from the workhouse over a year ago. Lucy, with her sharp tongue and sharper wits, who'd always seemed to know how to navigate the harsh realities of their world. Oh, how Emma longed for her friend's guidance now. Where was Lucy? Had she found a better life beyond the workhouse walls, or had the unforgiving streets of London claimed her too?

Hunger gnawed at Emma's belly, a constant, aching companion. She closed her eyes, leaning her head back against the rough stone. "Lord, please watch over them. Keep Sarah and Hannah safe. And Lucy... wherever she may be."

After the rabble of men had passed, Emma began to trudge through the winding alleys again, her feet aching with each step on the uneven cobblestones. The stench of open sewers assaulted her nostrils, a foul mixture of human waste and rotting refuse that made her stomach churn.

Towering tenements loomed on either side of the narrow street, their facades crumbling and stained with soot. Windows, many with broken panes hastily patched with scraps of cloth or paper, stared down at her like hollow eyes. The buildings leaned towards each other, nearly touching overhead, creating a claustrophobic tunnel that seemed to trap the pervasive smell of coal smoke and decay.

As she rounded a corner, Emma's heart clenched at the sight before her. A group of ragged children, their faces smudged with dirt and eyes hollow with hunger, huddled around a small fire burning in a rusted barrel. They stretched out thin hands, begging passersby for any morsel of food or spare coin. Emma's own empty stomach twisted with empathy.

Further down the street, a haggard woman with sunken cheeks stood at a corner, her trembling hands holding out a meagre collection of wilted flowers for sale. "Violets, miss?" she called out weakly to Emma, her voice cracking with desperation. "Only a penny a bunch."

Emma's gaze was drawn to an open doorway, where she caught a glimpse of a cramped room beyond. Multiple families seemed to share the tiny space, with pallets crowding the floor and laundry strung across the ceiling. The sound of a baby's cry mingled with harsh coughing, a stark reminder of the illness that lurked in these overcrowded conditions.

As she passed an alley, Emma overheard a heated argument. Two men, their clothes patched and worn, were fighting over a half-rotten apple they'd found in the gutter. The desperation in their voices made Emma's heart ache.

Emma's shoulders sagged. The once-vibrant flame of hope that had sustained her through years in Grimshaw's Workhouse flickered dangerously low, buffeted by the harsh realities of London's underbelly.

She found a small alcove between two crumbling buildings, barely wide enough for her thin frame. Emma wedged herself into the space, grateful for even this small shelter from prying eyes and the biting wind. Her body shook uncontrollably, teeth chattering as the cold seeped through her threadbare dress and into her very marrow.

The sights and sounds of misery surrounded her. A child's wail pierced the air, quickly muffled by a harsh adult voice. The stench of unwashed bodies and rotting refuse made Emma's empty stomach roil. She closed her eyes, trying to shut out the world, but the images of suffering were etched on the back of her eyelids.

"Lord..." The words caught in her throat as a tear slipped down her grimy cheek. "Please..." Emma's voice broke, the prayer dying on her lips.

For the first time since losing her parents, Emma felt her faith waver. The God who had been her constant companion through years of hardship seemed distant and silent in this moment of utter desolation. She squeezed her eyes shut, another tear joining the first as she struggled to find the words to pray for deliverance.

A KIND STRANGER

*E*mma huddled in the alcove, her body trembling from cold and hunger. The sounds of misery surrounding her seemed to grow louder, drowning out the faint whispers of hope she'd clung to for so long. She closed her eyes, trying to summon the strength to pray.

A gentle voice cut through the cacophony of the slums. "My dear, are you quite all right?"

Emma's eyes fluttered open, focusing on the figure before her. A woman stood there, her rich, jewel-toned dress a stark contrast to the drab greys and browns of the alley. Deep green eyes regarded Emma with concern, set in a face framed by an elaborate updo of auburn hair.

"I... I'm..." Emma's voice cracked, her words failing her.

The woman's expression softened. "You poor thing. You must be freezing." She knelt down, seemingly unconcerned about dirtying her fine dress. "I'm Mrs Joanna Hartley. What's your name, dear?"

"Emma," she managed to whisper. "Emma Grace Redbrook."

Mrs Hartley's low, melodious voice carried the refined accent of an educated background. "Well, Miss Redbrook, it simply won't do to leave you out here in this dreadful cold." She extended a gloved hand. "I run a boarding house not far from here. Would you like to come with me? Get warm, have something to eat?"

Emma hesitated. The offer of warmth and food was tempting beyond measure, but years in Grimshaw's Workhouse had taught her to be wary of unexpected kindness. She glanced around the alley, taking in the squalor and desperation that surrounded her.

Mrs Hartley seemed to sense her indecision. "I understand your caution, my dear. But I assure you, I mean you no harm. It would ease my conscience greatly to know you're safe and cared for, even if just for tonight."

Emma's gaze returned to Mrs. Hartley's face, searching for any sign of deceit. She found only warmth and concern in those captivating green eyes. Exhaustion weighed heavily on Emma's shoulders, and her empty stomach clenched painfully.

With a small nod, Emma reached out and took Mrs. Hartley's offered hand.

∼

Emma followed Mrs Hartley through the winding streets. The chill of the night air nipped at her exposed skin, making her shiver despite the warmth of Mrs Hartley's gloved hand guiding her along.

As they rounded a corner, a three-story townhouse came into view. Its facade, though showing signs of age, stood in stark contrast to the grimy streets they'd just traversed. Emma's eyes widened slightly, taking in the respectable appearance of the building.

Mrs Hartley led her up the front steps, producing a key from her reticule. The lock clicked open, and Emma found herself ushered into a dimly lit parlour. The warmth of the room

THE WORKHOUSE ORPHAN'S REDEMPTION

enveloped her immediately, a welcome change from the biting cold outside.

Emma's gaze darted around, taking in her surroundings. Overstuffed furniture filled the space, their rich fabrics a luxury she'd never known. Heavy velvet curtains hung at the windows, muffling the sounds of the street outside. For a brief moment, Emma allowed herself to relax into the comfort of the room, her tense muscles easing ever so slightly.

But as the initial relief faded, Emma's heart began to pound with a mixture of gratitude and suspicion. Her eyes continued to scan the room, noting details that seemed out of place in such a respectable-looking establishment.

A small door, barely noticeable, was set into one wall. Emma's gaze lingered on it, wondering what purpose such a hidden entrance might serve. As Mrs Hartley moved about the room, lighting lamps, Emma noticed several small compartments built into the furniture and walls. They were cleverly disguised, but Emma's keen eye, honed by years of watchfulness in the workhouse, picked them out easily.

These hidden spaces, clearly designed for concealment, sent a shiver down Emma's spine that had nothing to do with the cold she'd left behind.

Emma's stomach growled audibly as Mrs Hartley set a bowl of steaming soup before her. The aroma wafted up, making her mouth water instantly. She hesitated for a moment, looking up at Mrs. Hartley, seeking permission.

"Go on, child. Eat," Mrs Hartley urged, her voice softer than Emma had expected.

Emma didn't need to be told twice. She lifted the spoon with trembling hands and brought it to her lips. The warm broth slid down her throat, igniting a fire of hunger in her belly. It wasn't the richest fare – just a simple vegetable soup with a few chunks of potato and carrot – but to Emma, it tasted like ambrosia.

She ate ravenously, barely pausing between spoonfuls. The

warmth spread through her body, chasing away the chill that had settled in her bones during her day on the streets. When she finished, Emma looked up to find Mrs. Hartley watching her with an unreadable expression.

"Thank you," Emma murmured, suddenly self-conscious of her eagerness.

Mrs Hartley simply nodded and led her up a narrow staircase. They passed several closed doors before stopping at one near the end of the hall. Mrs. Hartley produced a key and unlocked it, ushering Emma inside.

The room was small, with peeling wallpaper and a threadbare rug on the floor. A narrow bed stood against one wall, covered with a thin blanket that had seen better days. A small dresser and a cracked mirror completed the sparse furnishings.

To most, it might have seemed a sorry excuse for a bedroom. But to Emma, who had spent years sleeping on the hard iron beds of Grimshaw's Workhouse, it was a palace. The mattress, though lumpy, yielded beneath her weight as she sat down. Emma ran her hand over the blanket, marvelling at its softness compared to the rough workhouse linens.

"Rest now," Mrs Hartley said, her tone businesslike once more. "We'll talk more in the morning."

With that, she left, closing the door behind her. Emma heard the key turn in the lock, but she was too exhausted to wonder about it. She lay down, pulling the blanket tightly around her shoulders.

As she lay there, Emma's mind raced with thoughts of Sarah and Hannah. Where were they now? Had they found shelter? Were they safe? She sent up a silent prayer for their protection, her lips moving wordlessly in the dim room. She also sent up a prayer of thanks to the Lord, for providing her a bed to sleep. Even though it was clear not everything was as simple at it seemed, at least she could sleep.

Despite her whirling thoughts, exhaustion soon began to

overtake her. Emma's eyelids grew heavy, the events of this miserable day catching up with her all at once. She fought against sleep for a few moments, but it was a losing battle. She drifted off into a fitful slumber, her dreams filled with fleeing shadows and the echoing laughter of her lost friends.

A NEW ROUTINE

*E*mma woke to sunlight streaming through the small window of her room. For a moment, she forgot where she was, the unfamiliar softness of the bed confusing her senses. Then reality rushed back, and she sat up, taking in her surroundings with fresh eyes.

Emma's fingers traced the small of her neck, where her silver crossed used to hang as she took in the room's details. The wallpaper, faded and peeling in places, spoke of better days long past. A rickety dresser stood against one wall, its mirror clouded with age.

A sharp rap at the door startled her. Mrs Hartley swept in, her presence filling the small space.

"Good morning, my dear. I trust you slept well?" Her voice was honey-sweet, but her eyes were sharp, assessing.

Emma nodded, not quite trusting her voice.

"Excellent. Come along then, we have matters to discuss."

Emma followed Mrs Hartley through a maze of corridors. The house seemed larger on the inside, full of twists and turns that left Emma disoriented. They finally reached a study, where Mrs Hartley settled behind an ornate desk.

"Now, child, tell me about your prospects. Family? Skills? Anything that might recommend you to a potential employer?"

Emma's throat tightened. "I... I have none, ma'am. My parents are gone, and I've no relatives to speak of."

Mrs Hartley's lips curved into a smile that didn't quite reach her eyes. "I see. And what of your education? Can you read? Write? Keep accounts?"

"I can read and write, ma'am. And I'm quick with figures."

"Hmm." Mrs Hartley tapped her fingers against the desk. "Well, it seems you're in quite the predicament. Fortunately for you, I find myself in need of an assistant. Someone to help with the day-to-day running of this establishment. Would that interest you?"

Emma hesitated. The offer seemed too good to be true, and something in Mrs Hartley's manner set her on edge. But the alternative was the street, with all its dangers and uncertainties.

"I... I would be most grateful for the opportunity, ma'am," Emma said.

～

OVER THE NEXT FEW DAYS, Emma fell into a routine at Mrs. Hartley's boarding house. She helped Fiona MacLeod with the laundry, her nimble fingers quickly adapting to the work. Fiona, a red-haired woman with sharp green eyes, taught Emma tricks to remove stubborn stains and how to press collars just so.

Rose Louson, the head girl, showed Emma how to polish silverware until it gleamed. Her elegant demeanour both intimidated and fascinated Emma, who found herself studying Rose's graceful movements.

Mr. Albert Jenkins, the butler, was a stern-faced man who rarely spoke. But Emma noticed how he slipped extra bread onto her plate at mealtimes, his gruff kindness warming her heart.

Nancy Miller, one of the maids, became a fast friend. Close to Emma's age, Nancy's infectious laugh and quick wit brought moments of lightness to Emma's days.

As the days passed, Emma began to feel a semblance of normalcy. The regular meals and warm bed were luxuries she'd almost forgotten. She found herself humming softly as she worked, surprising herself with the sound.

One evening, as Emma helped Mrs Hartley arrange flowers in the parlour, she found herself opening up. "I never thought I'd feel safe again," she admitted quietly, fingers tracing the soft petals of a rose.

Mrs Hartley's eyes softened. "We all need a refuge sometimes, child."

Encouraged, Emma spoke of her parents, her time in the workhouse, and her daring escape. She hesitated before mentioning Thomas, but found the words spilling out anyway. "He was so brave," she whispered, blinking back tears.

"And your faith?" Mrs. Hartley asked gently. "Has it sustained you through all this?"

Emma nodded. Even when everything else felt like it could disappear in an instant, she knew her faith would always remain.

WHISPERS IN THE DARK

*A*s Emma's days at Mrs Hartley's boarding house settled into a comfortable rhythm, an undercurrent of unease began to grow beneath the surface. As she polished silverware in the dining room one afternoon, a snippet of hushed conversation drifted through the partially open door.

"...can't risk exposure. The Inspector's getting too close."

Emma's hand stilled, the silver fork gleaming in her grip. She strained to hear more, but the voices faded as footsteps retreated down the hall.

Later that evening, as Emma hung freshly pressed linens, she noticed a gentleman in a top hat slip through the back door well past midnight. His furtive glances and hurried pace struck her as odd for a simple boarding house guest.

At breakfast the next morning, Emma caught Rose and Fiona exchanging meaningful looks over their porridge. When Emma asked if everything was all right, Rose's smile seemed strained.

"Of course, dear. Just a busy day ahead."

But Emma's sharp eyes didn't miss how Rose's fingers tightened around her spoon, or how Fiona's gaze darted to the closed parlour door.

As the days passed, Emma began to pay closer attention to the rhythms of the house. She noticed how Mr Jenkins would sometimes disappear for hours, returning with a briefcase he hadn't left with. How Mrs Hartley's ledger was always quickly shut when anyone entered her office.

One night, unable to sleep, Emma crept down to the kitchen for a glass of water. As she approached, she heard muffled voices and paused in the shadows of the hallway.

"...new shipment tomorrow night. We'll need to be discreet."

Emma's heart quickened. She recognised Mrs Hartley's voice, but the tone was different – harder, more impassioned than the business tone she usually employed.

Emma pressed herself against the wall. She strained to hear more, but Mrs Hartley's voice faded as footsteps retreated down the hallway. Slowly, Emma released the breath she'd been holding and crept back to her room, her mind racing with questions.

As she lay in her narrow bed, staring at the shadowy ceiling, Emma's thoughts drifted to Sarah, Hannah, and Lucy. A wave of guilt washed over her. She should have held on tighter to Sarah's hand in the chaos of their escape. She should have called out louder for Hannah when the crowd separated them.

Tears pricked at Emma's eyes as she imagined her friends huddled in some dark alley, cold and afraid. She curled onto her side. "I'm sorry," she whispered into the darkness. "I'm so sorry I couldn't keep us together."

And then there was Thomas…

Emma took a deep breath, steeling herself against the tide of despair. She couldn't change what had happened, but she could honour the memory of those she'd lost by staying true to their shared dream. With renewed resolve, Emma silently vowed to uncover the truth about Mrs Hartley's establishment, to find a way to help others as she and Thomas had once planned.

HIDDEN AGENDAS

*E*mma found herself drawn to the other girls at Mrs Hartley's establishment, their shared circumstances creating an unspoken bond. In quiet moments between chores, she'd catch snippets of their stories, each one a tapestry of hope and hardship.

Ava, a willowy blonde with tired eyes, spoke of a father lost to drink and a mother who couldn't feed her children. "Mrs Hartley offered me a way out," she murmured, her gaze distant. "Sometimes I wonder if I made the right choice."

Emma's heart ached for Ava, recognising the impossible decisions.

It was Nancy, though, a spirited girl with honey-blonde curls, who truly caught Emma's attention. One evening, as they folded linens together, Nancy leaned close.

"Don't let Mrs Hartley's kindness fool you," she murmured. "There's more going on here than meets the eye."

Emma's hands stilled on the crisp fabric. "What do you mean?"

Nancy glanced over her shoulder before continuing. "The

gifts, the fine clothes... they come at a price. One that's higher than you might think."

A chill ran down Emma's spine. She opened her mouth to ask more, but the sound of approaching footsteps silenced them both.

Mr Jenkins, the establishment's imposing butler, rounded the corner. His steel-grey eyes swept over the room, missing nothing. Emma straightened instinctively, feeling his scrutiny.

"Ladies," he intoned, his voice deep and controlled. "Mrs Hartley requests your presence in the parlour."

As they followed Mr Jenkins down the hall, Emma couldn't help but notice the military precision in his movements. His ramrod-straight posture and measured steps spoke of a man accustomed to discipline and order.

While his presence often brought a sense of security to the house, Emma now felt a flicker of unease. She recalled the way he seemed to materialise at the slightest hint of trouble, his watchful gaze always alert for any sign of dissent or disobedience.

Nancy's words echoed in Emma's mind as they entered the parlour. She found herself studying Mrs Hartley's benevolent smile with new eyes, wondering what secrets might lie behind that carefully crafted facade.

Emma's eyes darted between Mrs Hartley's composed features and the knowing glances exchanged by Nancy, Rose, and Fiona. The air felt thick with unspoken understanding, a language Emma couldn't quite decipher.

Mrs Hartley's voice, smooth as honey, filled the room. "Ladies, I'm pleased to announce that our little enterprise is expanding. With this growth comes new opportunities... and new responsibilities."

Emma's brow furrowed as she tried to make sense of Mrs Hartley's words. The woman's eyes gleamed with a mixture of pride and calculation that sent shivers down Emma's spine.

"Some of you will be taking on new roles," Mrs Hartley continued, her gaze lingering on each girl in turn. "I trust you'll rise to the occasion with the same... enthusiasm you've shown thus far."

Nancy's fingers twitched at her side. Rose's chin lifted slightly, a hint of ambition flashing in her eyes. Fiona remained still as stone, but Emma noticed the slight tightening of her jaw.

"Of course, with expansion comes increased risk," Mrs Hartley added, her tone deceptively light. "But I'm sure Mr Jenkins will see to our continued safety and discretion."

The butler inclined his head, a silent affirmation.

Emma's mind raced, trying to piece together the fragments of conversation she'd overheard in recent days. Whispers of late-night visitors, hushed discussions of shipments and clients – they swirled in her thoughts, refusing to form a clear picture.

"Emma, dear," Mrs Hartley's voice cut through her musings. "You've been with us for a short while now. I think it's time we discussed your... particular talents."

She met Mrs Hartley's gaze, searching for any hint of the woman's true intentions.

"Yes, ma'am," Emma replied, her voice steadier than she felt. "I'm eager to be of service."

Mrs Hartley's smile widened, but it didn't reach her eyes. "Excellent. We'll speak more on this later. For now, ladies, you may return to your duties."

As they filed out of the parlour, Emma caught Nancy's eye. The older girl's expression was a mixture of sympathy and warning, leaving Emma with a growing sense of unease about what lay ahead.

A GILDED CAGE

⁓

*E*mma's heart lurched as she crept down the darkened hallway, her footsteps muffled by the thick carpet. The boarding house slumbered around her, but sleep eluded Emma. Nancy's warning and Mrs Hartley's cryptic words had planted seeds of suspicion that refused to be ignored.

She paused at the corner, listening intently for any sign of movement. Satisfied that she was alone, Emma slipped into the parlour where she had first noticed the hidden compartments. Moonlight filtered through the heavy curtains, casting eerie shadows across the room.

Emma's fingers trembled as she ran them along the ornate wainscoting, searching for the catch she had glimpsed Mrs Hartley using days earlier. A soft click rewarded her efforts, and a small panel swung open.

Inside, Emma found a leather-bound ledger. She opened it carefully, squinting in the dim light to make out the cramped handwriting. Columns of figures and cryptic notations filled the pages. Emma's brow furrowed as she tried to decipher their meaning. Though the specifics eluded her, the sheer amount of money involved made her breath catch.

Replacing the ledger, Emma moved to another hidden compartment. This one revealed a stack of letters, some bearing official-looking seals. As she skimmed their contents, Emma's eyes widened. References to "shipments," "special merchandise," and "discrete clientele" painted a disturbing picture.

A floorboard creaked somewhere in the house, startling Emma. She hastily returned the letters to their hiding place, her heart pounding. As she prepared to close the compartment, something caught her eye. A small velvet pouch lay tucked in the back corner.

With trembling hands, Emma opened the pouch. Several gemstones spilled out onto her palm, glittering even in the muted moonlight. Emma stared at them in disbelief, remembering the whispered conversations about jewellery she had overheard among the other girls.

The pieces were beginning to fall into place, forming a picture far darker than Emma had imagined. Mrs Hartley's kindness, the fine clothes, the air of secrecy – it all pointed to something sinister lurking beneath the respectable facade of the boarding house.

Emma quickly crouched behind the heavy velvet curtains in Mrs Hartley's parlour. The sound of approaching voices had sent her scrambling for cover, as she had spent too long looking at the gemstones. Now, she held her breath, afraid even the slightest movement might betray her presence.

The door creaked open, and Mrs Hartley's melodious voice drifted into the room. "Lord Blackthorn, what a pleasure to see you again. Please, make yourself comfortable."

Emma peered through a gap in the curtains, her eyes widening as she took in the sight of the portly gentleman who entered. His silvering blonde hair was meticulously styled, and his waistcoat strained against his ample belly. But it was his eyes that caught Emma's attention – cold and calculating beneath his genial exterior.

"Mrs Hartley, always a delight," Lord Blackthorn replied, his cultured tones at odds with the predatory gleam in his gaze. "I trust everything is... in order?"

Mrs Hartley's laugh tinkled like crystal. "Of course, my lord. Your special requests have been accommodated, as always."

Emma's brow furrowed as she tried to make sense of their cryptic exchange. Before she could ponder further, another set of footsteps approached.

"Ah, Inspector Wilkins," Mrs Hartley purred. "How fortuitous. I believe you and Lord Blackthorn have some matters to discuss."

Emma's breath caught as a stocky man with a square jaw entered her field of vision. His dark eyes darted around the room, assessing every detail with a policeman's practiced gaze.

"Indeed," Inspector Wilkins grunted, his voice low and gravelly. "Your information has proven... most useful, Mrs Hartley."

"I'm pleased to hear it," Mrs Hartley replied smoothly. "Now, gentlemen, shall we retire to my private office? I believe we have much to discuss."

As the trio moved towards the hidden door Emma had discovered nights before, she caught fragments of their hushed conversation. Words like "shipment," "cover," and "payment" drifted back to her, each one adding to the growing knot of dread in her stomach.

∼

EMMA CREPT BACK to her small room, her mind reeling from the revelations of the night. The boarding house that had seemed a sanctuary now felt like a gilded cage, its walls hiding secrets darker than she could have imagined.

As she sat on the edge of her bed, memories of her mother came flooding back. Mary Redbrook's kind eyes and gentle voice seemed to whisper across the years, reminding Emma of the values she'd been raised with.

"What would you do, Mama?" Emma murmured. She could almost hear her father's deep chuckle, imagine John Redbrook's strong hands on her shoulders as he'd guide her through a difficult decision.

The weight of her situation pressed down on Emma. Mrs Hartley had offered her shelter, food, and a semblance of safety – things Emma had desperately needed after her harrowing escape from the workhouse. But at what cost? The ledgers, the jewels, the hushed conversations – they all pointed to a web of deceit and corruption that went against everything Emma believed in.

Thomas's face flashed in her mind, his determined expression as clear as if he were standing before her. Emma remembered their shared dreams of justice, the nights spent planning to expose Mr Grimshaw's cruelty. Thomas had been willing to risk everything for what was right, even when it led to his brutal punishment and separation from Emma.

"Oh, Thomas," Emma whispered, her eyes filling with tears. "What would you do if you were here?"

She knew the answer, even as she asked the question. Thomas would never compromise his principles, no matter how dire the circumstances. His unwavering dedication to justice had been a beacon of hope in the darkness of the workhouse, inspiring Emma to find strength she didn't know she possessed.

BOUND BY SILK AND STEEL

*E*mma's fingers traced the outline of her skin where her mother's silver cross used to lay.

A soft knock at the door pulled Emma from her reverie. Mrs Hartley's voice, smooth as honey, called out, "Emma, dear, might I have a word?"

Emma's heart quickened, but she steadied herself. "Of course, Mrs Hartley." She opened the door, revealing the older woman's impeccably coiffed figure.

Mrs Hartley seemed to glide into the room, her silk dress rustling softly. She perched on the edge of Emma's bed, patting the space beside her. "Come, sit with me, child."

Emma complied, her posture stiff with apprehension.

"You've been with us for some time now," Mrs Hartley began, her voice warm but her eyes sharp. "I hope you've come to see this place as a home of sorts."

Emma nodded cautiously. "You've been very kind to me, Mrs Hartley."

"And yet," Mrs Hartley continued, "I sense a... hesitation in you. A reluctance to fully embrace the opportunities we offer here."

Emma's throat tightened. She knew this moment would come, but facing it still sent a chill down her spine.

Mrs Hartley leaned in, her perfume enveloping Emma. "My dear, you must understand. The world is a cruel place for women like us. What we do here... it's a necessary evil. It provides security, a chance at a better life for girls who would otherwise be trapped in poverty or worse."

Emma's mind flashed to the workhouse, to Sarah and Hannah, to the countless faces of children ground down by a system that saw them as nothing more than cheap labour. She understood the allure of Mrs Hartley's words, the temptation to justify wrongdoing in the name of survival.

But as Mrs Hartley continued to speak, her tone shifted. The warmth in her voice cooled, replaced by something harder, more threatening. "Of course, my dear, this arrangement works both ways. We provide for you, protect you. But we also expect... loyalty. Discretion."

Mrs Hartley's hand closed over Emma's, her grip just a touch too tight to be comforting. "It would be such a shame if you found yourself back on the streets. Or worse, if certain authorities were to learn of your... colourful past."

Emma's heart raced as Mrs Hartley's words hung in the air, a veiled threat wrapped in silk and perfume. The older woman's grip on Emma's hand tightened, her eyes boring into Emma's with an intensity that made her want to shrink away.

"I trust we understand each other, my dear?" Mrs Hartley's voice was soft, but the steel beneath was unmistakable.

Emma nodded, not trusting her voice. Mrs Hartley released her hand and stood, smoothing her skirts. "Excellent. I look forward to seeing you blossom here, Emma." With a final, pointed smile, she stepped out of the room, leaving Emma trembling.

IN THE DAYS THAT FOLLOWED, Emma felt expectation pressing down on her. Meaningful glances from Mrs Hartley, whispered conversations that stopped when she entered a room, and the growing sense that she was being watched at all times set her nerves on edge.

One afternoon, as Emma scrubbed linens in the laundry room, Fiona MacLeod approached her. The Scottish woman's green eyes darted around the room before she leaned in close.

"Be careful, lass," Fiona murmured, her hands busy with folding sheets. "Mrs Hartley's patience has limits. Tread lightly."

Emma's hands stilled for a moment, surprise and gratitude washing over her. She'd thought herself alone in her unease. "Thank you," she whispered back, her voice thick with emotion.

Fiona gave a nearly imperceptible nod before moving away, leaving Emma to ponder her words.

Later that evening, as Emma tidied the parlour, Rose Louson cornered her. The head girl's auburn hair gleamed in the lamplight as she fixed Emma with an appraising look.

"It's time you learned the ropes properly, Emma," Rose said, her tone brisk but not unkind. "Let me show you how to make the most of your... assets."

Emma's stomach churned, but she kept her voice steady. "I appreciate your offer, Miss Louson, but I'm content with my current duties."

Rose's eyes narrowed. "Don't be a fool, girl. Mrs Hartley's generosity only extends so far. You need to pull your weight."

Emma stood straighter, meeting Rose's gaze. "I understand, Miss Louson. But I cannot compromise my principles. I hope you can respect that."

A PRAYER FOR JUSTICE

*E*mma had only meant to fetch a forgotten duster from the parlour, but the hushed voices drifting from Mrs Hartley's private study had caught her attention. She crept along the hallway, the carpet fortunately muffling her footsteps.

Pressing herself against the wall, Emma inched closer to the partially open door. The warm glow of lamplight spilled out, casting long shadows across the floor.

"Now, Lord Blackthorn," Mrs Hartley's silky voice purred, "I'm sure we can come to an arrangement that benefits us both."

Emma's breath caught in her throat as she peered through the crack. Mrs Hartley stood behind her desk, resplendent in a deep burgundy gown. Across from her, a portly gentleman with a thick moustache shifted uncomfortably in his seat.

"It's a delicate matter, Joanna," Lord Blackthorn muttered, mopping his brow with a handkerchief. "If word got out..."

Mrs Hartley's laugh was like tinkling crystal. "My dear Archibald, discretion is our specialty here." She moved around the desk, placing a hand on the lord's shoulder. "Your little indiscretions will remain our secret, provided you ensure that factory inspection bill never sees the light of day."

Emma's stomach churned as she watched Lord Blackthorn nod, relief washing over his features. Mrs. Hartley's smile was triumphant as she guided him to a hidden panel in the wall. It slid open, revealing stacks of banknotes.

"A token of our appreciation for your cooperation," Mrs. Hartley said smoothly. "I trust you'll find it most generous."

As Lord Blackthorn stuffed the money into his coat, Emma backed away, her mind reeling. She'd suspected illegal activities, but this blatant corruption and manipulation of those in power left her breathless.

She quickly took her leave, before her fast breathing could give her away, and she slipped off to bed.

Emma tossed and turned in her narrow bed, sleep eluding her as it had for nights on end. What she'd witnessed pressed down on her chest, making it hard to breathe.

"Lord," she whispered, "guide me. Show me the path of righteousness in this den of sin."

Her mind raced, replaying the scene she'd witnessed between Mrs Hartley and Lord Blackthorn. The casual way they'd discussed corruption and bribery made Emma's skin crawl. She thought of the other girls in the house, some even younger than herself, and her heart ached for their innocence lost.

As the first rays of dawn crept through her window, Emma's resolve solidified. She couldn't stand idly by while such wickedness flourished. But neither could she risk the safety of the other women who, like her, had found shelter here from even worse fates.

Emma slipped from her bed and knelt on the cold floorboards, bowing her head in fervent prayer. "Lord, grant me the wisdom of Solomon and the courage of David," she pleaded. "Help me find a way to bring light to this darkness without endangering those who are already so vulnerable."

As she rose, a plan began to form in Emma's mind. She

would need to be cautious, gathering evidence bit by bit. Perhaps there were others in the house who shared her misgivings – Fiona, with her sharp eyes, or even Mr Jenkins, who sometimes looked troubled when he thought no one was watching.

She would find a way to expose Mrs Hartley's corruption without putting herself or the other girls at risk. It would require patience, cunning, and above all, faith. But as she gazed out at the brightening sky, Emma felt a flicker of hope. God had not abandoned her in the workhouse, and He would not abandon her now.

THREADS OF REBELLION

Emma carefully made her way down the narrow servant's staircase. The early morning light had yet to penetrate the gloomy interior of Mrs Hartley's establishment, but Emma knew she had precious little time before the house stirred to life.

She found Fiona in the laundry room, already hard at work sorting through piles of linens. The Scottish woman's fiery red hair was tucked neatly beneath her cap, her green eyes sharp and alert despite the early hour.

"Mornin', Miss Emma," Fiona said softly, her accent thicker in the quiet of dawn. "You're up early."

Emma glanced over her shoulder before stepping closer. "Fiona, I need your help," she whispered urgently. "I've seen things... heard things. This place isn't what it seems."

Fiona's hands stilled on the sheets she was folding. For a moment, Emma feared she'd made a terrible mistake. But then Fiona's eyes met hers, a glimmer of understanding passing between them.

"Aye, I've had my suspicions," Fiona murmured. "What do you need?"

Emma's relief was palpable. "Information. Access to Mrs Hartley's study when she's out. Anything you can find without raising suspicion."

Fiona nodded, her movements swift and sure as she resumed her work. "I'll do what I can. But be careful, lass. Mrs Hartley's eyes and ears are everywhere."

As if to emphasise Fiona's point, footsteps echoed in the hallway outside. Emma quickly grabbed a pile of linens, feigning work as Mary, one of the newer girls, entered the laundry room.

Mary's eyes were red-rimmed, her face pale with fatigue or worry – perhaps both. She offered a wan smile to Emma and Fiona before settling into her own tasks.

Emma watched her for a moment, noting the tremor in Mary's hands as she sorted through soiled tablecloths. Sensing an opportunity, Emma moved closer, keeping her voice low.

"Are you all right, Mary?" she asked gently.

Mary's lip quivered, and she shook her head almost imperceptibly. "I... I don't know if I can do this," her voice thick with unshed tears. "The things they want us to do... it's not right."

Emma's heart ached for the girl. She reached out, squeezing Mary's hand reassuringly. "You're not alone," Emma said, her voice steady and warm. "We'll find a way out of this, I promise."

Mary's eyes widened, hope and fear warring in her expression. "How?"

Emma glanced at Fiona, who gave an almost imperceptible nod. "Trust me," Emma said. "And stay strong. God hasn't abandoned us, even here."

THE WORK BEGINS

Nimble fingers worked quickly to unlock the hidden compartment, as Emma slipped into Mrs Hartley's study. The house was quiet, most of its occupants still abed, but Emma knew she had precious little time.

Her hazel eyes, sharp and alert despite the early hour, scanned the room for any sign of disturbance. Satisfied she was alone, Emma carefully extracted a leather-bound ledger from its hiding place. She settled into a corner, angling herself to catch the weak morning light filtering through the heavy curtains.

The ledger's pages were filled with neat columns of figures and cryptic notations. Emma's brow furrowed as she deciphered the entries, her quick mind connecting seemingly disparate pieces of information. Here, a record of "donations" from prominent names she recognised from overheard conversations. There, notations of shipments with dates and coded locations.

Emma's fingers trembled slightly as she turned the pages. She longed to confide in Thomas, to seek his steady counsel, but she pushed the thought aside. This was her burden to bear, her mission to see through.

A floorboard creaked in the hallway outside, and Emma froze. She held her breath, straining to hear any approaching footsteps. After a moment of tense silence, she exhaled slowly, her heart still pounding.

With practiced efficiency, Emma copied key details onto a scrap of paper she'd hidden in the hem of her dress. Her handwriting was small and neat, cramming as much information as possible into the limited space. As she worked, Emma's mind raced, piecing together the larger picture of Mrs Hartley's operation.

It was more extensive than she'd initially believed, reaching into the highest echelons of London society. The realisation both thrilled and terrified her. Emma knew she was sitting on a powder keg of information, one that could bring down not just Mrs Hartley, but countless others who benefited from her illegal activities.

THE TIGHTENING GRIP

*E*mma's world at Mrs Hartley's establishment began to shrink. The freedom she'd once enjoyed to move about the house diminished day by day. No longer was she permitted to assist Fiona in the laundry or help Mr Jenkins with his errands. Instead, Emma found herself confined to her small room more often than not, her meals brought up by a stern-faced Rose.

At first, Emma tried to convince herself it was mere coincidence. Perhaps there was simply less work to be done. But as the days wore on, the truth became undeniable. Mrs Hartley was tightening her grip.

One evening, as Emma sat on her narrow bed, Mrs Hartley swept into the room unannounced. Her usually composed features were tight with barely concealed frustration.

"My dear Emma," Mrs Hartley began, her voice syrupy sweet but with an edge that made Emma's skin prickle. "I fear you've misunderstood the nature of our arrangement."

Emma met Mrs Hartley's gaze steadily, though her heart raced beneath her calm exterior. "I'm not sure I take your meaning, ma'am."

Mrs Hartley's smile thinned. "Let me be plain, then. Your continued... reluctance... to fully embrace the opportunities I've presented is becoming problematic. I've been patient, but my patience has limits."

The threat, though veiled, hung heavy in the air between them. A chill ran down Emma's spine, but she kept her expression neutral. "I'm grateful for all you've done for me, Mrs Hartley. Truly, I am."

"Gratitude is all well and good, child," Mrs Hartley replied, her tone hardening. "But it doesn't pay the bills, does it? I took you in when you had nothing. I've clothed you, fed you, given you a roof over your head. And yet, you persist in this... stubbornness."

Emma's mind raced, searching for the right words to placate Mrs Hartley without compromising her principles or her secret mission. She knew she was walking a dangerous line, but the thought of Thomas, of the children still trapped in workhouses across London, steeled her resolve.

"I apologise if I've given offence, ma'am," Emma said softly. "I only wish to serve to the best of my abilities."

Mrs. Hartley studied Emma for a long moment, her eyes cold and calculating. "See that you do, Emma. For both our sakes."

∼

THE LEDGER she'd borrowed from Mrs Hartley's study felt heavy in Emma hands, its contents a damning testimony to the illegal activities that occurred within these walls. She'd nearly finished copying the most incriminating details, but she needed just a few more minutes to complete her task.

As she rounded the corner, a floorboard creaked beneath her feet. Emma froze. The unmistakable sound of approaching footsteps echoed from the adjacent corridor.

"Who's there?" Mr. Jenkins' gruff voice called out.

Panic surged through Emma's veins. She glanced around frantically, searching for a place to hide. Her gaze landed on a heavy velvet curtain draping a nearby window. Without a moment's hesitation, she ducked behind it, pressing herself against the cold glass.

The footsteps drew nearer, each one sending a jolt of fear through Emma's body. She clutched the ledger to her chest, silently praying that Mr. Jenkins wouldn't notice the slight bulge in the curtain.

"Strange," Mr Jenkins muttered to himself. "Could've sworn I heard something."

Emma held her breath as the butler's shadow fell across the curtain. She could see his silhouette through the thick fabric, mere inches away from her hiding spot. For a heart-stopping moment, she thought he might pull back the curtain and discover her.

But then, mercifully, Mr Jenkins turned away. "Must be getting old," he grumbled, his footsteps receding down the hallway.

Emma waited until the sound of his movements had faded entirely before she dared to emerge from her hiding place. Her legs trembled as she stepped out from behind the curtain, the ledger still clutched tightly to her chest.

That had been far too close. Emma's mind raced as she hurried back to her room, her heart still thundering in her ears. She'd have to be more careful, more strategic in her movements. The stakes were too high for careless mistakes.

AN UNEXPECTED ALLY

※

*E*mma sat on her bed, and she found herself yearning for guidance. As if in answer to her unspoken prayer, a soft knock sounded at her door.

"Come in," Emma called.

The door creaked open, revealing Rose Louson's elegant figure. Emma tensed, expecting another lecture on the virtues of compliance. But something in Rose's expression gave her pause.

"May I speak with you, Emma?" Rose asked, her voice uncharacteristically hesitant.

Emma nodded, shifting to make room on the bed. Rose closed the door behind her and perched on the edge, her usual poise momentarily shaken.

"I've been watching you," Rose began, her eyes meeting Emma's. "You're not like the others, are you?"

Emma remained silent, unsure of Rose's intentions.

Rose sighed, her shoulders sagging slightly. "I know what you've been doing, sneaking about and asking questions. It's dangerous, you know."

Emma's heart raced, but she lifted her chin defiantly. "Sometimes doing the right thing is dangerous."

A ghost of a smile flickered across Rose's face. "You remind me of myself, once upon a time. Before... well, before all this." She gestured vaguely at their surroundings.

"What do you want, Rose?" Emma asked, her voice low but firm.

Rose leaned in. "To help you. Mrs Hartley's grip on this place, on all of us... it needs to end. But I can't do it alone."

Emma's eyes widened in surprise. "You want to help me? But why? I thought you were loyal to Mrs Hartley."

"Loyalty born of fear and necessity isn't true loyalty," Rose replied, a hint of bitterness in her tone. "I've been here long enough to know that what goes on in this house isn't right. But you... you have the strength to do something about it."

The woman before Emma, once an intimidating figure of authority, now seemed vulnerable and human. She searched Rose's face for any sign of deception but found only sincerity in her eyes.

"I... I don't know what to say," Emma said, her voice thick with emotion.

Rose reached out and gently squeezed Emma's hand. "You don't have to say anything. Your actions, your unwavering spirit – they say everything for you. You've reminded me of something I thought I'd lost long ago."

Emma tilted her head, curious. "What's that?"

"The courage to stand up for what's right," Rose replied, a hint of shame colouring her words. "I've been complicit in this... this madness for so long, I'd forgotten there was another way."

Emma felt a surge of compassion for the older woman. She squeezed Rose's hand in return. "It's never too late to do the right thing."

Rose's eyes glistened with unshed tears. "Thank you, Emma.

For showing me – showing all of us – that we can still stand up for ourselves. That there's still hope."

Emma nodded, a lump forming in her throat. "What you're offering... it means more than you know."

"I'm willing to help you in any way you need," Rose said, her voice gaining strength. "Whatever it takes to bring Mrs Hartley's operation down."

"Thank you," Emma whispered, the words barely audible but filled with deep gratitude. "Truly, Rose. Thank you."

Rose stood, smoothing her skirts. "I should go before anyone gets suspicious. We'll talk more soon."

As Rose reached for the door handle, Emma called out softly, "Be careful."

Rose turned back, a sad smile playing on her lips. "You too, Emma. You too."

Emma paced her small room, her mind racing with possibilities and dangers. Rose's unexpected alliance weighed upon her, both a comfort and a new complication. She knew she couldn't waste this opportunity, but every step forward felt fraught with peril.

Emma closed her eyes, drawing in a deep breath. She needed help beyond these walls, someone with the authority and moral standing to confront Mrs Hartley's web of corruption.

Reverend Davies' kind face flashed in her memory. He had always been a beacon of hope in the darkness of the workhouse, his gentle words a balm to the children's weary souls. If anyone could be trusted with this delicate task, it was him.

But how to reach him without arousing suspicion? Emma's brow furrowed as she considered her options. Perhaps she could convince Mrs Hartley to allow her a visit to the nearby church, under the guise of seeking spiritual guidance. It wasn't far from the truth, after all.

Emma moved to the small, grimy window, her eyes scanning the tangle of streets below. The enormity of her task threatened to overwhelm her, but she pushed the fear aside. She thought of Thomas, of Sarah and Hannah, of all the children still trapped in places like Grimshaw's Workhouse. Their faces steeled her resolve.

She would find a way to get word to Reverend Davies. With his help and Rose's inside knowledge, they might just have a chance at exposing Mrs Hartley's operation and bring justice to those who had long escaped it.

The moon emerged from behind a cloud, casting a silvery glow over the city. Emma stood straighter, her chin lifting with determination. No matter the obstacles, no matter the danger, she would see this through. For Thomas, for her parents, for all those who couldn't fight for themselves – she would be the change this world so desperately needed.

∽

FIONA, Mary and Rose were working in the dimly lit laundry room when Emma approached them. The hum of the machines provided cover for their hushed conversation. She glanced over her shoulder, ensuring they were alone before speaking.

"I need your help," Emma whispered, her eyes darting between the three women. "But what I'm about to tell you... it's dangerous."

Fiona's brow furrowed, her green eyes sharp with concern. "We're in this together, lass. Go on."

Mary placed a comforting hand on Emma's arm. "We're with you, Emma. This place... it's taken enough from all of us."

Rose nodded in agreement. "Tell us what you need."

Relief washed over Emma as she outlined her plan. "We need to time our actions carefully. There's a ledger in Mrs Hartley's study that records everything. If we can copy its contents when important clients are here, during large transactions..."

"I can help with that," Fiona interjected. "I hear things, notice patterns in the coming and goings."

Rose's eyes narrowed in thought. "And I can create diversions if needed. Keep Mrs Hartley and the others distracted."

Emma felt a surge of hope. "We'll need to be extremely careful. If we're caught..."

"We won't be," Mary said firmly. "We've survived this long. We'll see this through."

The four women huddled closer, their voices dropping even lower as they began to flesh out the details of their plan. Fear and determination tinged the conversation as they spoke, knowing that the path ahead was fraught with danger, but also with the possibility of justice and freedom.

THE REVEREND'S WISDOM

Emma slipped out of the boarding house's back door, the cool night air a welcome relief from the stifling atmosphere inside. Fiona, Rose, and Mary huddled around her, their faces etched with worry and determination.

"Remember, stick to the alleys and avoid the main streets," Fiona whispered, her eyes darting nervously.

Rose pressed a small pouch of coins into Emma's hand. "For a cab, if you need it. Be safe, dear."

Mary squeezed Emma's arm. "God be with you, Emma."

With a nod of gratitude, Emma melted into the shadows of the London night. She moved swiftly, her feet carrying her through a maze of narrow backstreets and dingy passageways. The familiar routes that might lead back to Grimshaw's Workhouse – if it still stood after the fire – were strictly avoided. Emma couldn't risk running into Silas or any other ghosts from her past.

The journey felt endless, each sound making her flinch, every passing shadow a potential threat. But Emma pressed on, driven by the urgency of her mission and the faces of those she sought to help.

At last, the modest spire of Reverend Davies's church came into view. Emma paused, catching her breath and steeling her nerves before approaching the small rectory beside it.

Her knuckles had barely grazed the door when it swung open, revealing the concerned face of Reverend Davies. His eyes widened in recognition.

"Emma? Good heavens, child, come in quickly," he ushered her inside, glancing warily at the empty street before closing the door.

In the warm glow of the rectory's humble sitting room, relief washed over Emma. Reverend Davies settled into a worn armchair, his kind eyes fixed on her with rapt attention.

"Now then, my dear," he said gently, "tell me everything."

Emma began her tale, her words tumbling out in a rush. She spoke of her escape from the workhouse, her time at Mrs Hartley's establishment, and the web of corruption she had uncovered. Reverend Davies listened intently, his brow furrowing deeper with each revelation.

When Emma finished, silence hung heavy in the air. The Reverend leaned forward, his hands clasped tightly.

"This is grave indeed, Emma," he said at last. "But you've done the right thing in coming to me. We must tread carefully, but rest assured, I will help you see this through."

Reverend Davies's words sank in. The weight Emma had been carrying seemed to lift, if only for a moment.

"My child," Reverend Davies said, his voice gentle, "remember that even in the darkest of times, the light of God's love shines through. Your compassion and courage are testament to that light."

He reached for his well-worn Bible, its pages soft and yellowed with age. As he opened it, Emma's eyes were drawn to the familiar text, memories of her mother's teachings flooding back.

"'Let us not become weary in doing good, for at the proper

time we will reap a harvest if we do not give up,'" Reverend Davies read, his finger tracing the words. "Galatians 6:9. Emma, your heart for justice and your care for others is a reflection of God's own heart."

Emma nodded, feeling the truth of his words resonate within her. "But Reverend," she whispered, her voice trembling slightly, "sometimes it feels as though the darkness is too great."

Reverend Davies leaned forward, his eyes kind but intense. "That, my dear, is precisely when we must hold fast to our faith and our principles. It is in the face of great evil that our light shines brightest."

As they prayed together, Emma felt a warmth spreading through her chest. The fears and doubts that had plagued her began to recede, replaced by a quiet determination.

When Emma finally rose to leave, she felt as though a great burden had been lifted from her shoulders. The path ahead was still fraught with danger, but she no longer felt alone in facing it.

"Go with God, Emma," Reverend Davies said as he saw her to the door. "And remember, you carry His light within you."

Emma stepped out into the night, her heart lighter than it had been in weeks. The streets of London, which had seemed so menacing before, now felt less daunting.

A PLAN IN MOTION

Emma's fingers trembled as she stitched the final thread, securing the small notebook within the hem of her dress. The incriminating evidence pressed against her leg, a constant reminder of the perilous task ahead. She took a deep breath, steadying herself as she smoothed out the fabric.

The floorboards creaked softly as Fiona appeared in the doorway. "It's time," she whispered, her eyes darting nervously down the hallway.

Emma nodded, her heart pounding so loudly she feared it might give them away. She followed Fiona down the servants' stairs, each step feeling like a small eternity. At the bottom, Mary and Rose waited, their faces pale with anxiety but eyes bright with determination.

"Remember," Rose murmured, "if anyone asks, we're running an errand for Mrs Hartley."

The cool night air hit Emma's face as they slipped out the back door. London's streets were eerily quiet, the fog muffling their footsteps as they hurried through the winding alleys.

As they neared the meeting point, a shadow detached itself from a doorway. Emma's heart seemed to stop until she recognised Reverend Davies's kind face. Beside him stood a tall man in a policeman's uniform, his expression grave but not unkind.

"Emma," Reverend Davies said softly, "this is Sergeant Alan Fairchild. He's here to help."

Emma curtsied slightly, her eyes meeting the Sergeant's steady gaze. "Thank you for coming, sir," she whispered.

Sergeant Fairchild nodded, his voice low and reassuring. "You're very brave, Miss Redbrook. We'll see this through together."

Emma gazed up at Sergeant Alan Fairchild. His broad shoulders and steady stance spoke of years of police work, but it was his warm brown eyes that truly caught her attention. They radiated kindness and trustworthiness, a stark contrast to the cold, calculating looks she'd grown accustomed to at Mrs Hartley's establishment.

"Miss Redbrook," Sergeant Fairchild said, "please, tell me everything."

Emma took a deep breath. She began to speak, her voice barely above a whisper at first but growing stronger as she recounted her harrowing journey from the workhouse to Mrs Hartley's boarding house. She described the hidden ledgers, the suspicious meetings, and the pressure she faced to participate in illicit activities.

Sergeant Fairchild listened intently, his brow furrowing with concern as Emma detailed the extent of Mrs Hartley's operation. He didn't interrupt, save for the occasional nod or gentle prompt when Emma's voice faltered.

When she finished, Emma felt drained yet oddly relieved. She'd carried this burden alone for so long, and now, standing before this kind-eyed policeman, she dared to hope that justice might finally be served.

Sergeant Fairchild placed a reassuring hand on Emma's shoulder. "Miss Redbrook, I want you to know that your bravery in coming forward is commendable. I give you my word that we will do everything in our power to expose Mrs Hartley's illegal activities and bring her to justice."

Emma's eyes widened. "But sir, what about the other girls? They're not bad people, they're just trapped, like I was."

The sergeant's expression softened. "I understand your concern, Miss Redbrook. Rest assured, our primary goal is to dismantle the criminal operation without harming those who've been exploited. We'll do our utmost to ensure the safety and well-being of the innocent women involved."

Emma's hands shook as she lifted the hem of her dress, her fingers brushing against the rough edges of the small notebook. With a deep breath, she withdrew it, the weight of its contents far greater than its physical form. She extended it towards Sergeant Fairchild, her eyes never leaving his face.

"Here, sir," she said. "Everything I've managed to gather is in here."

Sergeant Fairchild took the notebook gently, his calloused hands a stark contrast to the delicate evidence they now held. Relief washed over her, as if a great burden had been lifted from her shoulders.

Reverend Davies stepped forward, placing a comforting hand on Emma's arm. His warm green eyes twinkled with pride and support as he spoke softly, "You've done well, my child. Your courage in the face of such adversity is truly inspiring."

A lump formed in her throat at the Reverend's kind words. She blinked back tears, overwhelmed by the gravity of the moment and the realisation of how far she had come since her days in the workhouse.

Sergeant Fairchild flipped through the pages of the notebook, his brow furrowing as he absorbed the details Emma had so carefully recorded. With each turn of a page, his expression grew more serious, the lines around his eyes deepening.

After what felt like an eternity to Emma, Sergeant Fairchild looked up, his warm brown eyes meeting hers. "Miss Redbrook," he began, his voice filled with admiration, "I cannot express how truly brave you've been. The information you've gathered here... it's more than we could have hoped for."

Emma felt a flush of pride mingled with fear. "Will it be enough, sir?" she asked.

The sergeant nodded solemnly. "More than enough, I should think. You have my word, Miss Redbrook, that justice will be served. Mrs Hartley and her accomplices will answer for their crimes."

THE FALL OF HARTLEY'S HOUSE

*E*mma stood in the shadows across the street from Mrs Hartley's boarding house. Sergeant Fairchild had insisted she stay back for her own safety, but she couldn't bear to be anywhere else. This was the moment she had risked everything for.

The night was eerily quiet as a group of plainclothes officers approached the building. Emma held her breath. She watched as Sergeant Fairchild knocked on the door, his broad shoulders tense with anticipation.

Mr Jenkins answered, his usual stoic expression faltering at the sight of the policemen. Before he could react, Sergeant Fairchild pushed past him, his men flooding into the house. Emma could hear muffled shouts and the sound of running feet from within.

Moments later, Mrs Hartley appeared at the door, flanked by two officers. Her normally impeccable appearance was in disarray, her hair falling loose from its usual tight bun. Emma had never seen the woman look so dishevelled, so utterly human.

"This is preposterous!" Mrs Hartley shrieked, her voice shrill with panic. "I demand to know the meaning of this!"

Sergeant Fairchild stepped forward, his voice steady and authoritative. "Mrs Joanna Hartley, you are under arrest for running a house of ill repute, blackmail, and corruption."

Emma watched as the colour drained from Mrs Hartley's face. The woman's eyes darted around wildly, as if searching for an escape route. For a moment, her gaze locked with Emma's across the street. Emma saw the flash of recognition, followed quickly by a look of utter betrayal.

As Mrs Hartley was led away in handcuffs, Emma saw other officers emerging from the house, carrying ledgers and boxes filled with documents. She recognised some of the papers – copies of the very ones she had risked so much to uncover.

The quiet night erupted into a flurry of activity as more police carriages arrived, their wheels clattering on the cobblestones.

Her heart raced as she recognised some of the figures being led out in handcuffs. Lord Archibald Blackthorn, his face flushed with indignation, stumbled down the steps. His usual air of aristocratic superiority had vanished, replaced by a look of sheer panic.

"This is outrageous!" Lord Blackthorn bellowed, his voice cracking. "Do you know who I am?"

Emma's eyes widened as she spotted Inspector Alistair Wilkins among the arrested. The corrupt policeman's face was ashen, his eyes darting about like a cornered animal. He seemed to have aged years in mere moments, his crimes etched into every line of his face.

As the night wore on, Emma noticed a shift in the atmosphere. The initial shock and chaos gave way to a tense quiet, punctuated by whispers and furtive glances. She could almost feel the ripples of change spreading outward, knowing that come morning, the news would rock London's elite to its core.

Emma watched as the police escorted the last of the arrested out of the boarding house. The night air was thick with tension, the quiet punctuated only by the occasional shout or clatter of hooves on cobblestones.

As the commotion began to die down, Emma's eyes were drawn to movement near the house's entrance. Fiona emerged, her usually composed face a mask of conflicting emotions. Close behind her came Rose, her shoulders slumped as if a great weight had been lifted from them. Mary followed, her eyes wide and searching.

The three women huddled together on the steps, speaking in hushed tones. Emma hesitated, unsure if she should approach. But then Fiona's eyes met hers across the street, and a flicker of recognition passed between them.

Fiona nudged Rose and Mary, gesturing towards Emma. The three women made their way across the street, their steps hesitant but determined.

"Emma," Fiona whispered as they drew near. "I can hardly believe it."

Rose reached out, grasping Emma's hand in her own. "You did it," she said, her voice thick with emotion. "You actually did it."

Mary's eyes shone with unshed tears. "Thank you," she murmured, her words carrying the years of suppressed hope.

Emma felt a lump form in her throat. "I couldn't have done it without your help," she said softly. "All of you."

The four women stood in silence for a moment, the enormity of what had transpired washing over them. The future stretched out before them, uncertain but filled with possibility.

"What happens now?" Mary asked, her voice trembling slightly.

Rose squared her shoulders, a hint of her old strength returning. "We start over," she said firmly. "We make better lives for ourselves."

Fiona nodded, a small smile playing at the corners of her mouth.

Emma suddenly felt something she hadn't experienced since before the workhouse. It was hope, she realised. Hope for a better future, not just for herself, but for all of them.

A HAPPY REUNION

*E*mma stood in Reverend Davies' small study, her fingers tracing the worn edges of his desk. The events of the past few days swirled in her mind like leaves caught in a whirlwind. She could scarcely believe how much had changed since that fateful night at Mrs Hartley's boarding house.

"You're safe here, Emma," Reverend Davies said, his kind eyes crinkling at the corners. "Sergeant Fairchild and I will make sure of it."

Emma nodded, tears pricking at her eyes. "Thank you, Reverend. I don't know what I would have done without your help."

Sergeant Fairchild cleared his throat, his usually gruff demeanour softened by a hint of warmth. "You've done a brave thing, Miss Redbrook. Your testimony will be crucial in bringing Mrs Hartley and her associates to justice."

A small spark of pride flickered in Emma's chest. She had made a difference, just as she and Thomas had once dreamed of doing. The thought of Thomas sent a pang through her heart, but she pushed it aside, focusing on the present.

"There's something else," Reverend Davies said, a smile

playing at the corners of his mouth. "We've managed to locate Sarah and Hannah."

Emma's heart leapt into her throat. "Sarah and Hannah? They're all right?"

The door to the study creaked open, and Emma turned, her breath catching in her chest. There, standing in the doorway, were Sarah and Hannah, their faces a mixture of joy and disbelief.

"Emma!" Hannah cried, rushing forward to throw her arms around Emma's waist.

Sarah followed close behind, her eyes brimming with tears. "We thought we'd never see you again," she whispered, joining the embrace.

Emma held them tightly, her own tears falling freely. Worries she'd carried for so long began to lift, replaced by an overwhelming sense of relief.

As they pulled apart, Emma noticed the changes in her friends. Both girls looked healthier, their cheeks fuller and their eyes brighter. "You both look well," she said, her voice thick with emotion.

Sarah nodded, wiping her eyes. "We've been lucky. We found work as maids in different houses. It's not easy, but it's better than... before."

Hannah squeezed Emma's hand. "We never forgot what you taught us, Emma. It's helped us so much."

Emma felt a warmth spread through her chest, a feeling of pride and love for these girls who had become like sisters to her. They had survived, they had found safety.

Emma's heart swelled with emotion as she held Sarah and Hannah close. The familiar scent of soap and clean linen clung to them, a stark contrast to the harsh smells of the workhouse they'd once known. She pulled back slightly, her eyes roaming over their faces, drinking in every detail.

"I've missed you both so much," Emma said, her voice thick

with unshed tears. "Every day, I wondered where you were, if you were safe."

Sarah's lip quivered as she spoke. "We thought about you too, Emma. Your lessons... they saved us. We were able to read signs, to write our names. It made all the difference."

Hannah nodded eagerly, her eyes shining. "I even taught some of the younger maids to read in secret, just like you taught us!"

Pride surged through Emma, mixed with a bittersweet ache. These girls had grown so much, had faced the world with the tools she'd given them. She cupped Hannah's face gently, marvelling at the confidence that now radiated from the once-timid girl.

"You've both been so brave," Emma whispered, pulling them close once more. The warmth of their embrace seemed to chase away the lingering chill of fear and loneliness that had haunted her since their separation.

As they stood there, holding each other, a thought suddenly struck Emma. She pulled back, her eyes bright with an idea. "What if... what if we went back? To see the workhouse?"

Sarah's brow furrowed. "The workhouse? But why?"

Emma took a deep breath, her mind racing. "It burned down, didn't it? Maybe... maybe seeing it might help us put it all behind us. To really believe it's over."

Hannah's eyes widened, a mix of fear and curiosity flickering across her face. "Do you think it would be safe?"

Emma glanced at Sergeant Fairchild, who had been watching their reunion with a soft expression. He nodded slightly, understanding her unspoken question.

"I think it might be good for us," Emma said softly, squeezing their hands. "To face it together, one last time."

Sarah and Hannah exchanged a look, a silent communication passing between them. Finally, Sarah nodded. "All right, Emma. If you think it will help... we'll go with you."

FAITH AMONG RUINS

Emma stood before the charred ruins of Grimshaw's Workhouse, her heart heavy with memories. The once-imposing structure now lay in crumbling heaps, its walls blackened and skeletal. Sarah and Hannah flanked her, their hands clasped tightly in hers.

Emma closed her eyes, remembering the countless souls who had suffered within these walls. She thought of the children who had never known kindness, of the dreams that had been crushed beneath Mr Grimshaw's cruel regime.

No one knew where Mr Grimshaw and his cruel wife had gone, or if they had even escaped the fire. It seemed to Emma like they may never truly know, but the memories and scars of their wrath and oppression remained, this burnt carcass of a building the largest scar.

"Let us pray," Emma said softly.

The three young women bowed their heads, and Emma's words rose into the still air. "Lord, we ask for Your mercy on all those who endured hardship and pain in this place. May they find peace in Your loving embrace. We remember those who did not survive, and we honour their memory."

As she spoke, Emma's thoughts turned to Thomas. Her heart ached with the memory of his kind eyes and rebellious spirit. She prayed silently for his safety and well-being, wherever he might be.

"And Lord," Emma continued, her voice growing stronger, "we thank You for Your guidance and protection. You have led us through dark times and brought us into the light. May we always remember Your love and carry it with us as we move forward."

When the prayer ended, Emma opened her eyes. She gazed at the ruins, no longer seeing a place of despair, but a testament to survival and hope. Her journey had been fraught with danger – from the desperate days following her parents' deaths to the perilous escape from the workhouse, and the moral quagmire of Mrs Hartley's establishment.

Yet through it all, her faith had been her anchor. It had given her strength when she felt weak, courage when she was afraid, and hope when all seemed lost.

Emma turned to Sarah and Hannah, her deep hazel eyes shining with renewed purpose. She saw in their faces the same strength and resilience that had carried them through their trials. They had all grown, not just in years, but in spirit.

PART III
THE CRUCIBLE OF KINDNESS

She openeth her mouth with wisdom; and in her tongue is the law of kindness.
– Proverbs 31:26

AUNT AGATHA'S PROPOSAL

*E*mma's act of courage in exposing Mrs Hartley's illegal activities sent ripples through London's high society. The story of a young woman who had overcome the horrors of Grimshaw's Workhouse, only to find herself ensnared in another web of corruption, captivated the imagination of the upper classes. It was a tale of resilience, faith, and unwavering moral conviction that stood in stark contrast to the scandals and frivolities that often occupied their gossip.

At Aspendale Manor, the news reached the ears of Aunt Agatha during one of her visits. The spinster aunt, known for her shrewd judgement and keen eye for potential, found herself intrigued by Emma's story. As she sat in the drawing room with her brother, Lord Edmund Aspendale, Aunt Agatha delicately broached the subject.

"I've heard the most fascinating account, Edmund," she began, her voice measured and refined. "A young woman who exposed quite a sordid affair in that boarding house scandal."

Lord Aspendale raised an eyebrow, his interest piqued. "Indeed? I recall hearing something of the sort. Hartley, wasn't it?"

Aunt Agatha nodded, her grey eyes sharp with purpose. "Yes, and the girl responsible – Emma Grace Redbrook, I believe – seems to be quite remarkable. Orphaned, survived that dreadful Grimshaw's Workhouse, and still maintained her principles in the face of temptation and threat."

She paused, allowing her words to sink in. Lord Aspendale's brow furrowed slightly, sensing there was more to his sister's interest than mere gossip.

"Such strength of character is rare these days, wouldn't you agree?" Aunt Agatha continued. "I was thinking... perhaps we might consider offering her a position here. As a laundress, perhaps. It would be a charitable act, of course, but I suspect she could prove to be quite an asset to the household."

∼

Emma Grace Redbrook stood before the wrought-iron gates of Aspendale Manor with the cold nipping at her cheeks. The long, tree-lined driveway stretched before her, leading to a sight that took her breath away. The Manor itself loomed in the distance, a magnificent Georgian mansion that dwarfed any building Emma had ever seen.

As she approached, the manicured gardens came into view. Perfectly trimmed hedges lined winding paths, and vibrant flower beds burst with colour. Fountains tinkled merrily, their water sparkling in the sunlight. Emma's eyes widened, drinking in every detail of this new world.

Tall windows reflected the afternoon sun, and intricate stonework adorned every corner. Emma's footsteps faltered as she reached the grand entrance, suddenly aware of her threadbare dress and worn shoes. She felt her grip unconsciously tighten on the letter of invitation she held tightly in her hand. She had a right to be here... She hoped.

With a deep breath, she pushed open the heavy gate and

knocked on the solid oak door. As she stepped into the entry hall, the grandeur within nearly overwhelmed her senses. A sweeping staircase dominated the space, its polished banister gleaming. Crystal chandeliers hung from the high ceiling, casting prismatic light across the marble floor. Family portraits lined the walls, stern faces peering down at her from ornate gilt frames.

"Miss Redbrook, I presume?"

The crisp voice startled Emma from her awe. She turned to find a tall, dignified man regarding her with a measured gaze. His silver hair was impeccably groomed, and his black tailcoat was without a wrinkle.

"Yes, sir," Emma managed, as she held up the letter. "I was invited here."

"So you were. I am Mr Forthworth, the butler," he said, his tone softening slightly. "Welcome to Aspendale Manor."

Before Emma could respond, a warm voice called out from a nearby doorway. "There you are, my dear!"

A plump, matronly woman bustled towards them, her face creased in a kindly smile. "I'm Mrs Tibbs, the housekeeper," she said, taking Emma's hand in both of hers. "We're so pleased to have you join us."

Emma's cheeks flushed at the unexpected kindness.

"Your actions were most commendable, Miss Redbrook," Mr Forthworth said, his crisp tone tinged with warmth. "It takes great courage to stand up for what's right, especially in the face of such... unsavoury characters."

Mrs Tibbs nodded vigorously, her plump hands still clasping Emma's. "Oh yes, dear. We've all heard about how you exposed that dreadful Mrs Hartley. It's not every day we see such bravery in one so young."

Emma's gaze dropped to the polished marble floor, overwhelmed by their kind words. She'd spent so long fighting just to survive, the idea of being praised for her actions felt foreign.

"Thank you," she murmured. "I only did what I thought was right."

Mrs Tibbs patted her hand reassuringly. "And that's exactly why you'll fit in perfectly here, my dear. Once you've learned the ropes, of course." She chuckled warmly. "There's quite a bit to get used to in a house like this, but don't you worry. We'll have you settled in no time."

Mr Forthworth cleared his throat, his posture straightening even further if that were possible. "Indeed. Aspendale Manor has high standards, Miss Redbrook, but I have no doubt you'll rise to meet them. Your determination speaks for itself."

A small spark of hope ignited within Emma. After all she'd been through – the workhouse, Mrs Hartley's establishment, the constant struggle to maintain her principles – could she finally have found a place where she truly belonged?

"Righty then." Mrs Tibbs said. "Shall we give you a tour of the place then?"

FIRST IMPRESSIONS

*E*mma followed Mrs Tibbs through the grand hallways of Aspendale Manor, her eyes wide as she took in the opulent surroundings. Silk wallpaper adorned the walls, interspersed with priceless works of art. Crystal chandeliers cast a warm glow over polished wood floors, each step echoing in the vast space.

As they rounded a corner, Emma's breath caught. There, in a beautifully appointed drawing room, stood Lord Edmund Aspendale himself. His broad-shouldered frame cut an imposing figure, his salt-and-pepper hair neatly combed back. Steel blue eyes fixed upon Emma, studying her with a mixture of curiosity and appraisal.

"My Lord," Mrs Tibbs said with a small curtsy, "may I present Miss Emma Grace Redbrook."

Emma dipped into an awkward curtsy, her cheeks flushing. "It's an honour, my Lord," she managed.

Lord Aspendale's gaze remained steady, but not unkind. "Miss Redbrook," he said, his deep voice resonating through the room. "We've heard much about your... recent experiences. I trust you'll find Aspendale Manor a more suitable environment."

Before Emma could respond, a rustle of silk announced another presence. Lady Victoria Aspendale seemed to glide into the room, the very picture of elegance and refinement. Her honey blonde hair, touched with subtle silver streaks, was perfectly coiffed. Emerald eyes, capable of both warmth and steely determination, swept over Emma.

"Ah, this must be our new addition," Lady Victoria said, her cultured tones measured and polite. She extended a gloved hand towards Emma. "Welcome to Aspendale Manor, Miss Redbrook."

Emma took the proffered hand, marvelling at its softness. "Thank you, my Lady," she said, willing her voice not to tremble. "I'm most grateful for this opportunity."

Lady Victoria's smile was pleasant but distant, a carefully crafted expression that revealed little. "Yes, well, we do hope you'll settle in nicely. Mrs Tibbs will see to your needs, I'm sure."

Emma felt acutely aware of her humble origins in their grand presence. She smoothed her hands over her simple dress, grateful for its cleanliness but painfully conscious of its worn fabric against the backdrop of such luxury.

"We understand you have some experience in laundry work," Lord Aspendale said, his tone matter-of-fact. "Mrs Tibbs will show you to your duties shortly."

Emma nodded, finding her voice. "Yes, my Lord. I'll do my utmost to meet the standards of Aspendale Manor."

A flicker of something – approval, perhaps? – passed across Lord Aspendale's face. Lady Victoria, however, maintained her polite but distant demeanour.

"Very good," Lady Victoria said. "We expect diligence and discretion from all our staff. I trust you understand the importance of that, given your... previous circumstances."

A flush crept up her neck at the veiled reference to Mrs

Hartley's establishment. "Of course, my Lady. You have my word."

Mrs Tibbs cleared her throat softly. "If you'll excuse us, my Lord, my Lady, I'll show Miss Redbrook to her quarters and acquaint her with her duties."

As Emma followed Mrs Tibbs from the room, she caught sight of a figure lingering in the doorway – an older woman with sharp, perceptive grey eyes. The woman's gaze seemed to pierce right through Emma, assessing and calculating. Emma realized this must be Aunt Agatha, the one who had advocated for her employment.

Aunt Agatha gave a small nod, almost imperceptible, before turning away. Emma felt a strange mix of gratitude and unease as she followed Mrs Tibbs towards the servants' quarters, wondering what lay ahead in this new chapter of her life.

THE ART OF LAUNDRY

Emma's fingers moved deftly over the fine linen, her touch gentle yet precise. The laundry room of Aspendale Manor hummed with activity, but Emma remained focused on her task. She'd quickly learned the intricacies of caring for the Aspendales' exquisite wardrobe, each garment requiring specific attention.

As she worked, Emma's mind wandered to her past experiences in laundry work. The harsh conditions of Grimshaw's Workhouse seemed a lifetime away now, yet those skills had laid the foundation for her current position. She took pride in her efficiency, tackling even the most stubborn stains with determination.

Emma's deep hazel eyes narrowed as she examined a delicate lace collar. With utmost care, she applied a mixture of lemon juice and salt, a trick she'd learned from Fiona back at Mrs Hartley's establishment. The yellowed fabric gradually brightened under her ministrations.

Unbeknownst to Emma, Aunt Agatha stood in the doorway, her sharp grey eyes observing the young woman's work. Aunt Agatha's angular face remained impassive, but approval crossed her features as she watched Emma meticulously press a silk evening gown.

Lady Victoria appeared beside Aunt Agatha, her eyebrow raised in silent inquiry. Aunt Agatha leaned in, her voice low but clear.

"I must say, Victoria, the girl has proven quite adept. Her attention to detail is... commendable."

Lady Victoria's gaze swept over Emma, noting the neat pile of freshly laundered and pressed garments. "Indeed," she murmured, her tone measured. "It seems your recommendation was not misplaced."

Emma, oblivious to the scrutiny, continued her work. She carefully hung the evening gown, smoothing out any remaining creases with a practiced hand. Her movements were efficient yet graceful, each action performed with quiet competence.

Emma's days at Aspendale Manor fell into a comfortable rhythm, each one bringing her closer to the household staff. As she worked tirelessly in the laundry room, she found herself under the watchful eye of Mr Forthworth, the butler. His stern demeanour initially intimidated her, but Emma soon discovered a wealth of knowledge and support beneath his formal exterior.

One afternoon, as Emma struggled with a particularly stubborn stain on Lord Edmund's waistcoat, Mr Forthworth appeared at her side. "Allow me to demonstrate, Miss Redbrook," he said, his voice measured. With deft movements, he showed her a technique she'd never seen before. "There's an art to preserving fine fabrics," he explained, a hint of pride in his tone.

From that day forward, Mr Forthworth made a point of sharing his expertise with Emma. He taught her the intricacies of caring for different materials, the proper way to press a gentleman's shirt, and even the correct method for folding napkins for formal dinners. Emma absorbed every lesson eagerly, her eyes bright with interest.

Mrs Tibbs, the housekeeper, took a different approach in her guidance. Her warm, motherly presence was a balm to Emma's spirit, reminding her of the kindness she'd known so briefly with her own mother. "You're doing well, my dear," Mrs Tibbs would say, patting Emma's hand. "Don't be afraid to ask for help if you need it. We're all family here, in a way."

These words touched Emma deeply. She'd known so little true kindness in her life that Mrs Tibbs' gentle encouragement brought tears to her eyes more than once. The housekeeper seemed to sense when Emma was feeling overwhelmed, appearing with a cup of tea or a reassuring smile just when she needed it most.

As the days passed, Emma's quiet diligence and unfailing politeness began to win over the other staff members. In the servants' hall, she found herself included in conversations and inside jokes. The cook's assistant, a cheerful girl named Betsy, often saved a sweet treat for Emma, slipping it to her with a conspiratorial wink.

THE CHILDREN OF ASPENDALE MANOR

Emma's hands moved methodically over the freshly laundered linens, her mind focused on the task at hand. The soft rustle of fabric filled the air as she carefully folded each piece, taking pride in her work. As she reached for another pillowcase, a gentle voice broke through her concentration.

"Miss Redbrook?"

Emma looked up, startled to find Miss Evelyn Aspendale standing in the doorway of the laundry room. The eldest daughter of the household cut an elegant figure in her pale blue dress, her chestnut hair neatly coiffed.

"Miss Aspendale," Emma said, quickly setting aside her work and dropping into a curtsy. "How may I assist you?"

Evelyn's warm brown eyes studied Emma for a moment before she stepped further into the room. "I was hoping we might speak privately for a moment, if you're not too busy."

Emma blinked in surprise but nodded. "Of course, Miss."

Evelyn glanced around the laundry room, her gaze lingering on the neat stacks of linens. "Your work is impeccable," she said softly. "I've noticed how diligently you approach your duties."

A faint blush coloured Emma's cheeks at the unexpected praise. "Thank you, Miss. I simply try to do my best."

Evelyn's lips curved into a small smile. "Your best is quite remarkable, Miss Redbrook. I wonder... would you mind terribly if I joined you for a few moments? There's something I'd like to discuss."

Emma nodded, her curiosity piqued. As Evelyn settled onto a nearby stool, Emma couldn't help but notice the way the young woman's shoulders seemed to relax, as if a weight had been lifted.

"I hope you don't find this too forward," Evelyn began in earnest, "but I've been meaning to speak with you for some time. Your story... your resilience in the face of such adversity... it's truly inspiring."

Emma's hands stilled on the linen she'd been folding. She met Evelyn's gaze, surprised by the genuine warmth she found there.

"Thank you, Miss," Emma said softly, her fingers tracing the edge of the pillowcase she held. "I'm afraid I don't see myself as particularly inspiring. I've simply done what I had to in order to survive."

Evelyn leaned forward, her emerald eyes bright with curiosity. "But that's precisely what makes your story so remarkable, Miss Redbrook. You've faced hardships that most in our circle could scarcely imagine, yet here you stand, unbroken."

A lump formed in Emma's throat. She thought of Thomas, of Sarah and Hannah, of all those who had suffered alongside her. "I wasn't alone," she said. "There were others who helped me along the way, who showed me kindness when the world seemed darkest."

Evelyn nodded, a look of understanding crossing her features. "I see. And yet, you were the one who found the courage to expose Mrs Hartley's illegal activities. That must have been terrifying."

Emma let in a short breath. "It was," Emma admitted. "But I couldn't stand by and watch others suffer when I had the power to help. My faith... it gave me strength when I felt I had none left."

A moment of silence fell between them, broken only by the distant sounds of the household beyond the laundry room door. Emma watched as Evelyn seemed to wrestle with some inner conflict, her brow furrowing slightly.

"Miss Redbrook," Evelyn said at last. "I wonder if you might be willing to share more of your experiences with me. I find myself... rather sheltered in many ways, and I believe I could learn a great deal from someone with your perspective."

Emma blinked, surprised by the request. She studied Evelyn's face, searching for any sign of insincerity, but found only genuine interest and a hint of vulnerability.

Emma hesitated, her mind racing as she considered Evelyn's request. The young woman's sincerity was evident, but years of caution and hardship had taught Emma to be wary of unexpected kindness.

"I'm... honoured by your interest, Miss Aspendale," Emma said carefully, her fingers fidgeting with the edge of a pillowcase. "But I'm not sure my experiences would be of much value to someone in your position."

Evelyn leaned forward, her emerald eyes bright with determination. "On the contrary, Miss Redbrook. I believe your experiences are invaluable. You've seen a side of life that I can scarcely imagine, and yet you've maintained your dignity and your faith. That's... remarkable."

Emma thought of the countless nights in the workhouse, of the desperate moments in Mrs Hartley's establishment, of the strength she'd found in her belief and in the kindness of others.

"It wasn't easy," Emma admitted softly. "There were times when I wanted to give up, to let the darkness win. But I remembered my mother's words, her faith in me. And I thought of the others who needed help, who had no one else to speak for them."

Evelyn nodded, her expression thoughtful. "That's precisely why I'd like to learn from you, Miss Redbrook. Your perspective could help me understand how to use my own position to make a difference."

Emma studied Evelyn's face, searching for any sign of deceit or condescension. But she found only genuine interest and a hint of vulnerability that resonated with her own experiences.

"I suppose," Emma said slowly, "I could share some of my story. But I'm not sure where to begin."

Evelyn's face lit up with a warm smile. "Perhaps you could start with what gave you the courage to stand up to Mrs Hartley? It must have been terrifying to challenge someone so powerful."

Emma took a deep breath, memories of those tense days flooding back.

～

Emma found herself growing more comfortable in the grand halls of Aspendale Manor as the days passed. Her interactions with the Aspendale children, each unique in their own way, began to soften the edges of her initial unease.

One afternoon, as Emma carried a basket of freshly pressed linens, she encountered Frederick Aspendale — the eldest son and the heir — in the corridor. His warm smile immediately put her at ease.

"Miss Redbrook," he greeted her, his voice friendly and earnest. "I hope you're settling in well?"

Emma nodded, a small smile tugging at her lips. "I am, thank you, Mr Aspendale. Everyone has been very kind."

Frederick's eyes crinkled at the corners. "I'm glad to hear it. You know, I've been meaning to ask you about your thoughts on the new factory regulations. I understand you have some... unique insights."

Emma felt a flutter of surprise at his interest. They fell into a brief but engaging discussion about workers' rights and conditions. Frederick listened intently, his questions thoughtful and genuine.

Later that week, Emma was in the library, dusting the shelves. Beatrice Aspendale lounged in a nearby armchair, a book dangling from her fingers.

"Oh, Emma!" Beatrice exclaimed, her hazel eyes twinkling with mischief. "You simply must hear this passage. It's absolutely ridiculous."

Emma paused in her work, listening as Beatrice read aloud, her dramatic inflections sending them both into fits of giggles. As their laughter subsided, Beatrice sighed contentedly.

"It's nice to have someone my own age to share these things with," she admitted. "Most of my acquaintances wouldn't appreciate the humour."

Emma was surprised at the unexpected camaraderie, but it was a welcome surprise.

As she made her way through the manor's winding corridors, Emma often felt Benjamin Aspendale's gaze following her. His bright sea-blue eyes, so similar to his twin sister's, held a mixture of curiosity and skepticism.

One day, as Emma passed him in the hall, Clarence spoke up. "Miss Redbrook," he said, his voice careful. "I saw you speaking with Frederick earlier. You seemed... well-informed on matters of industry."

Emma met his gaze steadily. "I've had some experience in that area, Mr Aspendale."

Clarence nodded slowly, admiration passing across his features. "I see. Perhaps we could discuss it further sometime."

Emma's encounters with Lillian Aspendale were always a breath of fresh air. The youngest Aspendale daughter seemed to appear wherever Emma worked, her eyes alight with enthusiasm.

"Emma!" Lillian exclaimed one afternoon, bounding into the laundry room. "I've just finished a new sketch. Would you like to see it?"

Emma smiled warmly, setting aside her work. "Of course, Miss Lillian. I'd be delighted."

As Lillian eagerly showed off her artwork, chattering about her latest adventure in the manor's gardens, a sense of belonging settled over Emma. It was a feeling both foreign and comforting, like the first rays of sunlight after a long, dark night.

BETWEEN PAGES AND POLISHING

Emma found herself in the manor's conservatory, surrounded by lush greenery and the gentle scent of blooming flowers. Evelyn Aspendale sat nearby, her emerald eyes fixed on a well-worn copy of "Pride and Prejudice." Emma paused in her task of polishing the brass fixtures, drawn in by the peaceful atmosphere.

Evelyn glanced up, a soft smile gracing her features. "Emma, have you read any of Jane Austen?"

"I have, Miss Evelyn," Emma replied, her voice warm with fondness. "Though it's been some time."

Evelyn's eyes lit up. "Oh, which is your favourite?"

"'Persuasion,' I think," Emma admitted. "There's something about Anne Elliot's quiet strength that speaks to me."

Evelyn nodded thoughtfully. "I can see why. You know, I've always dreamed of writing my own novel someday. Something that captures the complexities of human nature, like Austen does."

Emma felt a surge of admiration for the young woman. "I think you'd write beautifully, Miss Evelyn. You have such a keen eye for detail."

Evelyn's cheeks flushed with pleasure. "Thank you, Emma. That means a great deal coming from you. You've seen so much of life... I often wonder what stories you could tell."

As Emma resumed her work, she felt a warmth in her chest. The reserved Miss Evelyn had opened up to her, sharing a piece of her heart. It was a gift Emma treasured, another small thread weaving her into the fabric of Aspendale Manor.

Later that week, Emma struggled with a heavy basket of linens in the laundry room. Suddenly, Frederick appeared at her side, his strong hands reaching for the load.

"Allow me, Miss Redbrook," he said, easily lifting the basket.

"Thank you, Mr. Frederick," Emma said, grateful for the assistance.

As they worked together to hang the sheets, Frederick's curiosity got the better of him. "Emma, if you don't mind me asking, what were your aspirations before... well, before everything?"

Emma paused, considering her answer. "I suppose I dreamed of being a teacher, Mr Frederick. To help children learn and grow, to give them hope for a better future."

Frederick's eyes softened with understanding. "That's a noble aspiration, Emma. And one I believe you're still fulfilling, in your own way. The impact you've had on this household... it's quite remarkable."

Pride fluttered through Emma at his words. "Thank you, Mr. Frederick. That means a great deal to me."

As they continued their task, Emma found herself sharing more about her past experiences and the lessons she'd learned. Frederick listened intently, his respect for her growing with each word.

When Emma had first arrived at the Manor, she couldn't help but notice the shy glances Beatrice cast her way during family dinners. At first, she'd thought nothing of it, but as the days passed, those glances turned into secret smiles and stifled giggles. It was during one particularly tedious dinner, filled with Lord Edmund's droning about business affairs, that Emma caught Beatrice's eye across the table as she was filling Lady Aspendale's glass. The young woman's lips quirked into a mischievous grin, and Emma returned it before she could think better of it.

From that moment on, a silent understanding bloomed between them. Emma would catch Beatrice's gaze during dull moments, and they'd share a look of amusement or exasperation.

One afternoon, as Emma polished silverware in the kitchen, she felt a presence at her elbow. Turning, she found Clarence, the youngest Aspendale son, watching her work with curious eyes.

"May I help?" he asked.

Emma nodded, handing him a soft cloth. They worked in companionable silence, the only sound the gentle clinking of silver. As days passed, Clarence began to seek her out more often, joining her in small tasks around the manor. Their shared silence gradually gave way to quiet conversations.

"Do you ever wonder what's beyond the manor walls, Emma?" Clarence asked one day as they folded linens.

Emma paused, memories of her past flashing through her mind. "I've seen a bit of what's out there, Master Clarence. It can be beautiful, but also very harsh."

Clarence nodded thoughtfully. "I want to invent things that could make life easier for people. Do you think that's possible?"

Emma smiled, touched by his earnest desire to help others. "With determination and a kind heart like yours, I believe anything is possible."

It was a few weeks later when Lillian, the youngest Aspendale daughter, approached Emma in the garden. The girl clutched a sketchbook to her chest, her eyes bright with excitement.

"Emma, would you mind terribly if I sketched you while you work?" Lillian asked. "You have such graceful movements, and I'm trying to capture people in motion."

Touched by the request, Emma agreed. As Lillian sketched, she chattered about her art and her dreams of becoming a renowned painter. Emma listened, offering encouragement and sharing her own experiences of finding beauty in unexpected places.

Their time together became a regular occurrence, with Lillian often seeking Emma's opinion on her latest creation or asking for help in arranging flowers for her still life studies. Emma began looking forward to these moments, cherishing the bond that was forming between them.

OBSERVATIONS AND APPROVALS

⁓

*E*mma's diligence in her duties at Aspendale Manor did not go unnoticed. As the weeks passed, she found herself becoming an integral part of the household, her presence a quiet but steady force that seemed to bring a newfound harmony to the grand estate.

Aunt Agatha's sharp eyes often followed Emma as she moved through the Manor, a thoughtful expression on her face. During afternoon tea with Lady Victoria, Aunt Agatha would casually mention Emma's latest accomplishment or a particularly insightful comment the young woman had made. "That girl has a remarkable spirit," Aunt Agatha would say, her voice carrying just the right hint of admiration. "It's not often one finds such moral fortitude in these trying times."

Lord Edmund, usually so absorbed in his business affairs, began to take note of Emma's unwavering dedication. One afternoon, as Emma polished the silver in the dining room, Lord Edmund entered unexpectedly. He paused, watching her work with meticulous care.

"Miss Redbrook," he said, his voice less gruff than usual. "I must commend you on your attention to detail. It's... refreshing to see such respect for our family's traditions."

Emma looked up, startled but pleased. "Thank you, my Lord. It's an honour to care for such beautiful pieces of your family's history."

A flicker of warmth passed through Lord Edmund's eyes, softening his stern countenance for a brief moment before he nodded and continued on his way.

Even Lady Victoria, who had initially regarded Emma with cool indifference, began to appreciate the young woman's contributions. One morning, as Emma arranged fresh flowers in the drawing room, Lady Victoria entered, her eyes scanning the room critically.

"Well done, Miss Redbrook," Lady Victoria said, her tone carrying a hint of approval. "Your eye for colour is quite... adequate."

Emma curtsied, her heart swelling with pride at the unexpected praise. "Thank you, my Lady. I've learned much from observing your impeccable taste."

Lady Victoria's lips curved into the barest hint of a smile, her steely gaze warming ever so slightly. "Yes, well... carry on," she said, sweeping out of the room with her usual grace.

A GOOD OPPORTUNITY

One morning, as Emma sorted through the day's laundry, she overheard two of the younger maids, Alice and Beth, arguing in hushed tones.

"I told you, it's my turn to serve tea in the drawing room," Alice hissed, her face flushed with anger.

Beth rolled her eyes. "No, it's not. Mrs Tibbs specifically asked me to do it today."

Emma sighed quietly, recognising the potential for this small disagreement to escalate. She approached the girls, her voice soft but firm. "Ladies, perhaps we can find a solution that works for everyone. Alice, why don't you assist Beth with the tea service today? That way, you'll both have a chance to impress Mrs Tibbs, and I'm sure the extra help will be appreciated."

The girls exchanged glances, their anger deflating. "I suppose that could work," Alice mumbled.

"Thank you, Miss Emma," Beth added, a small smile on her face.

Emma nodded, pleased to have diffused the situation. As she turned back to her work, she caught Mrs Tibbs watching from the doorway, an approving nod on the housekeeper's face.

Later that week, Emma found herself face-to-face with a potential disaster. Lady Evelyn burst into the laundry room, her eyes wide with panic. In her hands, she clutched a delicate silk gown, now marred by an ugly ink stain.

"Oh, Emma!" Evelyn cried. "It's ruined! And I'm meant to wear it to Lady Pennington's garden party this afternoon. Whatever shall I do?"

Emma's mind raced, recalling a trick her mother had once shown her. "My Lady, if you'll allow me, I believe I can help."

With steady hands, Emma mixed a paste of salt and lemon juice, carefully applying it to the stain. As she worked, she spoke soothingly to Evelyn, calming the young woman's frayed nerves. After several tense minutes, the ink began to lift.

"There," Emma said, holding up the dress. "It may need a quick press, but the stain is gone."

Evelyn's face lit up with relief and gratitude. "Emma, you're a miracle worker! I don't know what we'd do without you."

∾

EMMA COULDN'T SHAKE the feeling of being watched as she went about her duties in Aspendale Manor. It wasn't an uncomfortable sensation, but rather one that made her stand a little straighter, move a little more deliberately. She'd catch glimpses of Aunt Agatha's sharp grey eyes following her progress, a hint of approval in their depths.

One afternoon, as Emma polished the silver in the dining room, Aunt Agatha approached her with measured steps. "My dear," she said, her voice crisp and refined, "I wonder if you might assist me with a small matter in the library."

Emma's heart quickened. She'd seen the impressive room from afar but had never dared to enter. "Of course, Miss Agatha," she replied, setting aside her polishing cloth.

Aunt Agatha led her through the Manor's winding corridors,

finally pushing open a heavy oak door. The scent of leather and paper enveloped them as they stepped inside. Emma's eyes widened, taking in the floor-to-ceiling shelves laden with books of every size and colour.

"I find myself in need of a particular volume," Aunt Agatha said, her eyes twinkling with something akin to mischief. "Perhaps you could help me locate 'An Inquiry into the Nature and Causes of the Wealth of Nations' by Adam Smith?"

Emma's brow furrowed in concentration as she scanned the shelves, her fingers tracing the spines of books. After a few moments, she located the tome in question, carefully pulling it from its place.

"Well done," Aunt Agatha nodded, taking the book. "Tell me, Emma, are you fond of reading?"

"Very much so, Miss Agatha," Emma replied, her voice soft with reverence for the knowledge surrounding them. "Though I've had little opportunity for it in recent years."

"Then perhaps we should remedy that," Aunt Agatha said, gesturing to the vast collection. "You're welcome to borrow any book that catches your interest, provided it doesn't interfere with your duties."

Emma's heart soared at the prospect. "Thank you, Miss Agatha. I... I don't know what to say."

"Say nothing, my dear. Simply make good use of the opportunity."

A GODSEND

*E*mma's days at Aspendale Manor took on a new rhythm, one that felt increasingly familiar and comforting. She moved through the grand halls with growing confidence, her steps no longer hesitant but purposeful. The Aspendale family's eyes, once curious and distant, now held warmth when they fell upon her.

Lady Victoria's nod of approval as Emma arranged fresh flowers in the drawing room sent a thrill of pride through her chest. Lord Edmund's gentle nod when she brought him his freshly pressed coat spoke volumes. Even young Master Clarence sought her out, eager to share his latest adventure in the gardens.

One evening, as Emma folded linens, she overheard Mrs Tibbs speaking to Mr Forthworth in the corridor.

"That girl's a godsend, I tell you," Mrs. Tibbs said, her voice warm with affection. "Never seen someone take to the household so quickly."

Mr Forthworth's deep chuckle followed. "Indeed. The family's quite taken with her, aren't they?"

Emma's cheeks flushed with pleasure, her heart swelling

with a sense of belonging she'd long thought lost. She hugged the crisp sheets to her chest, breathing in the clean scent that now represented home.

Later that week, as Emma dusted the library shelves, a soft knock at the door drew her attention. Little Lillian Aspendale stood in the doorway, her hands clutched behind her back, a shy smile playing on her lips.

"Miss Emma," Lillian said. "I've something for you."

Emma set aside her feather duster, kneeling to meet Lillian's eye level. "For me? Why, Miss Lillian, you shouldn't have."

Lillian's smile widened as she revealed a small, carefully wrapped package. "It's to say thank you. For being so kind and... and for making Aspendale feel more like home."

With trembling fingers, Emma unwrapped the gift. Inside lay a delicate watercolour painting of the manor's rose garden, Lillian's favorite spot. The colours danced on the paper, capturing the essence of summer blooms and dappled sunlight.

Emma's deep hazel eyes glistened with appreciation as she gazed at the heartfelt gift. "Oh, Miss Lillian," she breathed, her voice thick with emotion. "It's beautiful. Thank you."

∼

EMMA STOOD IN THE LIBRARY, carefully dusting the leather-bound tomes that lined the shelves. The scent of old paper and polished wood filled her nostrils, a far cry from the harsh soap and damp of the workhouse laundry. As she reached for a particularly high shelf, a soft cough behind her made her turn.

Aunt Agatha stood in the doorway, her piercing eyes studying Emma with an intensity that made the young woman's cheeks flush.

"Miss Emma," Aunt Agatha said, her voice crisp yet not unkind. "A moment of your time, if you please."

Emma set down her duster and smoothed her apron. "Of course, Miss Aspendale."

Aunt Agatha seemed to float into the room, her silver-grey hair gleaming in the afternoon light. She ran a gloved finger along the spine of a nearby book, nodding approvingly at its pristine condition.

"I've been observing you, Miss Emma," Aunt Agatha began, her gaze sharp. "Your work is exemplary, of course, but it's not just your diligence that's caught my attention."

Emma's heart quickened. Had she overstepped somehow? "I hope I haven't caused any displeasure, Miss Aspendale."

A rare smile tugged at Aunt Agatha's lips. "Quite the contrary, my dear. I've noticed your keen mind, your quick wit. The way young Master Clarence seeks you out for conversation, how Miss Evelyn values your literary opinions."

Emma stood still, barely daring to breathe as Aunt Agatha continued.

"You have a gift, Miss Emma. One that could benefit this family in ways beyond your current... station." Aunt Agatha's eyes gleamed with something Emma couldn't quite place. "I believe there may be opportunities for you to contribute more significantly to the Aspendale household. To use that intellect of yours in service of greater things."

Emma's mind whirled. "I... I'm not sure I understand, Miss Aspendale."

Aunt Agatha patted Emma's arm, an uncharacteristically gentle gesture. "You will, my dear. In time. For now, continue as you are. But keep your eyes and ears open. There's much to learn in this house, for those clever enough to see it."

With that, Aunt Agatha swept from the room, leaving Emma standing amidst the books, her thoughts a tumult of confusion and hope.

Later that evening, as the sun dipped low on the horizon,

Emma found herself in the Manor's gardens. She stood on the gravel path, gazing out at the sprawling estate before her. The manicured lawns stretched into the distance, dotted with ancient oaks and vibrant flowerbeds.

TALK OF TROUBLE

Emma rose before dawn, her small attic room bathed in the soft glow of first light as she dressed in her simple grey frock and crisp white apron.

As she moved through the grand halls of the manor, Emma's keen mind absorbed every detail of her surroundings. Her eyes, always observant, caught the subtle shifts in atmosphere – a tightness in Lady Victoria's smile at breakfast, a furrow in Lord Edmund's brow as he read the morning paper.

Emma's duties took her from the kitchen to the grand bedrooms, her hands never idle. She polished silver until it gleamed, arranged fresh flowers in crystal vases, and tended to the endless piles of laundry with meticulous care. Yet even as she worked, her ears remained attuned to the ebb and flow of conversation around her.

One crisp autumn afternoon, as Emma folded freshly pressed linens in the laundry room, she caught the sound of hushed voices drifting through the partially open door. Mr Forthworth's low baritone mingled with Mrs. Tibbs' worried whisper.

"...trouble brewing in the factories," Mr. Forthworth

murmured, his usual composure tinged with concern. "The workers are restless, Amelia. There's talk of strikes."

Mrs Tibbs clucked her tongue softly. "Lord have mercy. Does his Lordship know?"

Emma's fingers stilled on the crisp linen, her ears straining to catch every word of the hushed conversation beyond the door. Mr Forthworth's usually steady voice carried an undercurrent of worry that sent a chill down her spine.

"I've heard whispers from the stables," he continued, his words barely audible. "The grooms speak of their cousins and brothers in the factories. Conditions are worsening, and the workers grow desperate."

Mrs Tibbs let out a soft sigh. "Those poor souls. Working from dawn to dusk for a pittance, with hardly enough to feed their families."

Emma's heart clenched, memories of her own desperate days in the workhouse flooding back. She could almost feel the ache in her hands from endless hours of scrubbing, the gnawing emptiness in her belly.

"It's not just the low wages," Mr Forthworth added, his tone grave. "The machinery is dangerous, poorly maintained. There was an accident at the Millbank factory last week – a young lad lost his arm."

Mrs Tibbs gasped softly. "Good heavens. No wonder they're talking of strikes."

"Strikes might be the least of our worries," Mr Forthworth replied, his voice dropping even lower. "There's talk of more... drastic measures. Sabotage, Amelia. Some of the more radical elements are whispering about destroying the machines, burning down factories."

Emma's breath caught in her throat. The sheet slipped from her fingers, falling to the floor in a soft whoosh. She froze, her heart pounding, praying they hadn't heard.

"Lord have mercy," Mrs Tibbs whispered, her voice trembling slightly. "I understand their anger, truly I do. But violence will only make things worse for everyone."

Emma's mind raced, her thoughts a whirlwind of concern. She thought of the Aspendale children, of Frederick's passionate discussions about social reform. Of Evelyn's kind heart and Lillian's gentle spirit. How would they be affected if the unrest spread?

Later that evening, Emma sat on the edge of her narrow bed in the attic room. The fading light of dusk filtered through the small window, casting long shadows across the floorboards.

Her mind drifted to Thomas Hawkins, a face she hadn't allowed herself to dwell on in so long. Those deep brown eyes, once so full of warmth and mischief, had hardened with determination in their final days together at Grimshaw's. She could almost hear his voice, passionate and unwavering as he spoke of justice for the downtrodden.

"We'll change things, Emma," he'd promised, his jaw set with conviction. "One day, we'll make sure no child suffers like we have."

Emma's heart ached with a mixture of longing and worry. Where was Thomas now? What had become of the boy who'd shared his meagre rations and whispered dreams of freedom on the workhouse roof?

The murmured conversation she'd overheard earlier echoed in her mind. Talk of strikes, of desperate workers pushed to the brink. Of sabotage and burning factories. Emma's stomach twisted with anxiety.

"Oh, Thomas," she whispered into the gathering darkness. "Are you caught up in all this?"

She didn't know which city Thomas had been sent to for his blacksmith apprentice-ship. The memory of his departure, bruised and defiant in the back of that wagon, still haunted her. But surely, the unrest wasn't limited to London. If conditions were as dire as Mr Forthworth suggested, wouldn't workers everywhere be feeling the same desperation?

Emma closed her eyes, picturing Thomas as he might be now. Taller, broader from the blacksmith's work, but with that same fire burning in his gaze. Would he be leading the calls for change? Standing at the forefront of angry crowds, his voice raised in righteous fury?

Emma took a deep breath. The day's revelations and her tumultuous thoughts pressed down on her, threatening to overwhelm her usually steadfast spirit.

She glanced at the small clock on her bedside table, its soft ticking a reminder of the late hour. The Manor had fallen silent, the hustle and bustle of the day giving way to the quiet of night. Emma knew she should try to rest, to gather her strength for whatever challenges tomorrow might bring.

With a soft sigh, she rose from the edge of the bed and moved to the window. The grounds of Aspendale Manor stretched out before her, bathed in moonlight. The manicured gardens and stately trees seemed a world away from the grime and desperation of the factories she'd overheard Mr Forthworth discussing.

Emma's eyes drifted to the distant horizon, where the faint glow of London's lights painted the sky. Somewhere out there, beyond the safety of these walls, unrest was brewing. Workers pushed to their limits, families struggling to survive, and perhaps... Thomas.

She shook her head, forcing herself to turn away from the window. There was nothing she could do about it tonight, standing here in her nightgown and letting her imagination run wild. Whatever was happening out there, whatever role Thomas might be playing in it all, she couldn't change it by worrying herself sick.

Emma moved back to her bed, smoothing the covers before slipping beneath them. The sheets were cool against her skin, a small comfort as she settled her head on the pillow. She closed her eyes, willing her racing thoughts to slow.

"Lord," she whispered into the darkness, "please watch over Thomas, wherever he may be. Keep him safe, and... and guide his path." She paused, her next words catching. "And help me find the strength to face whatever comes."

With that final prayer, Emma took another deep breath and tried to relax. She knew sleep might not come easily, but she had to try. Tomorrow was another day, and she would need all her wits about her to navigate the uncertain waters ahead.

UNREST IN THE AIR

~~~

*E*mma's day off arrived, a rare respite from her duties at Aspendale Manor. She made her way through London's bustling streets, her heart quickening as she approached the small cafe where she'd arranged to meet Fiona and Rose. The familiar scents of coffee and freshly baked bread wafted through the air as she pushed open the door.

Fiona's sharp green eyes spotted Emma immediately. "There you are, love," she called, waving Emma over to their corner table.

Rose greeted Emma with a warm smile, pulling out a chair for her. "It's good to see you, Emma. How's life in the grand manor treating you?"

Emma settled into her seat, grateful for the company of her friends. "It's... different," she admitted. "But I'm managing. How are things with you both?"

As they caught up, Emma carefully steered the conversation towards the rumours she'd overheard. "I've been hearing whispers," she began, her voice low. "About unrest in the factories. Have either of you heard anything?"

Fiona's eyes narrowed, her posture straightening. "Aye,

there's been talk," she said, glancing around before leaning in closer. "Workers pushed to their limits, wages that can't feed a family. It's brewing into something fierce, mark my words."

Rose nodded gravely. "The girls at the laundry where I work now, they're all abuzz with it. Husbands and brothers ready to take a stand, they say."

Emma absorbed their words, her concern growing. She thanked them for their insights, making a mental note to seek out Sarah next. Perhaps her friend would have a different perspective to offer.

Later that week, Emma managed to arrange a meeting with Sarah during her lunch break. They sat on a park bench, the sounds of passing carriages providing cover for their hushed conversation.

"Sarah," Emma began, "what have you heard about the troubles in the factories?"

Sarah's eyes lit up with a mixture of excitement and concern. "Oh, Emma, it's all Mr Hawthorne — that's the carriage driver I've told you about, the one who just knows everything about politics nowadays! Anyways, talks about these days. He says the workers are at their breaking point."

As Sarah spoke, Emma was struck by the depth of her friend's knowledge. Gone was the timid girl from the workhouse; in her place sat a young woman with a keen understanding of the world around her.

"The conditions are terrible," Sarah continued, her voice low but passionate. "Sixteen-hour days, children as young as six working dangerous machines, lungs choked with cotton dust. And the wages? Barely enough to keep a roof over their heads."

Emma listened intently, her heart heavy with Sarah's words. She thought of Thomas, wondering if he faced similar hardships in his apprenticeship. The world beyond Aspendale Manor's walls suddenly seemed so much darker, so much more complex than she'd realised.

HEADLINES AND WORRIES

⁓

*E*mma sorted through the morning's delivery of newspapers and correspondence, her eyes darting across the bold headlines. The words "LABOUR UNREST GROWS" and "WORKERS DEMAND REFORMS" leapt out at her, causing her heart to quicken. She paused in her task, glancing furtively around to ensure no one noticed her lingering gaze.

As she distributed the papers and letters to their proper recipients, Emma's mind whirled with the implications of what she'd read. The tensions she'd discussed with Fiona, Rose, and Sarah were no longer mere whispers; they'd become front-page news.

Her duties complete, Emma passed by the drawing room. The door stood slightly ajar, and Lord Edmund's deep voice carried through the gap. Curiosity overcame her, and she slowed her steps, straining to hear.

"Agatha, these reports are deeply troubling," Lord Edmund said, his tone uncharacteristically grave. "If this unrest spreads to our factories, the disruption could be catastrophic."

Emma risked a glance through the crack in the door. Lord

Edmund stood by the fireplace, his tall frame silhouetted against the morning light. He was usually so assured, but now a flicker of worry passed over him that Emma had never seen before.

Aunt Agatha's voice came in response, measured and calm. "Now, Edmund, let's not get ahead of ourselves. Surely there are steps we can take to address the workers' concerns before it comes to that."

Later that day, Emma found herself in the family library, dusting the shelves with careful precision. Her mind still buzzed with the morning's overheard conversation, her hands moving almost mechanically as she pondered the implications of the growing unrest.

She was so lost in thought that she didn't hear Frederick Aspendale enter the room. His voice, warm and curious, startled her from her reverie.

"Emma? Is everything all right? You seem rather preoccupied."

Emma turned, nearly dropping her feather duster. Frederick stood there, his blue eyes filled with genuine concern. She hesitated, unsure how much to reveal.

"I... It's nothing, Master Frederick. Just lost in thought, I suppose."

Frederick's brow furrowed slightly. "Come now, Emma. I'd like to think we've become friends of a sort. If something's troubling you, I'd be glad to lend an ear."

Emma bit her lip, weighing her words carefully. The young heir's kindness had always struck her, so different from the cold indifference she'd known in the workhouse. Still, she was acutely aware of the vast gulf between their stations.

"Well, sir," she began hesitantly, "I couldn't help but notice the headlines in the morning papers. All this talk of unrest in the factories... it's rather unsettling."

Frederick's expression softened. He moved to a nearby

armchair, gesturing for Emma to sit as well. After a moment's hesitation, she perched on the edge of a reading chair, her back straight and hands folded in her lap.

"I understand your concern, Emma," Frederick said, his voice reassuring. "Rest assured, the family is well aware of the situation. Father's been in meetings about it all week."

Emma nodded, feeling a small measure of relief. "It's just... I can't help but worry. Some of my friends, they work in factories, and the conditions they describe..."

Frederick leaned forward, his elbows on his knees. "We're doing all we can. Change is slow and hard, especially with old men with old money, but we will work it out, I'm sure of it."

Emma wished Frederick's words reassured her more, but they did very little in soothing her worries.

As the evening shadows lengthened across Aspendale Manor, Emma arranged flowers for the dinner table in the conservatory. The glass walls reflected the warm glow of the setting sun, casting a golden hue over the room.

"Those arrangements are lovely, Emma," Evelyn said, her voice soft and warm.

Emma turned, a small smile gracing her features. "Thank you, Miss Evelyn. I hope they'll please your mother."

Evelyn moved closer, her emerald eyes reflecting the fading sunlight. "I'm sure they will. But I was hoping we might talk, if you have a moment?"

Emma nodded, setting aside her work. "Of course, Miss."

Evelyn settled onto a nearby bench, gesturing for Emma to join her. As Emma sat, she noticed a furrow in Evelyn's brow, a sign of the young woman's troubled thoughts.

"I couldn't help but overhear your conversation with Frederick earlier," Evelyn began, her voice low. "About the unrest in the factories. It's been weighing on my mind as well."

Emma's heart quickened. "It's a troubling situation, Miss."

Evelyn nodded, her eyes serious. "Indeed it is. The more I

learn about the conditions these workers face, the more I realise how desperately change is needed."

As they talked, Emma began to open up about her own experiences and the stories she'd heard from Sarah and her other friends. Evelyn listened intently, her expression a mix of shock and sympathy.

"It's not right," Evelyn said firmly. "Something must be done."

Their conversation was interrupted by the arrival of Beatrice, her dark curls bouncing as she entered the conservatory.

"There you are!" Beatrice exclaimed. "I've been looking everywhere for you both."

Beatrice's eyes sparkled with curiosity as she joined them. "What are you discussing so seriously?"

Evelyn shared a glance with Emma before answering. "We were talking about the factory workers and their struggles."

Beatrice's expression grew solemn. "Oh, yes. It's dreadful, isn't it? I was just reading about it in the papers. How can people be treated so poorly?"

Emma felt a warmth in her chest at the sisters' genuine concern. She'd never imagined finding such understanding among the upper classes.

"It reminds me of that passage in 'North and South,'" Beatrice mused. "Where Margaret confronts Mr Thornton about the treatment of his workers. Do you know it, Emma?"

Emma nodded, pleasantly surprised. "I do, Miss Beatrice. It's a powerful scene."

As they delved into a discussion about literature and its reflections of social injustice, a growing sense of connection with the Aspendale sisters started to form. Their compassion and desire for change resonated deeply with her own beliefs.

A GATHERING STORM

Emma's heart skipped a beat as she overheard two kitchen maids whispering fervently near the scullery. Their hushed tones carried fragments of a name she hadn't heard in years – Thomas Hawkins. Her hands trembled slightly as she continued folding linens, straining to catch every word without appearing to eavesdrop.

"...right here in London," one maid murmured, her eyes wide with excitement. "A right firebrand, he is. Stirring up the workers something fierce."

Emma's breath caught in her throat. Could it truly be her Thomas? The boy who had stood by her side in Grimshaw's Workhouse, who had shared her dreams of a better world?

As days passed, more whispers reached her ears. Fragments of conversations among the household staff, snippets overheard as she served tea to Lord Edmund and his business associates. A new voice in the workers' movement, they said. A blacksmith with eyes that burned with revolutionary fire.

One morning, as Emma arranged flowers in the conservatory, she caught sight of a discarded newspaper. Her gaze was drawn to a small article tucked away on the third page. It spoke of growing unrest in the factories, of a charismatic leader emerging from the ranks of the workers. Though no name was mentioned, Emma's heart knew. It had to be him.

Her daily routines took on a new rhythm, punctuated by moments of anticipation and anxiety. As she hung laundry in the manor's sprawling gardens, her deep hazel eyes would often drift toward the bustling London streets beyond the iron gates. Each passing carriage, each distant shout from a newsboy made her pulse quicken.

In quiet moments between her duties, Emma murmured fervent prayers for Thomas's safety, her lips moving silently as she polished silverware or swept the grand staircase.

At night, in the solitude of her small attic room, Emma's thoughts turned to reunion. She imagined Thomas's face, no longer the boy she had known but a man hardened by years of toil and injustice. Would he remember her? Would he still carry the faith they had once shared?

A SURPRISE VISIT

The creak of the laundry room door startled Emma. She looked up from her work to see Mr Forthworth's tall, dignified figure in the doorway. His expression, usually so composed, held a hint of something Emma couldn't quite place.

"Miss Redbrook," he said, "there is someone here to see you."

Emma's brow furrowed in confusion. Who could possibly be calling on her? She had no family, and her few friends knew better than to visit her at work.

"Me, Mr Forthworth?" she asked, setting aside the sheet she'd been folding.

"Indeed," he replied with a slight nod. "If you'll follow me, please."

Heart quickening, Emma smoothed her apron and followed the butler through the winding corridors of the Manor. He led her not to the main entrance, but to a discreet side door, one typically used for deliveries and tradesmen.

"Your visitor is waiting outside," Mr Forthworth said, his hand on the doorknob. He paused, studying Emma's face for a moment before adding, "Take as much time as you need, Miss Redbrook."

With that, he opened the door, and Emma stepped out into the grey afternoon.

There, standing beneath the shelter of a gnarled oak tree, was a figure Emma knew instantly, despite the years that had passed. Thomas Hawkins stood before her, his body hardened by years of labour at the forge. His clothes were rough and worn, a far cry from the polished world Emma now inhabited.

But it was his eyes that truly captured Emma's attention. Those deep brown eyes that had once looked at her with such kindness and hope now burned with an intensity that almost frightened her. In them, Emma saw the fire of revolution, of barely contained anger at the injustices of the world.

"Thomas," Emma breathed.

REUNION

Emma took in the sight of Thomas. The boy she'd known had vanished, replaced by a man hardened by years of toil and injustice. His broad shoulders and calloused hands spoke of countless hours at the forge, while the set of his jaw hinted at a stubbornness that had only grown with time.

"It's been a long time," Emma said. She fought the urge to reach out and touch him, to make sure he was real and not some fevered dream conjured by her longing.

Thomas's eyes darted past her, taking in the grand manor behind. "Looks like you've done well for yourself," he said, a hint of bitterness creeping into his tone.

Emma flinched at his words. "I've been fortunate," she admitted, "but Thomas, I've never forgotten—"

"Save it," Thomas cut her off, his voice sharp. "I didn't come here for a trip down memory lane."

Emma's hand instinctively went to her throat, feeling for the silver cross that no longer hung there. She'd given it to Thomas all those years ago, a symbol of hope and faith. Now, she noticed its absence around his neck as well.

"Why did you come, then?" Emma asked, steeling herself for his answer.

Thomas's gaze locked onto hers, and for a moment, Emma caught a glimpse of the boy she'd known—vulnerable, searching for connection. But it vanished as quickly as it had appeared, replaced by a hardness that made her heart ache.

"Things are changing, Emma," Thomas said intensely. "The workers are rising up. We're not going to take the abuse and exploitation anymore."

Emma had heard whispers of unrest, but to hear Thomas speak of it with such conviction made it all too real.

"Thomas," she began softly, her voice barely above a whisper, "what happened to you after... after they took you away?"

Thomas's jaw clenched, a muscle twitching beneath his skin. For a moment, Emma thought he might refuse to answer, but then he spoke.

"Master Jerome Grimm," he spat the name like a curse. "That's where they sent me. A blacksmith's apprentice, they said. More like a slave."

Emma's hand flew to her mouth, her eyes widening in horror. She'd known Thomas's fate wouldn't be easy, but the bitterness in his voice spoke of horrors beyond her imagination.

"He worked us from dawn 'til dusk," Thomas continued, his gaze distant. "No food if the work wasn't perfect. No rest until our hands bled and our backs broke."

Emma fought back tears, remembering the gentle boy who had shared his rations with her in the workhouse. That boy was still there, she realised, buried beneath layers of pain and anger.

"But I'm not here to talk about what happened to me," Thomas said, his voice firm. "I'm here about what's happening now."

Emma straightened, sensing the shift in Thomas's demeanour. She watched as he reached into his worn coat, pulling out a folded piece of paper.

"The workers are organising," Thomas continued, his eyes blazing with conviction. "We're demanding fair wages, safer conditions, and an end to child labour. But the factory owners, they're not listening."

He unfolded the paper, revealing a crudely printed flyer. Emma's eyes widened as she read the bold letters at the top: "WORKERS UNITE!"

"We're planning a strike," Thomas said, his voice low but intense. "Not just one factory, but all across London. We'll bring the city to its knees if we have to."

A chill ran down Emma's spine. She glanced back at the Manor, thinking of the Aspendale family inside, of Mr Forthworth and Mrs Tibbs, of the life she'd built here.

"Thomas," she began cautiously, "surely there must be a way to negotiate, to—"

"Negotiate?" Thomas scoffed, his eyes flashing. "We've tried that, Emma. They don't listen to words. But they'll listen when their profits dry up, when their machines stand idle."

Emma could see the passion in Thomas's eyes, the determination set in every line of his face. This was no idle threat or passing fancy. Thomas truly believed in this cause, was willing to risk everything for it.

"Why are you telling me this?" Emma asked.

Thomas's expression softened for a moment, and Emma caught a glimpse of the boy she once knew. "Because I remember who you were, Emma. The girl who stood up to Grimshaw, who taught others to read in secret. I thought... I hoped you might still be that girl."

Thomas's eyes blazed as he spoke of the workers' movement. "We're not alone anymore, Emma. There are thousands of us, all across London. In the factories, the mills, the docks. We're tired of being treated like machines, like we're less than human."

He described clandestine meetings in smoky taverns, whispered plans passed from hand to hand in the dead of night.

Emma listened, enthralled and terrified in equal measure, as Thomas recounted daring acts of sabotage – gears jammed with metal shavings, shipments mysteriously lost, foremen's ledgers altered.

"You should see their faces when we stand together," Thomas said, a fierce pride in his voice. "When we refuse to bow, to scrape, to beg for the crumbs they throw us. We're not asking anymore, Emma. We're demanding."

As Thomas spoke, Emma caught glimpses of the boy she had known. It was in the way his hands moved as he talked, in the passion that lit up his eyes. But those glimpses were fleeting, quickly swallowed up by the hardened man before her.

"Emma," Thomas said, his voice softening for a moment, "we need you. Your mind, your courage – they could make all the difference."

He reached out, his calloused hand hovering just inches from hers. "Join us," he urged. "Help us take down the industrial overlords who profit from our suffering. Together, we can build a better world."

Emma's mouth opened, but no words came out. Her mind whirled with conflicting thoughts and emotions. She thought of the stability and kindness she'd found here. But she also remembered the workhouse, the cruelty of Mr Grimshaw, and the countless children still trapped in a cycle of poverty and exploitation.

Thomas watched her, his expression shifting as the seconds ticked by. The hope in his eyes began to fade, replaced by a dawning realisation. A sadness crept over his features, etching lines into his face that made him look older than his years.

Emma wanted to protest, to explain the complexity of her situation, but the words wouldn't come. She stood there, frozen.

Thomas let out a sigh, as he pulled something small from his other coat pocket.

Emma felt the cool metal of the silver cross press into her

palm as Thomas placed it there. The weight of it seemed to increase tenfold as his words sank in. "This belonged to you," he said, his voice rough with emotion. "God is no longer with me, Emma. I can't carry this anymore."

Her eyes welled with tears, blurring her vision of Thomas's face. The cross had been her mother's final gift, a symbol of hope and faith that had sustained her through the darkest times. To see it returned, to hear Thomas renounce the faith they'd once shared, felt like a physical blow.

"Thomas," Emma's voice trembled. She closed her fingers around the cross, feeling its familiar contours. "God hasn't abandoned you. He's always with us, even in our darkest moments."

But Thomas's expression remained hard, unyielding. The boy who had once found comfort in shared prayers and whispered Bible verses was gone, replaced by a man whose faith had been beaten out of him by years of cruelty and injustice.

"Save your platitudes, Emma," Thomas said, his voice low and bitter. "I've seen too much, suffered too much, to believe in a benevolent God anymore."

Emma's heart ached at the pain she saw etched in every line of Thomas's face. She wanted to reach out, to offer comfort, but she sensed that any attempt would be rebuffed. Instead, she clutched the cross tighter, as if she could somehow transfer its strength to Thomas through sheer will.

"Faith isn't just about believing when things are easy," Emma said softly. "It's about holding on when everything seems darkest. I know you've been through so much, Thomas, but—"

"But what?" Thomas interrupted, his eyes flashing. "Should I thank God for the beatings? For the hunger? For watching children collapse from exhaustion in the factories?"

"Thomas," Emma began, "I understand you've seen terrible things, but—"

"No, Emma," Thomas cut her off, his eyes flashing with a mixture of pain and anger. "You don't understand. You can't."

Emma flinched at the harshness in his tone, but she pressed on. "I may not have experienced exactly what you have, but I remember the workhouse. I remember the cruelty, the hunger, the despair. My faith helped me through those times, and I believe it can still—"

"Your faith?" Thomas scoffed, shaking his head. "Where was your God when children were beaten for not working fast enough? Where was He when I watched a boy die from exhaustion, worked to death before he'd even seen his tenth year?"

Tears threatened to spill from Emma's eyes. She wanted to reach out to Thomas, to comfort him, but the gulf between them seemed insurmountable.

Thomas's voice softened slightly, though the bitterness remained. "I used to believe, Emma. I used to pray every night, hoping for some divine intervention. But it never came. The only change I've seen has come from people standing up for themselves, fighting back against injustice with their own hands."

Emma listened, her heart breaking for the boy she'd once known, for the faith he'd lost. She clutched the cross tighter, as if it could somehow bridge the gap between them.

"I'm not here to debate theology," Thomas continued, his voice growing firm once more. "I'm here because the world needs changing, and we can't wait for someone else to do it for us. We have to take action ourselves. And I thought you would want to be a part of that."

"Thomas, faith gave us strength. It connected us. Can't we find a way to fight for justice while holding onto hope?"

For a moment, Emma saw a flicker of the boy she once knew in Thomas's eyes. His fierce expression softened, and she dared to hope that her words had reached him. But as quickly as it appeared, the vulnerability vanished, replaced by a hardened resolve.

"Hope?" Thomas scoffed, shaking his head. "Hope is a luxury we can't afford, Emma. The world needs action, not prayers."

Emma's fingers tightened around the silver cross in her hand, its familiar weight a reminder of all they had endured together. She searched Thomas's face, looking for any sign of the gentle soul she had known in the workhouse.

"But Thomas," she pressed on, her voice gentle but firm, "isn't hope what drove us to survive in the workhouse? Isn't it what gave us the strength to stand up to Grimshaw, to dream of a better life?"

Thomas's jaw clenched, a muscle twitching beneath his skin. "Dreams and prayers didn't get us out of there, Emma. Action did. And action is what's needed now."

Emma took a step closer, her eyes never leaving Thomas's face. "I'm not saying we shouldn't act," she said softly. "But hope... hope is what gives our actions meaning. It's what keeps us going when everything seems darkest."

She held up the silver cross between them, its surface catching the fading light. "This isn't just about God, Thomas. It's about believing that we can make a difference, that our struggles aren't in vain."

Thomas's eyes flickered to the cross, and for a moment, Emma saw a shadow of doubt cross his face. But then his expression hardened once more.

"Pretty words won't feed hungry children or stop factory owners from exploiting workers," he said. "We need more than hope, Emma. We need change, and we need it now."

Though Thomas's words were harsh, Emma could see the pain behind them, the years of suffering that had shaped him into the man who stood before her now.

"I understand your anger, Thomas," Emma said softly. "And I

agree that change is needed. Perhaps... perhaps we can find a way to work towards that change, even if our methods differ."

Thomas's expression softened slightly, surprise crossing his face. He studied Emma for a long moment, as if seeing her anew. "You'd be willing to help?" he asked, his voice guarded but tinged with hope.

Emma nodded, her resolve strengthening. "We may not agree on everything, but we both want a better world. That's something we can stand together on."

A ghost of a smile tugged at Thomas's lips, the first Emma had seen since his arrival. It wasn't the carefree grin of their youth, but it was something. "I never thought I'd hear you say that," he admitted.

They stood together in the garden, the late afternoon sun casting long shadows across the lawn. For a moment, the years between them seemed to melt away, and they were once again two children dreaming of a brighter future.

No words were needed as they shared this moment of understanding. Emma's fingers curled around the silver cross, and she made a silent vow to support Thomas's cause in whatever way she could. She hoped that one day, through their combined efforts, Thomas might find the peace that had eluded him for so long. And perhaps, in time, he might even rediscover the faith that had once been their common ground.

PART IV
THE CRUCIBLE OF LOVE

Love is patient, love is kind. It does not envy, it does not boast, it is not proud.
– I Corinthians 13:4

FACES OF THE CAUSE

A gentle breeze rustled the leaves of the garden as Emma stood near the servant's entrance, her heart fluttering with a mixture of anticipation and trepidation. The silver cross hung heavy around her neck. She smoothed her simple dress, taking a deep breath to steady her nerves.

Thomas appeared at the gate, his broad shoulders silhouetted against the setting sun. The sight of him still sent a jolt through Emma, a complex tangle of emotions she couldn't quite unravel. He approached with purposeful strides, his eyes intense and focused.

"Emma," he said. "I need you to come with me. There are people you should meet, things you need to see."

Emma hesitated, her fingers unconsciously reaching for her cross. "What sort of things, Thomas?"

His jaw tightened, a muscle twitching beneath the skin. "The reality of what workers face every day. The conditions we're fighting against. I want you to understand why this cause is so important."

Emma studied Thomas's face, noting the lines of worry and determination etched there. She thought of the conversations she'd overheard in the Manor, the whispers of unrest that had reached even these gilded halls. A part of her longed to retreat to the safety of her faith, to the familiar routines of the Aspendale household. But a deeper part, the part that had always yearned for justice, urged her forward.

"All right," she said softly, squaring her shoulders. "I'll come with you."

Relief flickered across Thomas's face, quickly replaced by his usual intensity. "Good. We'll need to be careful. Some of these places... they're not what you're used to."

As they slipped out of the garden and into the gathering twilight, Emma's mind raced. She thought of the Aspendale family, of Mrs Tibbs and Mr Forthworth, wondering what they would think of her clandestine excursion. But more than that, she thought of the people she was about to meet, the harsh realities she was about to witness.

Emma's heart pounded as they made their way through increasingly unfamiliar streets. The grand houses gave way to more modest dwellings, then to crowded tenements and narrow alleys. The air grew thick with the smell of coal smoke and unwashed bodies.

Thomas led her down a winding path, his hand occasionally reaching back to steady her on the uneven cobblestones. Finally, they stopped before a nondescript door in a run-down building. Thomas knocked in a specific pattern, and Emma held her breath as they waited for a response.

The door creaked open, revealing a dimly lit room filled with a haze of pipe smoke. Emma's eyes adjusted slowly, taking in the scene before her. A group of people huddled around a makeshift table, their faces etched with weariness and determination. Thomas guided her forward, his hand a reassuring presence at the small of her back.

"Everyone," Thomas called out, his voice cutting through the murmur of conversation. "This is Emma."

A man with a shock of fiery red hair turned to face them, his intense green eyes locking onto Emma. He strode forward, his presence filling the small space.

"Welcome, Emma," he said, his voice carrying a melodious Irish lilt. "I'm Jack O'Malley, but most call me Firebrand." He grasped her hand warmly, a smile lighting up his face. "Thomas has told us about you. It's good to have you here."

Jack turned to address the room, his voice rising with passion. "Friends, Emma here has seen the injustice of this world firsthand. She knows the struggle of the workhouse, the exploitation of the vulnerable. Her presence reminds us why we fight!"

A murmur of agreement rippled through the crowd. A flush crept up Emma's neck, uncomfortable with the sudden attention.

A stern-faced woman approached next. Her gaze was appraising but not unkind. "Martha Steele," she said simply, offering a curt nod. "I worked the looms for twenty years before they replaced us with machines. Now I fight so others don't suffer the same fate."

Emma nodded back, feeling a mix of admiration and unease at the hardness in Martha's eyes.

A gruff voice spoke from her left. "Bert Clutterbuck, miss. Most call me One-Eye, for obvious reasons."

Emma turned to face a grizzled man with an eye patch, his remaining eye regarding her with a mix of curiosity and suspicion. He extended a calloused hand, which Emma shook, surprised by the gentleness of his grip despite his intimidating appearance.

"Lost this eye and my livelihood to the mines," Bert continued, a bitter edge to his voice. "Now I'm here to make sure it wasn't for nothing."

Emma's gaze settled on a young woman with striking features and an air of quiet determination. Her dark eyes sparkled with intelligence as she approached, offering a small smile.

"Lily Chen," she introduced herself, her accent a melodious blend of East and West. "It's a pleasure to meet you, Emma."

Emma felt an immediate connection. "The pleasure is mine, Lily. What brought you to this gathering?"

Lily's expression grew wistful. "Dreams of a better life, I suppose. I came to England for education, but reality had other plans." She gestured around the room. "Now I work in a laundry, but I haven't given up hope for more."

Emma nodded, understanding all too well. "I've worked in laundries too. It's hard work, but it doesn't define us."

"Exactly," Lily agreed, her eyes brightening. "We're capable of so much more, if only given the chance."

Their conversation was interrupted by the approach of a mountain of a man. Emma had to crane her neck to meet his eyes, which were a surprisingly gentle blue in his rugged face.

"Sam Blackburn," he rumbled, extending a hand that engulfed Emma's. "Most call me The Ox."

Emma could see why. Sam's massive frame spoke of incredible strength, yet there was a careful gentleness in how he shook her hand.

"Nice to meet you, Sam," Emma said, finding her voice. "How long have you been involved with... all this?" She gestured vaguely at the gathering.

A shadow passed over Sam's face. "Since I saw a man crushed by faulty machinery and the factory owner didn't even blink." His hands clenched into fists. "Sometimes it's hard not to want to crush something myself."

Emma felt a chill at his words, but also a deep sympathy. Before she could respond, a young woman with fierce eyes approached, practically vibrating with energy.

"Rachel Flowers," she said, grasping Emma's hand. "Thomas

told us you worked in a workhouse. I started in the factories when I was ten."

Emma's heart clenched. "I'm so sorry, Rachel. No child should have to endure that."

Rachel's eyes flashed. "Exactly why I'm here. We have to stop it, for all the children still suffering."

Emma nodded, feeling a surge of kinship with this passionate young woman. "You're absolutely right. It has to end."

An older man with weathered hands joined their small circle. "George Tinker," he introduced himself, his voice gravelly but kind. "Watchmaker by trade, or at least I was."

"All right everyone!" Thomas clapped his hands together. "That's all the time we have for introductions. Let us begin."

FIRE WITH FIRE

◈

Jack O'Malley's impassioned words filled the cramped room. His fiery red hair seemed to glow in the dim lamplight as he laid out the group's plans with meticulous detail. Emma found herself captivated by the intensity in his eyes, burning with a fervour that both awed and unsettled her.

"The Aspendale Mill," Jack declared, his voice rising, "is the symbol of everything we're fighting against. Its destruction will be our first strike against the oppressors!"

Emma's breath caught in her throat. The Aspendale Mill. The very family that had shown her kindness, that had given her a chance at a new life. She glanced at Thomas, hoping to see a hint of doubt, but his face was set with grim determination.

As Jack continued to outline the sabotage plans, Emma felt as if the floor was tilting beneath her feet. Her mind raced, recalling Frederick's passionate discussions about improving factory conditions, Evelyn's gentle encouragement, and even Aunt Agatha's subtle mentorship. These were not faceless oppressors, but real people with complexities and contradictions.

Yet, as she looked around the room at the hardened faces of those who had suffered so much, Emma couldn't deny the justice of their cause. The memory of her own time in Grimshaw's Workhouse rose unbidden, along with the faces of countless children still trapped in such hellish conditions.

Emma's fingers unconsciously sought the silver cross beneath her dress. The cool metal against her skin grounded her, even as her thoughts whirled in turmoil. How could she reconcile her loyalty to Thomas, her oldest friend and confidant, with her deep-seated belief that violence was not the answer? The faces of the Aspendale family flashed before her eyes, contrasting sharply with the determined expressions of Jack and his compatriots.

As the meeting progressed, Emma was torn between two worlds, struggling to find her place in either. The passion in the room was palpable, but so was the undercurrent of anger and potential for destruction. She knew she would have to make a choice, and soon.

Taking a deep breath, Emma stepped forward. Her legs trembled slightly, but her voice rang out clear and firm. "Please," she began, her eyes moving from face to face, "I understand your anger, truly I do. But have you considered the consequences of such actions?"

The room fell silent, all eyes turning to her. Emma swallowed hard, but pressed on. "I've seen the inside of that mill. There are good people working there, people just like us who are struggling to feed their families. If we destroy it, what becomes of them?"

She could feel Thomas's gaze burning into her, but she didn't dare look at him yet. Instead, she focused on Jack, whose fiery expression had turned to one of curiosity.

"There must be peaceful ways to make our voices heard," Emma continued, her voice gaining strength. "Ways that don't risk innocent lives or destroy livelihoods. What if we could speak directly to those in power, make them see the humanity in our struggle?

"I've seen both sides of this divide. There are those among the wealthy who would listen if given the chance. Destruction will only harden their hearts against us."

Finally, Emma turned to Thomas. His eyes, once so kind and full of hope, now blazed with a determination that both thrilled and terrified her. She held his gaze, silently pleading for him to understand.

Thomas stepped forward. "Emma," he said, "your heart is in the right place, as always. But you haven't seen what we've seen, haven't endured what we've endured. Peaceful methods have failed us time and time again. The time for talk is over."

He placed a hand on her shoulder, his touch both gentle and unyielding. "We need drastic action to achieve real change. It's the only language they understand."

Emma's heart raced as she looked around the room, gauging the reactions to her impassioned plea. The air felt thick with tension, a palpable mix of conflicting emotions swirling among the gathered workers.

Lily's eyes met Emma's, a flicker of doubt crossing her delicate features. The young woman twisted a loose thread on her sleeve, her brow furrowed in contemplation. "Perhaps," Lily began hesitantly, her accented voice soft but clear, "there is wisdom in Emma's words. Violence begets violence, does it not?"

Rachel nodded, her auburn hair catching the dim lamplight. "I've seen first-hand what happens when things turn ugly," she said, her voice tinged with remembered pain. "It's the women and children who suffer most when factories close."

But Jack O'Malley's fiery gaze hadn't dimmed. He paced the small room, his steps quick and agitated. "Peaceful measures?" he scoffed, his voice sharpening with frustration. "How many petitions have we signed? How many polite letters ignored? The bosses don't care about our words!"

Bert's gruff voice rumbled in agreement. "Aye, lass," he said, his one good eye fixed on Emma. "Your heart's in the right place, but you haven't been down in the mines. You haven't seen men crushed for a few extra pennies of profit. Sometimes, you've got to fight fire with fire."

Emma turned to Martha, hoping to find an ally in the older woman's weathered face. Martha's eyes softened as they met Emma's pleading gaze, but the set of her jaw remained firm. "I understand your fears, Emma," Martha said gently. "God knows I've had my fill of violence. But we've tried it your way for years, and where has it gotten us? Sometimes, drastic times call for drastic measures."

The room fell silent, the decision hanging heavy in the air. Emma could feel Thomas's presence beside her, solid and unyielding. She longed to reach for his hand, to find some remnant of the boy she once knew, but the stranger he'd become seemed miles away.

A DANGEROUS PATH

Emma felt a gentle tug on her sleeve and turned to find Rachel's sympathetic eyes meeting her own. The redhead tilted her head towards a quieter corner of the room, away from the heated debate still raging among the workers. With a quick nod, Emma followed, grateful for the momentary reprieve from the tension.

Rachel led them to a small alcove, partially hidden by a threadbare curtain. The din of raised voices faded to a muffled hum as Rachel turned to face Emma, her expression a mix of concern and understanding.

"It's not easy, is it?" Rachel said softly. "Standing up for what you believe in, when everyone around you seems so certain."

Emma exhaled, feeling some of the tightness in her chest loosen. "I just can't shake the feeling that violence will only breed more violence," she confessed, twisting her hands in the folds of her skirt. "But I understand their anger, truly I do. I've lived it myself."

Rachel nodded, a shadow passing over her face. "We all have, in one way or another," she said. "Sometimes I wonder if I've become too hardened, too willing to accept drastic measures."

She paused, her gaze distant. "But then I think of the children in the factories, their little hands raw and bleeding, and I feel that fire in my belly all over again."

Emma reached out, grasping Rachel's work-roughened hand in her own. "I feel it too," she said earnestly. "The injustice, the suffering – it burns inside me. But I can't help but believe there must be another way, a way that doesn't risk innocent lives."

Rachel squeezed Emma's hand, a small smile tugging at the corners of her mouth. "Your faith gives you strength," she observed. "I admire that, even if I can't always share it."

For a moment, they stood in companionable silence, each lost in their own thoughts. A wave of gratitude washed over Emma. Here, in this dingy room filled with anger and desperation, she had found a kindred spirit.

"Whatever happens," Rachel said at last, her voice low but firm, "I'm glad you're here, Emma. We need voices like yours, reminding us of our humanity even in the darkest times."

Emma nodded, feeling a lump form in her throat. "And I'm grateful for you, Rachel," she replied. "For understanding, for listening. It means more than you know."

Thomas's voice cut through the quiet moment between Emma and Rachel. "Emma, Rachel! We need you back here." His tone was urgent, brooking no argument.

Emma exchanged a glance with Rachel, drawing strength from their shared understanding. With a deep breath, she straightened her shoulders and made her way back to the table, Rachel close behind.

The group had spread out a crude map of the Aspendale Mill, marking potential entry points and weak spots. Thomas's finger traced a path along the paper, his voice firm and strong as he outlined their plan of attack.

"We'll need someone to distract the night watchman," Thomas said, his eyes scanning the faces around the table. "Lily, you're our best bet for that. Use that silver tongue of yours."

Lily nodded, her expression grim but determined.

As Thomas continued assigning roles, Emma felt her stomach twist. The reality of what they were planning crashed over her like a wave. These weren't just abstract ideas anymore; these were concrete steps towards destruction.

"Jack and Sam, you'll be responsible for setting off the machines," Thomas declared. "Those things are so old, and so poorly maintained, we set them off to work at their full capacity, and..." Thomas indicated an explosion with his fingers.

Emma's searched his face for any sign of hesitation. But his jaw was set, his eyes hard with resolve. This wasn't the boy she had known in the workhouse; this was a man forged in the fires of injustice and hardship.

"Emma," Thomas voice snapped her attention back to the present. "You know the layout of the Manor. We need information on the family's movements, potential weak points in security."

Emma felt all eyes turn to her, a mix of expectation and suspicion in their gazes. Her throat felt dry as she nodded. "I... I can do that."

As the meeting continued, Emma's mind raced. Why had she agreed to help them? To betray the family that had done so much for her?

She realised why. She had to find a way to steer them from this path of destruction, to show them that violence would only beget more violence. And the best way to do that, was from inside their operation. It was risky and dangerous, but she would find a way.

THE WEIGHT OF CHOICES

*E*mma's mind whirled as she moved through her duties at Aspendale Manor. The weight of her knowledge pressed down on her, making even the simplest tasks feel monumental. As she polished the silver in the dining room, her eyes kept darting to Lord Edmund's study door, guilt gnawing at her insides.

Lord Edmund's voice drifted through the crack beneath the door, his tone hushed but urgent. "We must increase security at the mill, Agatha. These whispers of unrest... I fear they may turn to action."

Emma's hand trembled, nearly dropping the silver candlestick she was polishing. She steadied herself, drawing a deep breath as she strained to hear more.

Aunt Agatha's measured tones followed. "Perhaps it's time we considered some of those reforms Frederick has been pushing for. A gesture of goodwill might—"

"Goodwill?" Lord Edmund scoffed. "These rabble-rousers don't want goodwill, they want to tear down everything we've built."

Emma's heart clenched. If only they knew the full extent of

the danger, the plans being laid even now. She longed to burst into the study, to confess everything she'd learned. But the faces of Thomas, of Rachel, of all those desperate workers flashed before her eyes, staying her hand.

As she moved to the library to dust the shelves, Emma caught sight of her reflection in a gilded mirror. Her deep hazel eyes, usually so warm and full of life, now seemed shadowed, haunted. She barely recognised the woman staring back at her.

In a quiet corner of the library, hidden behind a towering bookshelf, Emma sank to her knees. Her fingers found the silver cross hanging beneath her dress, clutching it like a lifeline.

"Please," she whispered. "Give me strength. Show me the path to justice without violence. Help me protect both the innocent and the desperate."

A tear slipped down her cheek as she prayed, her shoulders shaking with the effort of containing her turmoil. For a moment, she allowed herself to be that scared little girl from the workhouse again, seeking comfort in her faith when all else seemed lost.

∽

As she dusted the ornate mantelpiece in the drawing room, Emma's ears pricked at the sound of raised voices from Lord Edmund's study. She inched closer, her feather duster moving in a steady rhythm to mask her true intent.

"Father, you can't simply ignore the workers' demands!" Frederick's impassioned plea carried through the heavy oak door.

Lord Edmund's response was muffled, but the frustration in his tone was unmistakable.

Emma's heart raced, torn between her duty to the family that had shown her kindness and the desperate faces of Thomas and his compatriots. She forced herself to move on, lest she be caught eavesdropping.

In the library, she found Evelyn bent over a stack of newspapers, her brow furrowed in concentration.

"Everything all right, Miss Evelyn?" Emma asked, careful to keep her tone light.

Evelyn looked up, her eyes troubled. "Oh, Emma. I was just reading about these factory strikes. It's all so... unsettling."

Emma nodded, her throat tight. "Indeed, miss. Troubling times for all."

As she arranged fresh flowers in the conservatory, Lillian appeared at her elbow, eyes wide with curiosity. "Emma, is it true what they're saying? About the angry workers wanting to burn down papa's mill?"

Emma's hands trembled, nearly dropping a delicate rose. "Where did you hear such a thing, Miss Lillian?"

"Clarence overheard the stable boys talking," Lillian said, her voice tinged with fear.

Emma forced a reassuring smile. "I'm sure it's just idle gossip, miss. Nothing to worry about."

Later, as Emma folded linens in the laundry room, she felt a presence behind her. Turning, she found Aunt Agatha watching her with keen eyes.

"You seem troubled, my dear," Aunt Agatha said softly, her voice free of accusation.

Emma swallowed hard, smoothing non-existent wrinkles from a pillowcase. "Just... concerned about all this unrest, ma'am."

Aunt Agatha's gaze softened. "These are difficult times, Emma. One often finds oneself caught between competing loyalties." She paused, laying a gentle hand on Emma's arm. "Remember, child, that a clear conscience is the surest shield."

With that cryptic remark, Aunt Agatha gracefully strode

from the room, leaving Emma to ponder her words and the choices that lay before her.

ADVICE

---

*E*mma's heart raced as she scrubbed the kitchen floors, her mind a whirlwind of conflicting loyalties. The weight of her silver cross necklace seemed to grow heavier with each passing moment.

She paused, resting on her heels, and closed her eyes. The faces of those she cared for flashed before her: Thomas, his eyes burning with revolutionary fervour; the Aspendale family, who had shown her such kindness; the desperate workers, their voices crying out for justice.

"Lord, give me strength," Emma whispered, her fingers tracing the outline of her cross through the fabric of her dress.

As she resumed her work, Emma's resolve crystallised. She needed guidance, a voice of reason amidst the chaos of her thoughts. There was only one person she could turn to, someone who had always been a beacon of wisdom and compassion.

That evening, as the household settled into its nightly routine, Emma slipped out the servants' entrance. The cool night air kissed her flushed cheeks as she hurried through the darkening streets, her destination clear in her mind: Reverend Davies' church.

The familiar silhouette of the modest chapel soon came into view. Emma's steps slowed as she approached, doubt gnawing at her. Was she betraying Thomas by seeking counsel? Was she putting the Aspendales at risk?

Taking a deep breath, Emma steeled herself and knocked on the church door. After a moment, she heard footsteps approaching from within.

The door creaked open, revealing Reverend Davies' weathered face. His eyes widened in surprise, then softened with concern as he took in Emma's troubled expression.

"Emma, my child. What brings you here at this hour?"

Emma opened her mouth, the words of warning on the tip of her tongue. But something held her back. Instead, she heard herself asking, "Reverend, how does one ask God for guidance when feeling utterly lost?"

The old priest's brow furrowed as he ushered her inside. The chapel was dim, lit only by a few flickering candles near the altar. Their footsteps echoed in the empty space as they made their way to a pew.

Reverend Davies sat beside Emma, his hands folded in his lap. "The Lord speaks to us in many ways, Emma. But there is wisdom in the scriptures that can light our path when we feel most adrift."

He reached for a nearby Bible, its leather cover worn smooth by years of use. With practiced ease, he turned to a passage and read aloud, "Trust in the Lord with all your heart and lean not on your own understanding; in all your ways submit to him, and he will make your paths straight."

Emma let the words wash over her, feeling their weight settle in her chest.

"The path of righteousness is often narrow and difficult,"

Reverend Davies continued softly. "But if we place our trust in God and walk in His ways, He will guide us true."

Emma nodded, her throat tight with unspoken words. She thanked the Reverend and rose, making her way back to the church entrance. There, she paused, her hand on the heavy wooden door.

The city sprawled before her, a tapestry of flickering lights and long shadows. Emma's heart felt as heavy as the door beneath her palm, burdened with the knowledge of what was to come and the choices that lay before her.

PRETTY WORDS

The acrid smell of metal and oil filled her nostrils, as Emma made her way through the dimly lit warehouse. She found him in a secluded corner, hunched over a workbench, the rhythmic scrape of metal against stone echoing in the cavernous space.

For a moment, Emma hesitated. The boy she once knew seemed a lifetime away from this hardened man before her. But her silver cross, hidden beneath her dress, gave her strength. She took a deep breath, steeling herself for what was to come.

"Thomas," she called softly, her voice only just carrying over the sound of his work.

He looked up, his eyes narrowing as he recognised her. "Emma? What are you doing here?"

She stepped closer, wringing her hands nervously. "We need to talk, Thomas. About... about the plan."

Thomas set down his tools, wiping his hands on a rag as he turned to face her fully. "What about it?"

Emma swallowed hard, forcing herself to meet his gaze. "It's too dangerous, Thomas. There must be another way."

Thomas's jaw clenched, a hint of something – anger? disappointment? – passing across his face. "Another way? Emma, we've tried other ways. This is our only chance to make them listen."

"But at what cost?" Emma pressed, her voice trembling yet determined. "Surely there's a path that doesn't risk so many innocent lives."

Thomas's eyes hardened, his posture stiffening. "Innocent? The Aspendales and their ilk have never been innocent, Emma. They've profited from our suffering for far too long."

Emma took another step forward, her hands outstretched in a pleading gesture. "I understand your anger, Thomas. Truly, I do. But this plan... it's not the answer. We can find another way, a better way."

Emma's heart raced as she searched Thomas's face for any sign of the boy she once knew. The dim light of the warehouse cast deep shadows across his features, making him seem even more unfamiliar.

"Thomas, please," she implored. "Think of the children who work in those factories. Think of the families who depend on those wages, meagre as they are. If we destroy the mill, what becomes of them?"

Thomas's jaw clenched, his knuckles whitening as he gripped the edge of the workbench. "And what of their futures if we do nothing? How many more will suffer and die in those death traps?"

Emma steadied herself. "I'm not saying we do nothing. But if we do this... We'll lose the moral high ground, and with it, any chance of true change."

She reached out, her fingers stopping just short of touching his arm. "Remember what we dreamed of in the workhouse? A world where justice prevailed, where kindness conquered cruelty? This plan... it's not justice, Thomas. It's vengeance."

Thomas's eyes flickered, a hint of uncertainty breaking through his hardened exterior. "And what would you have us do instead, Emma? Write more petitions that go unread? Stage more protests that are violently suppressed?"

"We find another way," Emma insisted, her voice growing stronger. "We expose their corruption, we rally public support, we make it impossible for them to ignore us without losing everything."

Thomas shook his head, the fire rekindling in his gaze. "Pretty words, Emma. But words won't feed hungry bellies or heal broken bodies. We've tried peaceful methods for years, Emma. They don't listen. This is our only choice."

The faces of the Aspendale children flashed through Emma's mind – Evelyn's quiet determination, Frederick's earnest questions, Benjamin's sea blue eyes, Beatrice's shy smiles, Clarence's mischievous grin, and little Lillian's wide-eyed wonder.

"Thomas, please," she pleaded, her voice trembling with urgency. "Think of the people you'll hurt. Not just the Aspendales, but their children. Innocent souls who've shown nothing but kindness."

Thomas scoffed, his eyes glinting with a cold fire Emma had never seen before. "Kindness? From the very family that profits from our suffering? Emma, you've gone soft living in their world."

Emma felt a surge of indignation. "I haven't gone soft, Thomas. I've seen both sides now. The Aspendale children – they're not their parents. They're just as trapped in this system as we are, in their own way."

"Trapped in luxury, you mean?" Thomas sneered. "While children half their age break their backs in factories?"

"That's not fair," Emma protested. "They didn't choose to be born into privilege, just as we didn't choose to be born into poverty. But they can be allies if we show them the truth, not enemies to be destroyed."

Thomas shook his head, his jaw set in a hard line. "You don't understand, Emma. This isn't about individuals anymore. It's about dismantling a system that's been grinding us down for generations. If a few privileged children have to learn some hard lessons along the way, so be it."

A chill ran down Emma's spine at the coldness in his voice.

"And what of the workers' children?" she pressed. "What happens to them when their parents lose their livelihoods because we destroyed the mill?"

"Short-term pain for long-term gain," Thomas replied, his tone resolute. "We have to break the cycle, Emma. No matter the cost."

Emma shook her head, feeling tears prick at the corners of her eyes. "Thomas, please. There has to be another way. One that doesn't involve destroying lives and livelihoods."

But Thomas' expression remained unmoved, his eyes hard as flint. "You're being naive, Emma. This is the real world, not some fairy tale where everyone lives happily ever after. Sacrifices must be made for the greater good. If you can't see that, maybe you're not the ally I thought you were."

"Thomas, what happened to the boy who believed in justice and compassion? This isn't you. Please, don't do this."

The words hung heavy in the air between them, echoing off the warehouse walls. Emma's heart raced, hoping against hope that she might reach the friend she once knew.

Thomas's face contorted, a storm of anger and pain etched across his features. He stepped closer, his broad frame casting a shadow over Emma. When he spoke, his voice lowered to a harsh whisper.

"That boy died in the workhouse, Emma. The world isn't as simple as you want to believe. These men and women deserve better, and I'll fight for them, even if it means sacrificing everything."

Emma felt her breath catch in her throat. The intensity in Thomas's eyes frightened her, so far removed from the kindhearted boy she'd known.

"Thomas," she said over the distant clanging of machinery. "We once dreamed of changing the world through kindness and perseverance. Don't let your anger destroy that dream. There's still good in you, I know it.

"We can find another way. Together."

Thomas shook his head, his jaw set in a hard line. "There is no other way, Emma. Not anymore."

The finality in his tone sent a chill down Emma's spine. She reached out. "It's not too late to turn back."

Thomas's eyes flickered, a hint of something – regret? pain? – flashing across his face before disappearing behind the mask of determination. "It's been too late for a long time, Emma. You just couldn't see it."

Emma felt tears pricking at the corners of her eyes, her chest tightening. "I won't give up on you, Thomas. Or on finding a peaceful solution."

Thomas turned away, his shoulders hunching as he leaned over his workbench. When he spoke, his voice was low and bitter. "Go back to your safe life at the Aspendales, Emma. This isn't your fight anymore."

The dismissal stung, leaving Emma feeling hollow and lost. She opened her mouth to protest, to make one last plea, but the words died on her lips. Thomas's posture, rigid and unyielding, told her that any further attempts would be futile.

With a heavy heart, Emma took a step back. The distance between them seemed to stretch into an unbridgeable chasm, filled with unspoken words and shattered dreams.

RACE AGAINST TIME

*D*arkness settled over London as the appointed night arrived. Emma's breath quickened as she slipped out of Aspendale Manor, her footsteps muffled by the thick fog that cloaked the streets.

Desperation drove Emma forward, her deep hazel eyes flickering with determination and fear as she headed towards the mill owned by the Aspendale family. The cobblestones were slick beneath her feet, and she clutched her shawl tightly around her shoulders, shivering in the damp night air.

Every shadow seemed to loom larger than life, every distant sound causing Emma to start. She'd grown accustomed to the safety of Aspendale Manor, and now the familiar streets of London felt alien and threatening. But she pressed on, driven by the need to prevent the violence, Thomas and his compatriots had planned.

Emma's mind raced with memories of her conversation with Thomas in the warehouse. The hardness in his eyes haunted her.

As she neared the mill, Emma's pace quickened. The looming brick structure emerged from the fog, its windows dark and lifeless. She knew that soon, those windows might shatter under the force of angry fists and hurled stones. The thought made her stomach churn.

Emma paused in the shadow of a nearby building, her breath coming in quick, shallow gasps. She closed her eyes for a moment, her hand instinctively reaching for the silver cross. A quick prayer passed her lips, a plea for guidance and strength in the face of what was to come.

Emma spotted a group of workers congregated just outside the mill. She recognised a few of them from her visits to the mill with the Aspendales, and the sight of their familiar faces only heightened her sense of urgency.

"Excuse me," Emma whispered. The workers turned to look at her, curiosity and wariness mingling in their expressions. Emma swallowed hard, gathering her courage.

"You have to leave now," she said, her voice low and urgent. "Something terrible is going to happen. Please, trust me."

The workers exchanged glances, skepticism evident in their furrowed brows and tight lips. A burly man with calloused hands stepped forward, eyeing Emma suspiciously.

"And why should we believe you, miss?" he asked, his voice gruff but not unkind.

Emma met his gaze. "I know I'm asking a lot, but I swear on my life, I'm telling the truth. There's no time to explain, but you're all in danger if you stay here."

The urgency in Emma's voice seemed to penetrate their skepticism. The workers began to murmur among themselves, casting uncertain glances at the mill and then back at Emma. A woman with greying hair at her temples spoke up.

"I don't know about the rest of you, but I've got little ones at home. If there's even a chance she's right..."

Her words seemed to sway the group. The burly man who had questioned Emma nodded slowly. "Aye, perhaps it's best we don't take chances. Let's go, lads."

As the workers began to disperse, melting away into the foggy night, Emma felt a momentary surge of relief. But she knew her task was far from over. Thomas and his group were still coming, and she had to find a way to stop them before it was too late.

The cool night air nipped at her skin as she clasped her mother's silver cross, drawing strength from its familiar contours. "Lord, guide my steps," she prayed.

Emma's mind whirled with possibilities, each more desperate than the last. She couldn't risk alerting Thomas and his group, nor could she allow innocent workers to be caught in the crossfire of their misguided revolution. A memory flickered in her mind – a conversation overheard between Frederick and Lord Edmund about the mill's inner workings.

Her gaze settled on a small, unassuming door partially hidden by shadows. Emma recalled Frederick mentioning it as a shortcut to the machinery room, used by workers for quick maintenance. A plan began to form in her mind, risky but potentially effective.

Taking a deep breath to steady her nerves, Emma glanced around to ensure she wasn't being watched. The fog provided a welcome cover as she crept towards the side entrance, her footsteps muffled by the damp cobblestones. Her hand trembled slightly as she reached for the door handle, praying it would be unlocked.

To her relief, the door yielded with a soft creak. Emma slipped inside, enveloped by the warm, oily air of the mill's interior. The distant clanking of machinery grew louder as she navigated the narrow passageway, her heart pounding in her ears.

THE HEART OF THE MILL

The smell of oil and metal filled Emma's nostrils. The interior was a labyrinth of machinery, silent and imposing in the dim light. She moved with careful precision, her footsteps light on the worn wooden floors.

The low hum of dormant machines provided a constant backdrop, masking the sound of her movements. Emma's eyes darted from shadow to shadow, searching for any sign of movement. She passed towering looms and spinning jennies, their intricate mechanisms a testament to the industrial age that had brought both progress and strife.

As she navigated through narrow corridors, Emma's mind flashed back to her conversations with Frederick about the mill's layout. She silently thanked God for those moments of casual chatter that now proved so crucial. Her mission weighed heavily upon her as she slipped from one shadowy room to another.

Emma's senses were on high alert, her ears straining to catch any sound that might betray the approach of Thomas and his group. The creaking of old timber and the occasional drip of water from a leaky pipe made her pause, her breath catching in her throat. But each time, she pressed on, driven by the urgency of her task.

As she moved deeper into the heart of the mill, Emma's thoughts turned to the workers she had warned earlier. She prayed they had heeded her words and were now safe at home with their families. The image of Thomas's determined face flashed in her mind, and she quickened her pace, knowing time was of the essence.

Emma entered the machinery room, her eyes widening at the sight before her. The cavernous space stretched out, filled with an intricate network of gears, pulleys, and machinery that seemed to breathe with a life of its own. The low whirring of motors created an eerie ambiance, punctuated by the occasional clank of metal against metal.

Light from scattered lamps cast long shadows across the room, turning familiar shapes into looming monsters. Emma took a deep breath, steadying herself against the overwhelming sensory assault. The air felt even thicker here.

As her eyes adjusted to the gloom, Emma's gaze fell upon the crucial gears that controlled the mill's operations. Their imposing size made her feel small and insignificant, a mere speck in the grand machinery of industry.

Emma approached the gears cautiously, her footsteps echoing in the vast space. She reached out a tentative hand, feeling the cool metal beneath her fingers. The power contained within these mechanisms was palpable, and Emma understood with sudden clarity why Thomas and his group had chosen this target for their act of sabotage.

Emma knew she had little time. Her fingers brushed against the worn fabric of her shawl as she removed it. She remembered the plan involved turning on the machines to their maximum capacity, and from that causing an explosion. But if the machines couldn't run…

With careful movements, Emma climbed onto the machinery. Her hands trembled, but her resolve remained steady. The cool metal beneath her palms contrasted sharply with the warmth of her shawl as she began to wedge it into the gears. She worked methodically, ensuring the fabric was tightly jammed between the metal teeth.

Emma's breath came in shallow gasps as she focused intently on her task. The enormity of what she was doing – preventing Thomas's sabotage and potentially saving lives – wasn't lost on her. She silently prayed for strength and guidance as she worked.

Suddenly, muffled voices and footsteps echoed through the cavernous room. Emma's heart leapt into her throat, panic threatening to overwhelm her. But she forced herself to concentrate, her fingers working even more frantically to secure the shawl in place.

The voices grew louder, and Emma's entire body tensed with fear. She willed her breathing to steady as she made the final adjustments to her makeshift sabotage prevention. The gears were now thoroughly jammed.

THE HAMMER AND THE CROSS

Thomas Hawkins led his band of determined saboteurs through the shadowy streets of London. Their mission hung heavy in the air, each footstep a muffled echo of their resolve. Jack "Firebrand" O'Malley strode beside him, eyes ablaze with revolutionary fervour. Martha Steele's weathered face bore the scars of countless injustices, her lips pressed into a thin line of determination.

Bert "One-Eye" Clutterbuck limped along, his good eye darting warily from shadow to shadow. Lily Chen moved with quiet grace, her delicate features belying the steel in her spine. Sam "The Ox" Blackburn's massive frame loomed protectively over the group, while Rachel Flowers and George Tinker brought up the rear, their faces etched with a mix of anticipation and trepidation.

Thomas felt the familiar weight of his blacksmith's hammer against his leg, a reminder of the skills that had both enslaved and empowered him.

As they approached the looming silhouette of the mill, Thomas raised a hand, signalling the group to halt. He surveyed the building, its dark windows staring back like soulless eyes.

The machinery inside, usually humming with relentless activity, lay silent in the night.

"Remember," Thomas whispered, his voice rough with emotion, "we're not just destroying a building. We're striking a blow against a system that grinds us down, that treats us as less than human."

Jack nodded fiercely, his fingers tightening around a makeshift torch. Each member of the group carried their own tools of sabotage, chosen with care and forged in the fires of their shared anger.

"C'mon."

Thomas's heart leapt into his throat at the sight of Emma standing before them, her slender figure silhouetted against the dim light of the mill. Her auburn hair, once tied back in a neat bun, now fell in loose waves around her shoulders. The silver cross he'd returned to her glinted at her throat.

"Emma," Thomas breathed. The hammer at his side suddenly felt heavier, its purpose more sinister in the face of her unwavering gaze.

Emma's eyes locked onto his. "Thomas," Emma said, her voice carrying clearly in the night air. "This isn't the way. You know it isn't."

Thomas felt Jack stiffen beside him, the revolutionary fire in his eyes now tinged with confusion. Martha let out a low hiss of frustration, while Bert's good eye narrowed suspiciously.

"What are you doing here, Emma?" Thomas asked, fighting to keep his voice steady. He took a step forward, acutely aware of the group's eyes upon him.

Emma's chin lifted defiantly. "I'm here to stop you from making a terrible mistake. There are innocent lives at stake, Thomas. Workers who depend on this mill for their livelihood. Families who will suffer if you go through with this."

Thomas felt a flicker of doubt, quickly smothered by the anger that had fuelled him for so long. "And what about the suffering that's already happened? The lives ruined by greed and exploitation?"

"Violence isn't the answer," Emma pleaded, her eyes never leaving his. "It will only breed more violence, more pain. There's another way, Thomas. A better way."

Thomas's jaw clenched, torn between the pull of Emma's words and the weight of his convictions. He could feel the group's restlessness behind him, the tension mounting with each passing moment.

"I've jammed the main gears," Emma said, her voice steady despite the tremor in her hands. "Your plan won't work anymore, Thomas. The machinery's useless."

Thomas's jaw clenched, his fingers tightening around the hammer at his side. He could feel the others shifting restlessly behind him, their carefully laid plans crumbling before their eyes.

"We've got other ways," he growled, fighting to keep his voice level. "This place will still burn. We'll make sure of it."

Emma took a step forward, her face pale in the dim light. "And what about the children, Thomas? The Aspendale children who've shown nothing but kindness? What about the workers who'll be caught in the crossfire?"

Thomas flinched, memories of his own childhood flashing before his eyes. The workhouse, the cruel masters, the fleeting moments of joy he'd shared with Emma. He pushed the thoughts away, steeling himself against her words.

"You're talking about justice and compassion," Emma continued, her voice rising with passion. "But where's the justice in destroying lives? Where's the compassion in leaving families without a way to feed themselves?"

Thomas felt the smallest hint of doubt, quickly smothered by the anger that had fuelled him for so long. "And what about our families?" he shot back. "The ones who've suffered under this system for generations?"

Emma's eyes softened, a hint of the girl he once knew shining through. "We can fight for them without becoming the very thing we're fighting against, Thomas. Remember what we used to believe in? The principles we held dear?"

Thomas watched as Rachel and Lily stepped away from the group, their eyes filled with a mixture of uncertainty and resolve as they moved to stand beside Emma. The betrayal stung, but a small part of him understood their choice.

Jack's voice cut through the tense silence, sharp as a knife. "You can't be serious! After everything we've been through, you're gonna let this... this maid talk you out of it?"

Rachel lifted her chin, her voice steady despite the tremor in her hands. "She's right, Jack. We can't build a better world on the ashes of innocent lives."

Lily nodded, her delicate features set with determination. "There must be another way. One that doesn't compromise our principles."

Thomas felt every eye upon him, the group's unity fracturing before his very eyes. He glanced at Bert, hoping for support, but the older man's face was a mask of doubt and confusion.

"Thomas," Emma's voice was soft, almost pleading. "Remember who you were. Who we were together. This isn't you."

For a moment, Thomas allowed himself to remember. The shared dreams, the quiet moments of hope in the midst of despair. He felt the familiar weight of faith tugging at his heart, a sensation he'd thought long buried.

But the memories of pain and injustice surged forward, threatening to drown out Emma's words. Thomas's jaw clenched, his fingers tightening around the hammer at his side.

"You don't know me anymore, Emma," he growled, fighting to keep his voice steady. "You don't know what I've been through, what I've seen."

Sam's deep voice rumbled from behind him. "Maybe not, mate. But she knows what's right. And deep down, so do you."

Thomas watched in disbelief as his carefully assembled group began to crumble before his eyes. Sam's massive frame seemed to shrink as he stepped away, those kind blue eyes filled with a mixture of regret and understanding.

George, ever the thinker, stroked his chin thoughtfully. His weathered features softened as he gave a slow, deliberate nod. "The lass has a point," he muttered, his voice gravelly with age and wisdom. "There's more than one way to fight this battle."

Martha hesitated. Thomas saw the conflict in her eyes, the years of injustice warring with Emma's words of compassion. For a moment, he thought she might stand firm, but then her shoulders sagged slightly.

"I've seen too much suffering," Martha said. "Maybe... maybe it's time to try something different."

One by one, they turned away from him, acknowledging Emma's plea with nods and murmured agreements. The unity he'd worked so hard to build was unravelling before his eyes, leaving him feeling more alone than he had in years.

Thomas felt the world closing in around him. He clenched his jaw, a familiar anger rising in his chest, threatening to consume him. With a snarl, he shoved past Jack, his hammer raised.

"I won't let you stop me," he growled, pushing through the group that had once followed him so loyally. "Not when we're so close."

Emma stood her ground, her eyes never leaving his. "Thomas, please," she pleaded, reaching out to him.

He knocked her hand away, his breath coming in ragged gasps. The others moved to intervene, but Thomas was faster, his years of hard labour giving him an edge. He grabbed Emma's arm, yanking her towards him.

"You don't understand," he hissed, his face inches from hers.

"You've been living in their world, playing by their rules. You've forgotten what it's like for the rest of us."

Emma winced at his grip but didn't back down. "I haven't forgotten, Thomas. I'm trying to save you from becoming what you hate."

A scuffle broke out as Sam and Bert tried to pull Thomas away. In the chaos, Thomas's elbow caught Emma in the face, sending her stumbling backward. She hit the ground hard, a small cry escaping her lips.

The world seemed to slow as Thomas stood over her, his fist raised in blind fury. But as he looked down at Emma, her eyes brimming with tears yet still filled with that unwavering faith, something inside him shattered.

He froze, his arm trembling in mid-air. In that moment, Thomas saw himself reflected in Emma's gaze – not the man he'd become, but the boy he once was. The boy who'd dreamed of justice, not vengeance. The boy who'd found hope in the darkest of places.

Thomas stared at his raised fist, horrified at what he'd almost done. The anger that had fuelled him for so long drained away, leaving him feeling hollow and lost.

Thomas stumbled backward, his hammer clattering to the ground. His actions crashed over him like a tidal wave, threatening to drag him under. His chest heaved as he stared at Emma, sprawled on the ground, her eyes wide with fear and concern.

"What have I become?" The words tore from his throat, raw and agonised. Thomas barely recognised his own voice, so far removed from the boy who'd once dreamed of justice and hope.

He looked at his trembling hands, calloused and scarred from years of labour. Hands that had just struck the one person who'd always believed in him. The realisation hit him like a physical blow, driving the air from his lungs.

Thomas's gaze darted frantically between Emma and the

others. Jack's face was twisted with disgust, while Martha and Bert looked on with a mixture of pity and disappointment. Even Sam, ever loyal, couldn't meet his eyes.

The silence stretched, broken only by the sound of Thomas's ragged breathing. He took a stumbling step backward, then another. The urge to flee, to escape the accusing stares and his own crushing guilt, overwhelmed him.

Without a word, Thomas turned and ran. His boots pounded against the cobblestones as he plunged into the darkness of London's streets. He ran blindly, with no destination in mind, desperate to outpace the shame that threatened to consume him.

Behind him, he could hear shouts and the sound of approaching footsteps. The rest of their group was arriving, ready to carry out the plan he'd so carefully crafted. A plan that now lay in ruins, along with whatever remained of his honour.

Thomas ran faster, his lungs burning and his eyes stinging with unshed tears. He'd lost everything – his purpose, his comrades, and worst of all, the last shred of the boy Emma had once known. The boy who'd believed in something greater than anger and revenge.

As he disappeared into the labyrinth of London's back alleys, Thomas Hawkins was nothing more than a shadow, fleeing from the light of truth that Emma had shown him.

THE EMBERS OF CHAOS

Emma's heart raced as she faced the crowd of angry workers flooding towards the mill: their faces, contorted with rage and desperation. She recognised the look in their eyes—the same fire that had burned in Thomas's gaze moments ago.

"Please, stop!" Emma shouted, her voice barely carrying over the din. "This isn't the way!"

Jack O'Malley stepped forward, his fiery red hair matching the intensity of the moment. "Listen to her, lads! We've had a change of heart."

Martha joined Emma's side. "Think of your families, your children. Violence will only breed more violence!"

But the crowd surged forward, their shouts drowning out reason. Emma felt herself being pushed back against the cold metal of a machine, as the crowd poured through the door, dragging her with them. Bert, his one good eye gleaming in the dim light, tried to hold back the tide of bodies.

"You're making a mistake!" Sam's deep voice boomed, but even his imposing frame couldn't stem the flow of angry workers.

Lily's voice, usually so calm and measured, rose in panic as she pleaded with her fellow immigrants in rapid Cantonese.

Rachel, her hair coming loose from its practical bun, grabbed Emma's arm. "We need to get out of here!" she yelled over the cacophony.

But before Emma could respond, a scuffle broke out near the center of the room. Bodies collided, fists flew, and suddenly, a sickening crash echoed through the mill. Emma watched in horror as a lantern toppled from its perch, spilling oil and flames across the floor.

For a moment, time seemed to stand still. Then, as if awakening from a trance, the crowd's anger transformed into terror. The small flame licked at the oil, growing with frightening speed. Smoke began to fill the air, thick and choking.

"Fire!" The cry went up, and panic took hold.

FORGED IN FLAMES

The chaos around Emma faded into the background as her mind focused on one thing: stopping the fire before it consumed them all.

"Rachel! Lily!" she shouted, her voice cutting through the panicked cries. "We need to put this out now!"

Without hesitation, Rachel and Lily rushed to her side. Emma's eyes darted around the room, searching for anything they could use to fight the flames.

"There!" she pointed to a stack of heavy woolen blankets in the corner. "Grab those!"

Lily dashed across the room, her nimble fingers snatching up the blankets. Rachel spotted a row of buckets near the wall and began filling them from a nearby water pump.

Emma's mind raced, recalling every scrap of knowledge she'd gleaned from her years in the workhouse and Mrs Hartley's establishment. "Smother the flames at the source!" she commanded, her voice steady despite the fear clawing at her insides.

The three women moved as one, their actions synchronized by a shared desperation. Emma grabbed a blanket from Lily, throwing it over the largest patch of flames. The heat seared her hands, but she pressed down, refusing to let go until the fire beneath was extinguished.

Rachel hefted a bucket, dousing the edges of the blaze where it threatened to spread to the wooden beams overhead. Lily, her face set in grim determination, used smaller cloths to beat out the scattered embers that danced across the floor.

Around them, others began to shake off their panic and join the effort. Jack's voice rang out, organising a line to pass buckets of water. Martha directed a group to clear flammable materials away from the spreading flames.

Sweat mingled with soot on Emma's face as she worked tirelessly, moving from one hotspot to another. The flickering flames cast grotesque shadows on the walls, transforming familiar machinery into looming monsters. But Emma refused to let fear paralyse her. She thought of Thomas, of the Aspendale family, of all the lives that would be affected if this mill burned. Her resolve hardened.

"Keep at it!" she encouraged, her voice hoarse from the smoke. "We're making progress!"

Emma's heart raced as she guided the last group of workers towards the exit. Her hazel eyes, reflecting the flickering flames, darted from face to face, ensuring no one was left behind. The acrid smoke burned her lungs, but she pushed through the discomfort, her resolve unwavering.

"This way!" she shouted above the crackling fire and panicked cries. "Stay low and follow me!"

As the workers stumbled towards safety, Emma noticed a young man trapped behind a fallen beam. Without hesitation, she turned back, her grey dress now stained with soot and sweat.

"Hold on!" she called out, her eyes locking with his terrified gaze.

Emma scrambled over debris, the heat intensifying with

each step. She reached a narrow railing, precariously balanced above the burning factory floor. Taking a deep breath, she began to inch her way across, her hands gripping the hot metal.

"I'm coming!" Emma reassured the trapped worker, her voice steady despite the danger.

The smoke thickened, obscuring her vision. Emma blinked rapidly, tears streaming down her face as she fought to keep her eyes open. The railing groaned beneath her weight, threatening to give way at any moment.

"Just a little further," she muttered, more to herself than anyone else.

Emma stretched out her hand, feeling the heat of the flames licking at her skin. The trapped worker reached for her, their fingers barely touching. With a final surge of effort, Emma lunged forward, grasping his hand firmly.

Emma's muscles strained as she pulled the young worker towards her, his weight threatening to drag them both down into the inferno below. With a final burst of strength, she hauled him onto the relative safety of the platform.

"Thank you," he gasped, his eyes wide with relief and fear. "I thought I was done for."

Emma nodded, her breath coming in short pants. "We're not out of danger yet. We need to move."

The worker didn't need to be told twice. He scrambled to his feet, casting one last glance at the roaring flames before rushing towards the exit. Emma watched him go, taking a moment to survey the scene, making sure there were no other trapped souls in need of rescue.

Satisfied that everyone else had made it out, Emma turned to follow the worker. Her legs felt like lead, exhaustion threatening to overtake her. But she pushed on, driven by the urgent need to escape the burning building.

As she moved, Emma's mind raced with thoughts of the others. Had Rachel and Lily made it out safely? What about Jack and Martha? And Thomas... where was he now? She shook her head, forcing herself to focus on the task at hand. There would be time for questions later. Right now, she needed to save herself.

Emma's fingers slipped from the railing, her heart leaping into her throat as gravity took hold. The world seemed to slow, the roar of the flames fading to a distant hum as she plummeted towards the inferno below. Her eyes, wide with terror, locked onto the blazing factory floor rushing up to meet her.

In that eternal moment, Emma's life flashed before her eyes. She saw her parents' faces, heard Thomas's laughter, felt her mother's silver cross against her chest. The faces of Sarah, Hannah, and Lucy swam before her, followed by the kind smiles of the Aspendale children. Each memory, each person who had touched her life, gave her a flicker of strength.

Emma's body twisted in the air, her arms flailing as she desperately sought something, anything to break her fall. The heat of the flames licked at her skin, growing more intense with each passing second. Smoke filled her lungs, making it hard to breathe, hard to think.

"God, please," she whispered, her voice lost in the chaos around her.

As the ground rushed up to meet her, Emma's hand brushed against something solid. Without thinking, she grasped at it, her fingers closing around a chain dangling from a piece of machinery. The sudden jolt sent pain shooting through her arm, but Emma held on with all her might, her teeth gritted against the agony.

She swung there, suspended above the flames, her grip already weakening from the strain and the slick sweat on her palms. Emma could feel the heat rising, singeing the hem of her dress. Her eyes darted around, searching for a way out, a path to safety that seemed increasingly out of reach.

Emma felt her grip slipping, her arms burning with the

effort of holding on. Just as her fingers began to lose their purchase on the chain, a strong hand grasped her wrist. She looked up, her eyes widening in surprise and relief as she saw Thomas's familiar face, etched with concern and determination.

With a grunt of effort, Thomas pulled Emma up, his muscles straining as he lifted her to safety. As soon as her feet touched solid ground, Emma collapsed against him, her body trembling from exhaustion and the fading rush of adrenaline.

Thomas's arms encircled her, holding her steady. Emma could feel the rapid beating of his heart against her cheek, matching the frantic rhythm of her own. For a moment, they stood there, surrounded by the chaos of the burning mill, yet somehow separate from it all.

When Emma finally looked up, she met Thomas's deep brown eyes. The hardness she had seen earlier was gone, replaced by a swirling mix of remorse and gratitude. His face, smudged with soot and glistening with sweat, showed every emotion he was feeling.

"I'm here, Emma. I'm so sorry," Thomas said, his voice trembling with emotion. The words seemed to catch in his throat, as if he were struggling to express the depth of his regret.

Emma searched his face, seeing the boy she had known in the workhouse peeking through the hardened exterior of the man he had become. Despite everything that had happened, despite the anger and hurt she had felt earlier, Emma felt a surge of relief at his presence.

THE RISING DAWN

The roar of the flames seemed to fade into the background as Thomas spoke, his words filled with conviction.

"I won't stop fighting for change, but I'll do it the right way. You showed me the light," Thomas swore, his voice trembling with emotion.

Hope rose within Emma. The boy she had known in the workhouse, the one who had stood up for others and dreamed of a better world, was still there beneath the hardened exterior. She saw it in the way his eyes softened, in the gentle touch of his hand on her arm.

Before Emma could respond, Thomas pulled her close. His lips met hers in a kiss that took her breath away. It was tender yet passionate, filled with years of unspoken feelings and shared history. Emma felt herself melting into the embrace, her hands instinctively moving to Thomas's shoulders.

The kiss spoke volumes where words had failed. Emma could feel Thomas's gratitude, his love, and his renewed sense of purpose. It was as if all the years of separation, all the hardships they had endured, had led to this moment of connection.

As they kissed, Emma's mind whirled with memories. She remembered the frightened boy she had first met in Grimshaw's Workhouse, the friend who had stood by her side through countless trials. She thought of the pain of their separation, the years of wondering and worrying. And now, here they were, reunited amidst the chaos of a burning mill, finding their way back to each other.

The kiss seemed to last an eternity, yet ended all too soon. As they parted, Emma's cheeks flushed with more than just the heat of the fire. She looked up at Thomas, seeing a familiar spark in his eyes – the same determination she had always admired, but now tempered with wisdom and compassion.

When they finally parted, Emma looked up at Thomas with a breathless smile. "We should probably get out of the burning building first," she grinned.

Thomas nodded, a ghost of a smile playing on his lips. "Right you are," he agreed, his voice husky with emotion.

Together, they turned to face the chaos around them. The mill's interior was a haze of smoke and flickering orange light. Shadows danced on the walls as workers scrambled for safety, their shouts echoing off the stone walls.

Emma's eyes darted around, searching for anyone who might have been left behind. "We need to make sure everyone's out," she said, her voice firm with determination.

Thomas squeezed her hand. "Lead the way," he said, falling into step beside her.

They moved through the smoky corridors, Emma's knowledge of the mill's layout guiding their path. She called out, her voice rising above the din, "Is anyone still here? Follow our voices!"

Thomas joined in, his deep baritone carrying through the thick air. "This way! We'll get you out!"

As they navigated the treacherous path, Emma spotted a

figure hunched in a corner, coughing violently. Without hesitation, she rushed over, Thomas right behind her.

"It's all right," Emma soothed, helping the worker to his feet. "We're getting out of here."

Thomas supported the man's other side, and together, they made their way towards the exit. The heat pressed in around them, sweat beading on their brows as they pushed forward.

∽

As the first rays of dawn broke through the smoky haze, Emma and Thomas emerged from the mill, their hands clasped tightly together. Behind them, a stream of workers and would-be saboteurs stumbled into the cool morning air, coughing and blinking in the pale light.

Emma's heart raced as she surveyed the scene. The once-imposing mill now stood silent, wisps of smoke curling from its windows. The fire that had threatened to consume everything was now little more than smouldering embers, thanks to their combined efforts.

She felt Thomas's hand squeeze hers, and she turned to meet his gaze. His face was streaked with soot, but his eyes shone with relief and newfound purpose.

Around them, the group began to gather. Jack O'Malley, his fiery rhetoric silenced by the night's events, slumped against a nearby wall. Martha Steele stood tall, her weathered face etched with lines of worry and relief. Bert Clutterbuck rubbed his good eye, as if trying to clear away the last vestiges of his anger along with the smoke.

Emma watched as Lily Chen helped Sam Blackburn tend to a small cut on his arm, their earlier animosity forgotten in the wake of their shared ordeal. Rachel Flowers caught Emma's eye and offered a small, grateful smile.

The tension that had fuelled their plans for destruction

seemed to have dissipated with the smoke. In its place, Emma sensed a fragile camaraderie, born from their narrow escape and the realization of how close they had come to tragedy.

"We... we could have died in there," George Tinker muttered, breaking the silence. His words hung in the air, heavy with what might have been.

Emma felt Thomas stiffen beside her, but before he could speak, she stepped forward. "But we didn't," she said firmly, her voice carrying across the group. "We chose a different path. We chose to save lives instead of destroying them."

CROSSROADS

～

The sound of approaching hoofbeats drew Emma's attention. She turned to see Lord Edmund Aspendale himself riding towards them, his face a mask of concern and confusion. As he dismounted, his eyes swept over the scene, taking in the blackened walls of the mill and the exhausted workers gathered around.

"What in world happened here?" Lord Edmund demanded, his voice sharp with worry.

Emma stepped forward, her chin held high despite her dishevelled appearance. "My lord, there was an accident. A fire broke out, but we managed to extinguish it and evacuate everyone safely."

Lord Edmund's gaze fell on Thomas, who stood beside Emma, his face streaked with ash and sweat. Recognition dawned in the nobleman's eyes. "You're the blacksmith's apprentice, aren't you? What's your part in this?"

Thomas straightened his shoulders, meeting Lord Edmund's gaze squarely. "My lord, I must be honest. I came here with intentions of sabotage, driven by anger at the injustices faced by the workers. But Emma..." He glanced at her, his eyes softening.

"Emma showed me the error of my ways. The fire was an accident, not our doing, and we worked together to save lives and your property."

Lord Edmund's brow furrowed as he processed this information. Emma held her breath, fear and hope warring within her. She watched as Frederick, who had arrived with his father, leaned in to whisper something in Lord Edmund's ear.

After a moment of contemplation, Lord Edmund spoke, his voice measured. "Your honesty is commendable, young man. And your actions in the face of danger speak to your character." He paused, his gaze moving between Thomas and Emma. "I won't press charges, on one condition: you will work as a blacksmith for the Aspendale company, to repay your debt to us."

Thomas nodded solemnly. "I accept, my lord. I will pay my debt however is needed."

Emma watched as Thomas turned to address the gathered workers and activists. His deep brown eyes, once filled with anger and resentment, now shone with a newfound earnestness. The transformation in his demeanour was palpable, and Emma felt a surge of pride and hope well up within her.

"My friends," Thomas began, his voice carrying across the mill yard, "I owe you all an apology. I've led you down a path of violence and destruction, believing it was the only way to achieve justice. But I was wrong."

He paused, his gaze sweeping over the faces before him.

"We must pursue our cause through peaceful protest and legal means," Thomas continued. "Violence only begets more violence, and in the end, it's the very people we're trying to help who suffer the most. I vow to you all that I will make amends for my misguided actions and work tirelessly for our rights through honourable means."

As Thomas's words settled over the crowd, Emma felt compelled to add her voice. She stepped forward, her deep hazel eyes shining with hope and conviction.

"We stand at a crossroads," Emma said, her voice clear and strong. "The path ahead won't be easy, but if we unite in our cause with courage and integrity, we can achieve the justice and fairness we all seek. Let us show the world that change can come through peaceful means, that our strength lies not in destruction, but in our unwavering spirit and solidarity."

UNDER THE EVENING SKY

※

*A*s the sun dipped below the horizon, casting long shadows across Aspendale Manor's grounds, Emma descended the narrow staircase to the gardens. The wooden steps creaked beneath her feet, a familiar sound that now brought comfort rather than anxiety. She stepped outside into the crisp air, and Thomas turned, smiling as he saw her.

"I was beginning to think you'd forgotten about me," Thomas said, a hint of a smile in his voice.

Emma's heart quickened at the sight of him. "Never."

They settled onto a bench, their shoulders touching. For a moment, they sat in comfortable silence, the day's work melting away in each other's presence.

"Do you remember," Thomas began, his voice warm, "that night on the workhouse roof? When we watched the stars and dreamed of a better life?"

Emma nodded, a small smile playing on her lips. "I do. It seemed so impossible then."

"And yet, here we are," Thomas mused, taking Emma's hand in his. His fingers, once calloused from the harsh labour of the workhouse, were now strong and sure from his work at the forge.

Emma's thumb traced the lines of Thomas's palm, marvelling at how far they'd come. "We've been through so much," she whispered. "Sometimes I can hardly believe it."

Thomas turned to face her. "Your faith never wavered, Emma. Even when mine did. You were my guiding light through the darkest times."

"I lost my way for a while, but I've found it again. Found my purpose... and you."

Their eyes met, and in that moment, Emma saw reflected in Thomas's gaze all the shared hardships, the triumphs, and the unwavering bond that had brought them to this point. Without a word, they leaned towards each other, their lips meeting in a gentle kiss that spoke of love, understanding, and shared dreams for the future.

THE CROSS

Emma watched Thomas with a quiet joy, her heart swelling as she observed the gradual change in him. In the weeks following the mill incident, she noticed subtle shifts in his demeanour. Where once his eyes had been clouded with doubt and anger, now they held a glimmer of something familiar – a light she recognized from their shared childhood.

One evening, as they walked hand in hand through the manor gardens, Thomas paused beneath an old oak tree. "Emma," he said, his voice soft, "would you... would you pray with me?"

Emma's breath caught in her throat. She nodded, unable to speak past the lump of emotion. They knelt together on the cool grass, and Thomas's voice, hesitant at first, grew stronger as he spoke to God for the first time in years.

In the days that followed, Emma often found Thomas deep in conversation with Reverend Davies. She'd catch snippets of their discussions – about faith, forgiveness, and finding one's way back to God. The Reverend's gentle guidance seemed to soothe something in Thomas, smoothing the rough edges that years of hardship had carved into his soul.

One afternoon, Emma noticed Thomas spending long hours at the forge. Curiosity piqued, she approached, the heat of the fires warming her face as she drew near. Thomas stood hunched over his workbench, his brow furrowed in concentration.

"What are you working on?" Emma asked, trying to peer around his broad shoulders.

Thomas turned, a shy smile playing on his lips. "It's a surprise," he said, his eyes twinkling with a secret. "You'll see soon enough."

As the days passed, Emma caught glimpses of Thomas at work – the rhythmic clanging of his hammer, the soft glow of metal in the forge. Each time she saw him emerge from the workshop, there was a peace about him that she hadn't seen in years.

One evening, as the sun dipped low on the horizon, casting long shadows across the Manor grounds, Emma found herself drawn to the forge. The warm glow spilling from its entrance beckoned her, and she approached with quiet steps.

Through the open doorway, she saw Thomas bent over his workbench, his strong hands moving with a delicate precision she'd never witnessed before. The firelight danced across his features, softening the hard lines that years of struggle had etched into his face.

She realised what Thomas was crafting. In his hands, a small silver cross took shape, its form achingly familiar. It was a mirror image of the one that hung around her own neck, the precious gift from her mother that had been her anchor through countless trials.

Thomas worked with painstaking care, his fingers tracing the delicate curves of the cross. Emma watched, transfixed, as he polished the silver until it gleamed in the firelight. There was a peace about him that she hadn't seen since their childhood days in the workhouse, before the world had hardened him.

As Thomas held the finished cross up to the light, a smile of quiet satisfaction spread across his face. Emma saw in that moment not just the man she loved, but the boy she had known – the one who had shared her faith and her dreams of a better world.

THE FIGHT FOR CHANGE

Emma's fingers traced the smooth surface of her mother's silver cross as she and Thomas made their way through the bustling streets of London.

As they approached the entrance of the textile mill, Emma noticed the sideways glances and hushed whispers of the workers gathering for their shift. A group of men huddled near the gates, their eyes narrowing as Thomas drew near.

"Well, if it isn't the reformed rebel," one of them sneered, spitting at Thomas's feet. "Come to preach about peaceful negotiations, have you?"

Thomas tensed beside her, but Emma placed a gentle hand on his arm. "We're here to speak with Mr Holloway about improving working conditions," she said, her voice calm but firm.

A woman in the crowd scoffed. "And what would a workhouse rat know about proper working conditions? You should be grateful for any work at all."

Emma felt the sting of the words, but she held her head high. "I may have come from Grimshaw's, but that doesn't make my desire for fair treatment any less valid."

As they pushed through the throng of skeptical faces, Emma overheard snippets of conversation.

"Can't trust a man who changes his tune so quickly."

"She's probably just using him to climb the social ladder."

"They'll never understand what it's really like for us."

Inside the mill, the foreman, Mr Garrett, eyed them suspiciously as they approached. "Mr Holloway won't see you today," he said gruffly. "We don't need troublemakers stirring up discontent among the workers."

Thomas stepped forward, his voice steady. "We're not here to cause trouble, Mr Garrett. We only want to discuss ways to improve conditions for everyone's benefit."

The foreman's laugh was harsh. "And why should we believe you? Last I heard, you were ready to burn a place like this to the ground."

Emma felt a flicker of doubt, but she pushed it aside. She thought of the Aspendale family, of Reverend Davies, of all those who had shown faith in them despite their pasts. Drawing strength from these memories, she spoke up.

"People can change, Mr Garrett. Thomas and I have seen the consequences of violence and know it's not the answer. We're here because we believe in a better way forward – for everyone."

Emma watched as Mr Garrett's stern expression wavered. His eyes darted between her and Thomas, searching for any sign of deception. For a moment, the only sound was the distant hum of machinery.

"Well," Mr Garrett said finally, his voice gruff but less hostile, "I suppose there's no harm in hearing you out. But mind you, any hint of trouble and you'll be out on your ear."

As they followed Mr Garrett through the factory floor, Emma noticed the curious glances from the workers. Some wore expressions of hope, while others remained skeptical. She felt Thomas's hand brush against hers, a silent gesture of support.

In Mr Holloway's office, Emma was surprised to find Lord Edmund Aspendale already present. His eyes met hers, and she detected a hint of approval in his nod.

"Miss Redbrook, Mr Hawkins," Lord Aspendale said, his tone measured but not unkind. "I've been discussing some of your proposals with Mr Holloway. I must admit, your dedication to improving conditions here is... commendable."

Emma's heart leapt at his words. She glanced at Thomas, seeing her own surprise mirrored in his face.

Mr Holloway, a portly man with a receding hairline, leaned forward in his chair. "Lord Aspendale tells me you have some ideas about how to increase productivity while also addressing workers' concerns. I'm interested to hear them."

As Emma began to outline their suggestions, she felt a surge of hope. The room's atmosphere shifted from tense to attentive. Even Mr Garrett, standing by the door with arms crossed, seemed to be listening intently.

By the time Emma finished speaking, a thoughtful silence had fallen over the room. Lord Aspendale was the first to break it.

"Well, Mr Holloway," he said, turning to the factory owner, "I believe Miss Redbrook and Mr Hawkins have presented some compelling arguments. Perhaps it's time we considered implementing some of these changes."

UNITY

Emma watched in awe as Lady Victoria Aspendale gracefully moved through the crowded drawing room, her honey blonde hair gleaming in the afternoon light. The elegant matriarch of the Aspendale family had transformed her usual social gatherings into a platform for change, inviting influential women from London's upper echelons to hear about workers' rights reform.

"Ladies, I'd like to introduce you to Miss Emma Grace Redbrook," Lady Victoria announced, her cultured tones commanding attention. "She has a most compelling story to share about the plight of our city's workers."

Emma stepped forward, her heart racing. She'd never imagined addressing such a gathering, yet here she was, standing before women draped in silks and adorned with jewels. She took a deep breath, remembering Thomas's encouraging words earlier that morning.

"Thank you, Lady Aspendale," Emma began, her voice steady despite her nerves. "I stand before you today not just as a former workhouse girl or a current employee of the Aspendale household, but as a voice for those who have none."

As Emma spoke, she noticed Evelyn Aspendale in the corner, furiously scribbling notes. The eldest Aspendale daughter had become a fierce ally, using her sharp intellect to craft powerful articles advocating for reform. Their eyes met briefly, and Evelyn gave an encouraging nod.

Later that evening, Emma found herself in Lord Edmund's study with Thomas, Frederick, and several other members of their growing coalition. Frederick, the Aspendale heir, leaned over a map of London spread across the mahogany desk.

"If we concentrate our efforts in these areas," Frederick said, pointing to several factory districts, "we can maximize our impact without stretching our resources too thin."

Thomas nodded, his brow furrowed in concentration. "Agreed. We'll need to coordinate with Jack and the others to ensure our message remains consistent across all the gatherings."

Emma marvelled at the unlikely alliance they'd formed. Here, in the opulent surroundings of Aspendale Manor, factory workers and aristocrats worked side by side, united in their pursuit of justice. She thought of Rachel and Lily, who'd become steadfast friends and invaluable strategists. Even Jack O'Malley, once so bent on destruction, now channelled his passion into inspiring peaceful change.

THE GATHERING TORCH

*E*mma watched with a mixture of pride and concern as Thomas addressed a crowd of workers gathered in a dimly lit warehouse. His voice, once hardened by anger, now rang with passionate conviction as he spoke of peaceful resistance and unity. The crowd hung on his every word, their faces a mix of hope and determination.

"We stand together, not to tear down, but to build up!" Thomas declared, his eyes shining. "Our strength lies in our solidarity, in our refusal to be silenced or divided."

As the crowd erupted in cheers, Emma noticed movement near the warehouse entrance. Her heart sank as she recognized Inspector Wilkins, his face twisted in a scowl. She nudged Rachel, who stood beside her, and nodded towards the door.

Rachel's eyes narrowed. "I'll handle this," she whispered, slipping away through the crowd.

Emma turned her attention back to Thomas, who was now fielding questions from the workers. She marvelled at how far they'd come, yet the constant threat of arrest loomed over them like a dark cloud.

Later that week, Emma found herself in the Aspendale

Manor library with Lily Chen, poring over newspaper clippings spread across a large oak table. The headlines screamed accusations of rabble-rousing and sedition, each article more vicious than the last.

"They're trying to discredit us," Lily said, her voice tight with frustration. "Look at this – they're painting Thomas as a dangerous radical, completely ignoring our peaceful approach."

Emma sighed, running a hand through her auburn hair. "We knew this wouldn't be easy. But we can't let them silence us."

The door burst open, and Jack O'Malley strode in, his face flushed with excitement. "You won't believe what's happening out there," he exclaimed. "Beatrice Aspendale's organised an art exhibition in the town square. It's drawing quite a crowd!"

Emma and Lily exchanged surprised glances before following Jack out of the library. As they reached the Manor's entrance, they saw Beatrice directing a group of young artists hanging paintings and sketches on makeshift displays.

Emma's eyes widened as she took in the scene before her. Beatrice Aspendale, usually so reserved, stood confidently in the center of the town square, directing a flurry of activity. Easels and wooden boards had been set up in a semicircle, each displaying paintings and sketches that depicted scenes from factory life.

The artwork was raw and honest, portraying the harsh realities of industrial labour alongside moments of human dignity and resilience. Emma recognised the style of several young artists she had met during her visits to the factories with Thomas. Their talent, nurtured in secret during stolen moments between gruelling shifts, now shone for all to see.

Beatrice caught sight of Emma and waved her over, her cheeks flushed with excitement. "What do you think?" she asked, gesturing to the exhibit. "I wanted to give these workers a voice beyond words."

Emma's heart swelled with pride. "It's incredible, Beatrice.

You've captured their struggles and their strength so beautifully."

As they spoke, Emma noticed Clarence Aspendale deep in conversation with a group of factory owners and workers. His hands moved animatedly as he explained something, pointing to a series of diagrams pinned to one of the displays.

"Clarence has been working on designs for improved ventilation systems," Beatrice explained, following Emma's gaze. "He's convinced several factory owners to implement them. The workers say it's made a world of difference."

Emma nodded, impressed by the young man's ingenuity and dedication. She had always known there was more to Clarence than his boyish enthusiasm for explosions and gadgets.

A commotion near the edge of the square drew Emma's attention. She spotted Lillian Aspendale surrounded by a group of children, their eyes wide with wonder as she spoke. As Emma drew closer, she could hear Lillian's clear voice.

"Remember, children, you have the right to safety and fair treatment," Lillian was saying, her tone gentle but firm. "If you see something wrong, don't be afraid to speak up."

Emma watched as the children nodded solemnly, hanging on Lillian's every word. It was a far cry from the timid girl Emma had first met upon arriving at Aspendale Manor. Lillian had found her voice, and she was using it to make a difference.

THE TURN OF THE TIDE

*E*mma stood beside Thomas at the head of the crowd gathering in front of the town hall. Workers from every factory in London stood shoulder to shoulder with aristocrats and shopkeepers, their faces a mix of determination and hope. The sight filled her with a sense of awe and purpose she'd never experienced before.

Thomas squeezed her hand, his eyes shining with pride. "Ready?" he whispered.

Emma nodded, drawing strength from the silver cross that hung around her neck. She stepped forward, her voice ringing out clear and strong across the square.

"We stand here today not as enemies, but as one people united in our desire for justice and dignity!"

The crowd erupted in cheers. Emma saw Frederick Aspendale nodding approvingly from the steps of the town hall, while Evelyn furiously scribbled notes in her ever-present journal. Even Lady Victoria, who had initially been skeptical of their cause, stood tall and proud among the protesters.

As Emma continued her speech, she noticed a flurry of activity near the edge of the crowd. Reporters from every major newspaper in London jostled for position, their pencils flying across notepads. The clacking of camera shutters punctuated her words as photographers captured the historic moment.

When Thomas took over, his impassioned words electrifying the air, Emma's gaze swept across the sea of faces before her. She saw Jack with his arm around Martha, both of them beaming with pride. Lily stood tall despite her small stature, her chin lifted defiantly. Even gruff old Bert had tears in his eyes as he listened to Thomas speak.

The protest stretched on for hours, but there was no violence, no unrest. Workers shared their stories of hardship and hope, while factory owners pledged to make meaningful changes. Emma watched in amazement as Lord Edmund Aspendale shook hands with Sam, the two men finding common ground despite their vastly different backgrounds.

As the sun began to set, casting a golden glow over the crowd, a shift in the air was palpable. Something had changed today. The seeds of reform they had planted were beginning to take root, and she could sense the tide of public opinion turning in their favour.

THE RING

*E*mma's heart swelled with joy as she and Thomas stepped into the tranquil sanctuary of Reverend Davies' church. The soft glow of candlelight danced across the worn pews, casting long shadows that seemed to embrace them. The air hung heavy with the scent of beeswax and old wood, a comforting reminder of countless prayers whispered within these walls.

Thomas guided her towards the altar, his hand warm and steady in hers. Emma's gaze lingered on the silver cross that now adorned his neck, a mirror of her own. The sight of it filled her with a quiet pride, a testament to how far they'd come.

As they knelt before the altar, Thomas turned to her, his eyes reflecting the flickering flames. "Shall we?" he asked.

Emma nodded, closing her eyes as Thomas began to pray. His words, once so full of anger and doubt, now flowed with a gentle reverence that brought tears to her eyes. She joined him, her own voice intertwining with his in a melody of gratitude and hope.

"Lord," Emma murmured, "we thank You for Your guidance

through the darkest of times. For the strength You've given us to fight for justice, and for the love that has sustained us."

Thomas squeezed her hand, his voice growing stronger. "We ask for Your continued blessing on our work, that we might be instruments of Your peace in this troubled world."

As their prayer continued, Emma felt a profound sense of peace wash over her. The weight of their responsibilities, the constant struggle for workers' rights, seemed to lift from her shoulders. In this moment, there was only Thomas, the warmth of his hand in hers, and the unwavering faith that had carried them both through so much.

As Thomas reached into his pocket, Emma's heart skipped two beats. The candlelight flickered across his face, illuminating the love and determination in his deep brown eyes. He produced a small, worn velvet box.

"Emma," Thomas began, "you've been my guiding light since we were children. Through the darkest times, your faith and strength have been my anchor."

He opened the box, revealing a simple silver band, with a small stone encased within it. The ring caught the light, sparkling with a brilliance that belied its humble appearance.

"I made this for you." Thomas explained, his voice thick with emotion. "I made it the day after you saved me at the mill. I've just been waiting for the right moment."

Emma's eyes welled with tears as Thomas took her hand in his. The roughness of his palm against her skin reminded her of all they'd endured together, all they'd fought for.

"Emma Grace Redbrook," Thomas said, his gaze never leaving hers, "will you continue this journey with me, as my wife?"

Emma's heart soared. "Yes," Emma voice trembled with joy. "Yes, Thomas, I will."

As Thomas slipped the ring onto her finger, Emma felt the

weight of its history, of all it represented. It was more than a symbol of their love; it was a testament to their shared struggle, their unwavering commitment to each other and to the cause they both held dear.

LASTING CHANGE

The air crackled with tension in the packed town hall, faces etched with skepticism and anger staring back at her. Emma felt Thomas's reassuring presence beside her, his strength bolstering her own.

A burly man with a thick moustache rose from his seat, his voice booming through the hall. "Who are you to speak for us? A former workhouse orphan and a blacksmith? What do you know of running a business or managing workers?"

Murmurs of agreement rippled through the crowd. Emma took a deep breath, her hand instinctively touching the silver cross at her neck.

"You're right," Emma began, her voice clear and steady. "I am an orphan who grew up in Grimshaw's Workhouse. I've known hunger, abuse, and despair. But I've also known hope, faith, and the power of unity."

She paused, her gaze sweeping across the room. "It's precisely because we've lived these experiences that we understand the true cost of injustice. We've seen firsthand the toll it takes on families, on communities, on the very fabric of our society."

Emma's voice grew stronger, passion infusing her words. "We're not here to destroy businesses or upend lives. We're here to build a future where every worker is treated with dignity, where every child has a chance to thrive, where prosperity is shared by all."

She turned to Thomas, drawing strength from his unwavering support. "Thomas and I have walked in the shoes of those we seek to help. We've also worked alongside factory owners, learning the complexities of running a business. Our goal is not to tear down, but to lift up – to create a system that benefits everyone."

Emma's eyes shone with conviction as she addressed the crowd once more. "We may not have fancy titles or prestigious educations, but we have something far more valuable – a deep understanding of the struggles faced by workers and a genuine desire to create positive change."

As Emma spoke, she noticed a shift in the atmosphere. Frowns began to soften, nods of agreement replacing looks of doubt.

Emma's heart swelled with hope as she watched the faces in the crowd soften. The tension in the room began to dissipate, replaced by a cautious curiosity. She glanced at Thomas, drawing strength from his steady presence beside her.

"We're not here to make empty promises," Emma continued, her voice clear and confident. "We're here to take action. With the support of the Aspendale family, we're establishing a foundation dedicated to workers' rights, education, and social justice."

A murmur of interest rippled through the crowd. Emma pressed on, her passion evident in every word. "This foundation will create programs to help those who have been exploited by the system, particularly former child labourers. We aim to ensure they receive the education and opportunities they've been denied for so long."

Emma's gaze fell on Rachel Flowers, who sat in the front row, her eyes shining with unshed tears. "I see before me individuals like Rachel, who started working in factories as children, robbed of their childhood and education. Our foundation will provide a path for them to reclaim what was taken, to learn, to grow, and to build better futures for themselves and their families."

Thomas stepped forward, his voice joining Emma's. "We've seen firsthand the cycle of poverty and exploitation. This foundation aims to break that cycle, to lift up those who have been pushed down for far too long."

As they spoke, Emma could see the spark of hope igniting in the eyes of those gathered. The skepticism was giving way to a cautious optimism. She felt a surge of determination, knowing that this was just the beginning of their journey to create real, lasting change.

TOGETHER

*E*mma stood on the balcony of Aspendale Manor, her eyes sweeping over the bustling city below. The late afternoon sun cast a golden glow over the rooftops, a far cry from the grimy streets she'd once called home. Beside her, Thomas's solid presence anchored her to the present.

She felt her silver cross against her skin, cool and comforting. Emma's fingers traced its familiar contours, a gesture that had become second nature over the years. Silently, she offered a prayer of gratitude, marvelling at the twists and turns that had led them here.

Thomas's arm slipped around her waist, pulling her close. Emma leaned into him. She turned to meet his gaze, finding herself lost in the depths of his soulful brown eyes. They held a fire she'd first glimpsed in the workhouse, now tempered by wisdom and unwavering faith.

"We've come so far, Emma," Thomas murmured, his voice filled with wonder. "And together, we'll go even further."

Emma nodded, her heart swelling with love and determination. She watched as Thomas lifted his own silver cross, a mirror image of hers. Without a word, they brought the two crosses together, the metal clinking softly.

In that moment, Emma saw their whole journey reflected in the joined crosses. From the despair of Grimshaw's Workhouse to the hope they now offered others, every step had led them here. Their shared faith had been their compass, guiding them through the darkest nights and the brightest days.

As they stood united, the crosses gleaming in the fading sunlight, Emma and Thomas silently renewed their commitment. To each other, to their cause, and to the divine purpose that had brought them together. Their wedding day approached, promising not just a union of two hearts, but a joining of two souls dedicated to bringing light to the shadows of injustice.

EPILOGUE

Who can find a virtuous woman? for her price is far above rubies.
  – Proverbs 31:10

THE DRESS

The Aspendale Manor hummed with activity as the day of Emma and Thomas's wedding drew near. Servants scurried through the halls, arms laden with flowers and ribbons, while the kitchen staff prepared a feast greater than any Emma could have dreamt of having. The air buzzed with excitement, a palpable energy that seemed to infuse every corner of the grand house.

Emma stood in Lady Victoria's private sitting room, surrounded by a sea of white fabric and lace. Her deep hazel eyes sparkled with joy and disbelief as she ran her fingers over the delicate materials. Lady Victoria and Beatrice moved around her, holding up various gowns and veils for consideration.

"What do you think of this one, Emma?" Beatrice asked, presenting a dress adorned with intricate beadwork and a sweeping train.

Emma's brow furrowed slightly. The gown was beautiful, but it felt... wrong. Too ostentatious, too far removed from the girl who'd scrubbed floors in Grimshaw's Workhouse. She shook her head gently.

Lady Victoria, observing Emma's reaction, stepped forward with another option. This dress was simpler, made of soft ivory silk with subtle lace accents. "Perhaps this would be more to your liking?" she suggested, her voice softer than Emma had ever heard it.

As Emma's fingers brushed against the silk, she felt a flutter in her chest. This dress spoke to her, reminding her of the strength she'd found in simplicity, the beauty that could arise from even the harshest circumstances.

"It's perfect," Emma whispered, her eyes meeting Lady Victoria's with genuine gratitude.

Beatrice clapped her hands in delight. "Oh, Emma! It suits you wonderfully. And look how it complements your cross!"

Emma's hand instinctively went to the silver cross at her throat. She smiled, imagining how she would look walking down the aisle to Thomas, this dress a symbol of both where she'd come from and where she was going.

THE INVITATIONS

*E*mma sat at the ornate writing desk in her room at Aspendale Manor, her brow furrowed in concentration as she carefully penned each invitation. The stack of envelopes beside her grew steadily, each name representing a chapter in the remarkable journey that had led her to this moment.

Her hand paused over an envelope addressed to Jack "Firebrand" O'Malley. Emma smiled, remembering the fiery activist's initial skepticism towards her and Thomas. Now, he was to be a guest at their wedding.

Next came invitations for Rachel Flowers and Lily Chen. Emma's heart swelled with affection for these women who had become dear friends and allies in the fight for workers' rights. Their presence would be a reminder of the cause that had brought her and Thomas together.

As she wrote out invitations for Fiona, Rose, and Mary, Emma's mind drifted back to Mrs Hartley's establishment. Those dark days had seemed hopeless, yet they had forged friendships that now shone brightly in her life.

Her hand trembled slightly as she addressed envelopes to

Sarah and Hannah. Tears pricked at Emma's eyes as she thought of the little girls they had once been, huddled together in Grimshaw's Workhouse. Now, they would stand beside her as bridesmaids, symbols of resilience and hope.

Emma's heart leapt as she penned an invitation to Lucy. After months of searching, they had finally found her working in a textile mill in Manchester. The joy of reconnecting with her old friend had been indescribable, and having Lucy as a bridesmaid felt like coming full circle.

As she worked, Emma marvelled at the diversity of the guest list. Workers would sit alongside aristocrats, former enemies would break bread together. Lord Edmund and Lady Victoria's names were written with the same care as those of the mill workers Thomas had befriended.

Each invitation represented more than just a wedding guest; it was a testament to the world Emma and Thomas were striving to create. A world where people from all walks of life could come together, united in their shared humanity.

THE GIFT

"*E*mma, my love," Thomas began tenderly. "I have something for you."

He revealed a beautifully bound leather journal, its cover embossed with intricate designs. Emma gently took it from him, running her fingers over the soft leather.

"Open it," Thomas urged softly.

Emma carefully lifted the cover, her eyes widening as she saw the first page. There, in Thomas's careful handwriting, was a detailed account of their first meeting at Grimshaw's Workhouse. As she turned the pages, she found more memories – their secret lessons on the rooftop, their daring escape, their reunion years later.

Interspersed with the memories were Thomas's hopes and dreams for their future together. Emma's vision blurred with tears as she read his heartfelt words about the family they would build, the changes they would make in the world, and the love that would sustain them through it all.

"Thomas," Emma whispered, her voice thick with emotion. "This is... it's beautiful."

Thomas took her hand, his fingers intertwining with hers. "I wanted you to have something that captures our journey – where we've been and where we're going."

Emma looked up at him, her heart overflowing with love for this man who had been her anchor through so much turmoil. Without a word, she reached for the pen tucked into the journal's spine and began to write.

Her hand moved swiftly across the page as she poured out her gratitude for Thomas's unwavering support and love. She wrote of her admiration for his strength, his kindness, and his determination to make the world a better place. Finally, she penned a solemn promise to cherish their journey together for all her days.

As Emma finished writing, she looked up to find Thomas watching her, his eyes shining with unshed tears. She closed the journal and pressed it to her heart, feeling as though it contained the very essence of their love.

THE WEDDING

Emma stirred as the first light of dawn filtered through the curtains of her room at Aspendale Manor. Her eyes fluttered open, and for a moment, she lay still, letting the realisation wash over her. Today was her wedding day.

A flutter of excitement mixed with a twinge of nervousness settled in her stomach as she sat up, her gaze falling on the simple ivory gown hanging by the wardrobe.

"Lord," she whispered, closing her eyes, "guide us through this day and all the days to come."

As she knelt by her bedside, Emma's thoughts drifted to Thomas. She wondered if he, too, was awake, perhaps offering his own prayers in the quiet of the morning. The image brought a smile to her lips.

Across town, Thomas stood by the window of his modest lodgings, watching the city slowly come to life. His calloused hands, evidence of years of hard work, were clasped behind his back. The silver cross he had crafted hung from his neck, a symbol of his rekindled faith and his love for Emma.

Thomas bowed his head, his voice barely audible as he prayed. "Father, grant us the strength to honour the vows we'll make today. Help us to be a light in this world, just as Emma has been a light in my life."

As the morning progressed, both Emma and Thomas made their way to the small church where Reverend Arthur Davies awaited them. The Reverend's warm grey eyes crinkled with joy as he greeted each of them in turn.

"Emma, my child," he said, taking her hands in his, "may God's love shine upon you today and always."

A sense of calm washed over Emma at his words. "Thank you, Reverend," she replied, her voice steady despite the emotions swirling within her.

To Thomas, Reverend Davies offered a firm handshake and a gentle pat on the shoulder. "Thomas, my boy, remember that love is patient and kind. It is a gift from God, to be cherished and nurtured."

Thomas nodded solemnly, feeling the weight and beauty of the commitment he was about to make.

~

EMMA'S HEART fluttered as she stood at the entrance of Reverend Davies's church, her arm linked with Lord Edmund Aspendale's. The gothic revival building, adorned with delicate white roses and ribbons, seemed to glow in the morning light. The soft murmur of voices and occasional laughter drifted out to greet her.

Lord Edmund patted her hand gently. "Are you ready, my dear?"

Emma took a deep breath, steadying herself. "Yes, I believe I am."

As they stepped inside, the conversations hushed for a moment before swelling into a warm chorus of greetings. Emma's eyes swept across the gathered guests, a tapestry of faces from every chapter of her life. There was Jack, his fiery red hair unmistakable, standing beside Martha and Bert. Lily and Sam were seated near the front, their faces beaming with joy.

Her gaze found Sarah and Hannah and Lucy, all three looking radiant in their simple dresses. Tears pricked at Emma's eyes as she remembered their shared struggles and triumphs. They had come so far from the grim days at Grimshaw's Workhouse. Fiona, Rose, and Mary sat beside them. Her two previous homes, brought together.

The Aspendale family occupied the front pews, a sight that still amazed Emma. Lady Victoria offered a small, approving nod, while Evelyn, Beatrice and Lillian waved enthusiastically. Frederick, Benjamin and Clarence stood tall and proud, looking every inch the gentlemen they were becoming.

As they made their way towards the aisle, Emma caught sight of Aunt Agatha, her usually stern face softened by a rare smile. The older woman's eyes held a hint of pride, and Emma felt a rush of gratitude for the chance Aunt Agatha had given her.

Emma's steps faltered slightly as they prepared to walk down the aisle, overwhelmed by the love and support surrounding her. Lord Edmund squeezed her arm reassuringly. "You've earned this happiness, Emma," he whispered. "Every bit of it."

The sound of organ music filled the air as Emma made her way towards the alter. Each step brought her closer to Thomas, who stood at the altar, his deep brown eyes filled with love and anticipation. Emma's gaze never left his, drawing strength from the warmth and devotion she saw there.

As she approached, Emma could see the slight tremor in Thomas's hands, a mirror of the nervous excitement coursing through her own body. He wore a simple but elegant suit, a far cry from the tattered workhouse uniforms of their youth. The silver cross he had crafted hung proudly around his neck, matching the one nestled against Emma's chest.

Reverend Davies stood between them. As she reached the altar, Thomas extended his hand, and Emma placed hers in his. The touch grounded her, steadying her racing heart.

"Dearly beloved," Reverend Davies began, his rich, melodious voice carrying through the church. "We are gathered here today in the sight of God to join Emma Grace Redbrook and Thomas James Hawkins in holy matrimony."

Emma listened as the Reverend spoke of love, commitment, and faith. She thought of the long journey that had brought them to this moment – the hardships they had endured, the challenges they had overcome, and the unwavering bond that had sustained them through it all.

When the time came for their vows, Emma's voice was steady and filled with emotion. "I, Emma Grace Redbrook, take you, Thomas James Hawkins, to be my lawfully wedded husband. I promise to love, honour, and cherish you, in sickness and in health, in plenty and in want, from this day forward, until death do us part."

Thomas's eyes glistened as he repeated the vows, his voice deep and resolute. "I, Thomas James Hawkins, take you, Emma Grace Redbrook, to be my lawfully wedded wife. I promise to love, honour, and cherish you, in sickness and in health, in plenty and in want, from this day forward, until death do us part."

As Reverend Davies pronounced them husband and wife, Emma's heart soared. She turned to Thomas, her eyes shining with love and joy. Their lips met in a tender, heartfelt kiss, sealing their vows and the journey that had brought them to this moment. The silver crosses around their necks clinked softly as they embraced.

The church erupted in applause and cheers, the sound washing over Emma like a wave of warmth and support. She felt Thomas's hand tighten around hers, and they turned to face their friends and family, their faces aglow with happiness.

Emma's gaze swept over the gathered crowd, lingering on the faces of those who had been with her through the darkest times. Rachel and Lily stood side by side, their eyes brimming with tears of joy. Fiona, Rose, and Mary beamed with pride, their presence a testament to the bonds forged in adversity. Sarah, Hannah, and Lucy, her sisters in all but blood, clapped and cheered, their faces radiant with shared triumph.

The sight of her friends, gathered to celebrate this moment, overwhelmed Emma with emotion. These people had seen her at her lowest, had shared in her struggles, and had stood by her side as she fought for justice and a better world. Their presence here, in this moment of joy, was a powerful reminder of how far they had all come.

Emma felt Thomas gently squeeze her hand, and she looked up at him, seeing her own happiness reflected in his eyes. Together, they began to make their way down the aisle, surrounded by the love and support of those who had been part of their extraordinary journey.

THE FIRST CHAPTER OF 'THE DOCKYARD ORPHAN OF STORMY WEYMOUTH'

The fog rolled in from the sea, blanketing Weymouth in a soft, eerie grey. Light from the rising sun struggled to penetrate the dense mist, casting a muted glow over the cobblestone streets.

Sarah Campbell stood on her tiptoes — as tall as her small nine year old legs could take her — straining to see over the windowsill of her family's bakery. Her light blue eyes, wide with curiosity, peered through the fog-shrouded street. The mist clung to everything, transforming familiar buildings into looming shadows.

She spotted her father's figure disappearing into the grey haze. His broad shoulders were hunched against the morning chill as he strode purposefully towards the railway construction site. Sarah's small hands pressed against the cool glass, leaving ghostly imprints as condensation formed around her fingers.

"Papa," she whispered, her breath fogging the window.

The scent of fresh bread filled the air, mingling with the damp earthiness seeping in from outside. Sarah inhaled deeply, savouring the comforting aroma that always reminded her of home and family.

She heard her mother bustling about in the kitchen, preparing Papa's lunch for the day. The familiar sounds of pots clanking and bread being wrapped in paper drifted through the bakery.

Sarah's heart fluttered with a mixture of excitement as she watched her father's familiar form recede into the mist. She pressed her nose against the cool glass, leaving a small smudge, her eyes never leaving the spot where he'd disappeared.

"Sarah, love, come away from the window," her mother called from the kitchen. "You'll catch a chill."

With a small sigh, Sarah reluctantly stepped back, her bare feet padding softly on the worn wooden floor. She turned towards the warm glow of the kitchen, where her mother stood kneading dough, her arms dusted with flour.

"Come now," her mother said, gesturing with flour-covered hands. "Help me shape these loaves. We've got a busy day ahead."

Sarah moved to join her mother, standing on her tiptoes to reach the countertop. As she worked the dough with small, determined hands, her thoughts drifted back to her father. She pictured him at the railway site, strong and capable, helping to build something grand and exciting.

A sudden gust of wind rattled the shop's sign outside,

drawing Sarah's attention back to the window. The fog seemed to have thickened, transforming the street into a dreamlike landscape. For a moment, Sarah imagined she could still see her father's silhouette in the distance.

Then, as if sensing her gaze, Thomas Campbell's figure emerged briefly from the mist. He glanced back towards the bakery, his weathered face breaking into a warm smile as he raised his hand in a reassuring wave. Sarah's heart swelled with love and pride.

Her father adjusted his flat cap, tucking away the strands of salt-and-pepper hair that had escaped in the damp air. With one last look, he turned and strode purposefully back into the fog, his broad shoulders soon swallowed by the grey veil.

Sarah strained her ears, listening to the fading sound of her father's heavy boots on the cobblestones. The rhythmic footfalls grew fainter and fainter until they were replaced by the distant clatter of horse-drawn carts, muffled by the thick mist.

Sarah turned away from the window. The warmth from the ovens enveloped her, chasing away the chill that had seeped into her bones while watching her father disappear into the fog.

Inside, her mother, Agatha Campbell, bustled about with practiced efficiency. Her apron was already dusted with flour, testament to the early morning's work. Sarah watched, mesmerised, as her mother's hands moved with grace and purpose, kneading dough and shaping loaves.

"Come, my little gift," Agatha called, her voice as warm as the ovens surrounding them. "Help me pack your father's lunch."

Sarah eagerly joined her mother at the worn wooden table. Agatha carefully selected thick slices of homemade bread, still warm from the oven. The crusty exterior gave way to a soft, pillowy interior as she arranged them on a clean cloth.

"Now, what else should we add?" Agatha asked, her eyes twinkling with affection.

"Cheese!" Sarah exclaimed, reaching for a wedge of sharp cheddar. "And an apple, Papa's favourite."

Agatha nodded approvingly, her smile crinkling the corners of her eyes. "That's right, love. Your father works so hard; we must make sure he has a good meal to keep him strong."

As they worked together, the aroma of freshly baked bread filled the small, warmly lit bakery. It mingled with the smell of yeast and sugar, creating a symphony of comforting smells that Sarah associated with home and love. She inhaled deeply, savouring the familiar fragrance.

"Mama," Sarah said, her voice tinged with curiosity, "will you take Papa his lunch today?"

Agatha paused in her wrapping, considering the question. "I think I shall, dear heart. It's been a while since I've visited the railway site, and I'd like to see how the work is progressing."

Sarah's eyes lit up at the prospect of visiting the railway site. Her heart raced with excitement as she imagined the bustling activity, the gleaming rails, and the towering machines that her father had described. The construction site had always held a mysterious allure for her, a place where dreams of progress and adventure seemed to come alive.

She turned to her mother, her small hands clasped together in anticipation. "Mother," Sarah began, her voice brimming with hope, "may I go with you to see Father and the railway?"

Sarah watched as her mother's expression softened, a familiar mix of love and gentle firmness settling across her features. Agatha's hands, still dusted with flour, paused in their work as she considered her daughter's request.

"Not today, my dear," Agatha said, her tone kind but resolute. "There is much to be done here, and I need your help."

Sarah's heart sank, disappointment clouding her face like the fog outside. She had so hoped to see the marvels her father spoke of, to breathe in the excitement of progress and change.

For a moment, she wanted to protest, to plead her case, but the sense of responsibility instilled in her by her parents won out.

With a small sigh, Sarah nodded reluctantly. "Yes, Mother," she said, her voice quiet but steady. She understood the importance of her duties at the bakery, the need to contribute to the family's livelihood.

Sarah's disappointment lingered for a moment, but she pushed it aside, focusing instead on the tasks at hand. The bakery was her home, filled with warmth and the comforting scents of fresh bread and pastries. She knew every nook and cranny, every utensil and ingredient, and took pride in her growing skills.

Agatha smiled softly at her daughter's resilience. "Come now, let's get you ready for the day's work."

Sarah nodded, her spirits lifting as she moved to fetch her small apron from its hook, a familiar routine. She carefully looped the apron strings around her waist, her small fingers working deftly to tie a neat bow at the back.

As she smoothed down the front of her apron, Sarah felt the rough texture of the fabric beneath her palms. It was worn soft in places from years of use, carrying the history of countless loaves and pastries. The apron had been her mother's when she was a girl, passed down like a cherished heirloom.

Once Sarah was properly attired, Agatha beckoned her over to the large wooden worktable. A substantial ball of dough sat waiting, its pale surface dusted with a fine layer of flour.

"Watch closely, love," Agatha instructed, her hands moving with practiced grace. She pressed her palms into the dough, pushing it away before folding it back on itself. The motions were fluid and rhythmic, almost hypnotic.

Sarah observed intently, marvelling at the way the dough transformed under her mother's expert touch. It seemed to come alive, stretching and folding with each movement.

After a few moments of demonstration, Agatha stepped back. "Now you try, Sarah. Remember, gentle but firm. Let the dough guide your hands."

With a small hint of trepidation, Sarah approached the worktable. She stood on her tiptoes, reaching out to place her small hands on the cool, sticky mass. The dough yielded beneath her touch, soft yet resistant.

Sarah began to knead, mimicking her mother's movements. She pushed the dough away, then pulled it back, feeling it stretch and compress beneath her fingers. The rhythmic motion was soothing, and she found herself falling into a steady pattern.

As she worked, a connection built within Sarah – to her mother, to the bakery, to the generations of bakers who had come before. Her small hands moved with increasing confidence, shaping the dough that would soon become nourishing bread for their customers.

As Sarah's small hands worked the dough, she felt a sense of pride growing within her. The sticky mass was slowly transforming under her touch, becoming smoother and more malleable with each push and fold. She glanced up at her mother, seeking approval, and was rewarded with a warm smile that made her heart swell.

Agatha began to hum softly as she moved about the bakery, preparing for the day ahead. The melody was familiar to Sarah, a gentle tune that her mother often sang at bedtime. It floated through the air, mingling with the comforting scents of yeast and warm bread.

Sarah closed her eyes for a moment, letting the sound wash over her. The notes seemed to weave themselves into the very fabric of the bakery, becoming part of the morning ritual. She found herself swaying slightly as she worked, her movements falling into rhythm with her mother's humming.

The familiar tune transported Sarah back to cosy evenings spent curled up in her bed, listening to her mother's soothing voice as she drifted off to sleep. Now, in the early morning light, it felt like a warm embrace, chasing away any lingering sleepiness and filling her with a sense of security.

As she continued to knead, Sarah became aware of the stark contrast between the warmth of the bakery and the chill that seeped in from outside. The fog still clung to the windows, transforming the street beyond into a mysterious, grey world. But inside, everything was golden and warm, filled with the promise of fresh bread and the comfort of family.

As Sarah finished kneading the dough, her small arms aching pleasantly from the effort, she stepped back to admire her handiwork. The once sticky mass had transformed into a smooth, elastic ball under her careful ministrations. Accomplishment swelled in her as she watched her mother gently lift the dough and place it in a large bowl, covering it with a damp cloth to rise.

"Well done, my little gift," Agatha said, her voice warm with pride. "God's given you quite the touch for baking."

Sarah beamed at the praise, her cheeks flushing with pleasure. She dusted the flour from her hands, leaving small white handprints on her apron. As her mother moved to tend to the ovens, Sarah found herself drawn back to the window.

The fog still hung heavy over Weymouth, transforming the familiar streets into a mysterious landscape. Sarah pressed her nose against the cool glass, her breath creating small patches of condensation. Her eyes strained to pierce the grey veil, imagining the railway construction site hidden somewhere beyond.

In her mind's eye, Sarah could see the bustle of activity her father had described. She pictured towering cranes reaching into the sky, their metal arms swinging to and fro as they lifted heavy loads. She imagined the rhythmic clanging of hammers on metal, the hiss of steam engines, and the shouts of workers coordinating their efforts.

Sarah's imagination painted a vivid picture of men in dusty

clothes and flat caps, much like her father's, scurrying about like ants on a great mound. In her fantasy, she could almost feel the rumble of the earth as massive machines carved out the path for the railway tracks.

The young girl's thoughts drifted to the trains themselves. She had seen pictures in books, but to see one in person, to hear its whistle and feel the rush of wind as it sped by – the very idea made her heart race with excitement. Sarah wondered how the railway would change their little town of Weymouth. Would it bring new faces, new stories from far-off places?

Sarah watched as her mother carefully wrapped the last slice of bread in a clean cloth, tucking it into the basket alongside the cheese and apple.

Agatha moved towards the door, her steps purposeful yet unhurried. She reached for the worn wool shawl that hung from a hook nearby, its familiar weave speaking of countless journeys through Weymouth's unpredictable weather. With practiced ease, she draped it over her shoulders.

Sarah's eyes followed her mother's movements, a mix of emotions swirling within her. Part of her still longed to accompany Agatha to the construction site, to see the marvels her father spoke of with such enthusiasm. Yet she understood her place was here, tending to the bakery.

Agatha turned back to Sarah, her eyes softening as they met her daughter's. She bent down, her face level with Sarah's, and placed a gentle kiss on the girl's forehead. The familiar scent of flour and vanilla enveloped Sarah.

"Be good, Sarah," Agatha said, her voice warm with affection. "I'll be back soon."

Sarah nodded, straightening her small shoulders as if to show her readiness for the responsibility ahead. She watched as her mother gathered the basket, preparing to step out into the fog-shrouded morning.

Sarah watched as her mother opened the bakery door,

letting in a swirl of cool, damp air. The fog seemed to reach its tendrils into the warm sanctuary of the shop, momentarily blurring the line between the cosy interior and the mysterious world beyond. Agatha's figure, wrapped in her familiar shawl, stood silhouetted against the grey backdrop for a moment before she stepped out onto the cobblestones.

"I will be good, Mother," Sarah promised, her voice steady despite the emotions swirling within her.

As the door swung shut behind Agatha, the bell above it giving a final, muted jingle, the bakery's atmosphere shifted. The space seemed larger somehow, emptier without her mother's comforting presence. The hum of the ovens and the lingering scent of fresh bread suddenly felt more pronounced in the quiet.

For a moment, Sarah stood still, her small frame dwarfed by the familiar surroundings that now felt slightly foreign. But then, as if shaking off a spell, she set her jaw with determination. Her mother and father were counting on her, and she would not let them down.

With purposeful steps, Sarah returned to the large wooden worktable. She pulled over the small stool her father had crafted for her, allowing her to reach the tabletop comfortably. Climbing up, she surveyed the array of ingredients before her: flour dusted the surface like a light snowfall, and a large ball of pastry dough sat waiting.

Sarah took a deep breath, inhaling the comforting scents of the bakery. She could almost hear her mother's gentle instructions guiding her actions. With careful movements, she began to roll out the dough, her small hands gripping the wooden rolling pin firmly.

Back and forth she worked, applying gentle pressure as she'd been taught. The dough slowly spread beneath the rolling pin, transforming from a lumpy mass into a smooth, even sheet. Sarah's tongue poked out slightly from the corner of her mouth as she concentrated, determined to achieve the perfect thickness.

As the morning progressed, Sarah managed to settle into a familiar rhythm. The bell above the door chimed, heralding the arrival of their first customer. Mrs Eliza Thompson, shuffled in, her face creasing into a smile as she spotted Sarah behind the counter.

"Good morning, little Miss Campbell," she said. "Where's your mother today?"

Sarah straightened her apron, pushing a stray lock of hair behind her ear. "Good morning, Mrs Thompson. Mother's gone to bring Papa his lunch at the railway site. How may I help you today?"

Mrs Thompson chuckled, her eyes twinkling. "Well, aren't you the proper little shopkeeper? I'll have two of your finest rolls, if you please."

Sarah nodded, her small hands carefully selecting the golden-brown rolls from the display. She wrapped them in brown paper with practiced ease, tying the package with a neat bow of twine. As she handed over the parcel, Mrs Thompson pressed a few coins into her palm.

"Thank you, Mrs Thompson," Sarah said, her voice clear and polite. "I hope you enjoy your breakfast."

As the morning wore on, more customers trickled in. Mr Browning, the owner of the general store, praised Sarah's neat plaits. Mr Heathcliff, the butcher, commented on how she was growing to be the spitting image of her mother. With each interaction, Sarah felt a little taller, a little more confident in her role.

Between customers, Sarah busied herself with the tasks her mother had set out.

Outside, the fog remained thick, transforming Weymouth into a ghostly landscape. But inside the bakery, all was warm and bright. The ovens radiated heat, keeping the chill at bay, while the golden glow of the lamps cast everything in a comforting light.

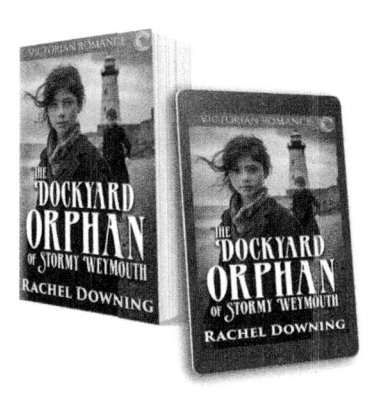

Click here to read the rest of
The Dockyard Orphan of Stormy Weymouth'

A lighthouse's beam. A fisherman's net. A love that defies the tide.

In the picturesque coastal town of Weymouth, Sarah Campbell's world crumbles when a tragic accident claims her parents' lives. Taken in by the gruff but kindly lighthouse keeper, she finds solace in the beam that guides ships to safety. But it's Matthew Fletcher, a young fisherman wrestling with his own loss, who truly captures her heart.

As Sarah and Matthew's bond deepens, a web of mystery and danger threatens to tear them apart. The arrival of a charming stranger from London adds fuel to the fire, tempting Sarah with glimpses of a world beyond her small coastal town.

With corruption lurking in the shadows and the sea hiding deadly secrets, Sarah must navigate treacherous waters. Can she uncover the truth before it's too late? And will her heart stay true to its first love, or be swept away by new possibilities?

From windswept cliffs to glittering ballrooms, this gripping tale of romance and intrigue will keep you spellbound. Watch as childhood promises collide with adult realities, testing the limits of trust, forgiveness, and the power of true love.

'The Dockyard Orphan of Stormy Weymouth'

OUR GIFT TO YOU

AS A WAY TO SAY THANK YOU WE WOULD LOVE TO SEND YOU THIS BEAUTIFUL STORY FREE OF CHARGE.

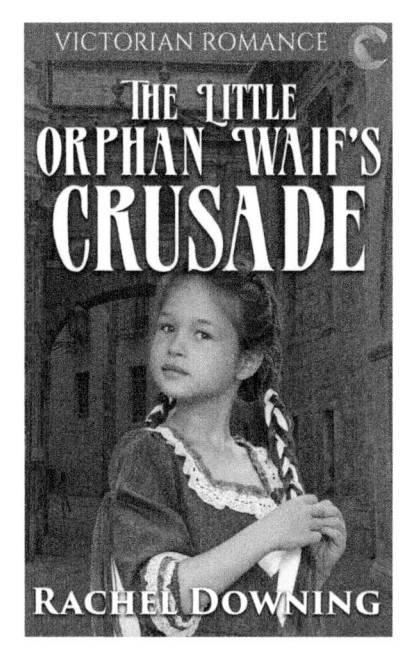

Click here for your FREE COPY of

'The Little Orphan Waif's Crusade'

CornerstoneTales.com/sign-up

In the wake of her father's passing, seven-year-old Matilda is determined to heal her sister Effie's shattered spirit.

Desperate to restore joy to Effie's life, Matilda embarks on a daring quest, aided by the gentle-hearted postman, Philip. Together, they weave a plan to ignite the flame of love in Effie's heart once more.

At Cornerstone Tales we publish books you can trust. Great tales without sex or swearing, but with all of the mystery and romance you expect from a great story.

Be the first to know when we release new books, take part in our fun competitions, and get surprise free books in your inbox by signing up to our free VIP Reader list.

As a thank you you'll receive a copy of 'The Little Orphan Waif's Crusade' straight away, alongside other gifts.

Click here to sign up for our mailing list, and receive your FREE stories.

CornerstoneTales.com/sign-up

LOVE VICTORIAN ROMANCE?

Other Rachel Downing Books

The Orphan's Christmas Hymn

Seven-year-old Clara Winters' world shatters when tragedy strikes days before Christmas. Sent to St. Mary's Church Orphanage, she finds her only solace in the hymns that once filled her happy home. When her angelic voice catches the attention of the kind-hearted Reverend Thornton and his musically gifted son Edward, Clara dares to dream of a brighter future.

Get 'The Orphan's Christmas Hymn' Here!

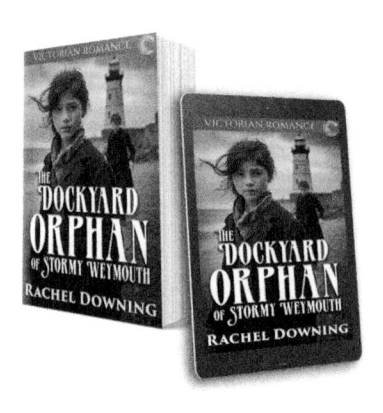

The Dockyard Orphan of Stormy Weymouth

Sarah Campbell's world crumbles when a tragic accident claims her parents' lives. She finds solace in the lighthouse's beam that guides ships to safety. But it's a young fisherman wrestling with his own loss, who truly captures her heart.

Get 'The Dockyard Orphan of Stormy Weymouth' Here!

The Workhouse Orphan Rivals

Childhood sweethearts torn apart. A promise broken. A love that refuses to die.

Get 'The Workhouse Orphan Rivals' Here!

The Orphan Prodigy's Stolen Tale

When ten-year-old Isabella Farmerson's world shatters with the tragic loss of her parents, she's thrust into a life of hardship and uncertainty.

Get 'The Orphan Prodigy's Stolen Tale' Here!

The Lost Orphans of Dark Streets

Follow the stories of Elizabeth and Molly as they negotiate the dangerous slums and find their place in the world.

Get 'The Lost Orphans of Dark Streets' Here!

Two Steadfast Orphan's Dreams

Follow the stories of Isabella and Ada as they overcome all odds and find love.

Get 'Two Steadfast Orphan's Dreams' Here!

And from our other Victorian Romance Author Dorothy Wellings...

The Moral Maid's Unjust Trial

Matilda must fend for herself when her father is wrongfully accused for a crime he didn't commit.

Get 'The Moral Maid's Unjust Trial' Here!

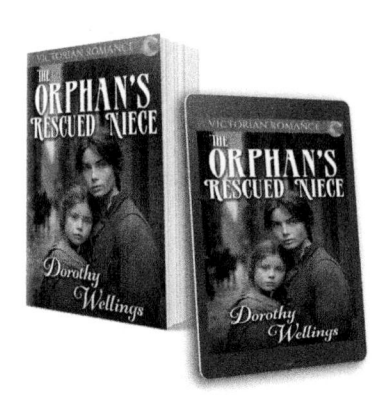

The Orphan's Rescued Niece

As Beatrice grows from a wide-eyed child into a resilient young woman, she finds herself caught between her love for her troubled brother and her desire for a life free from poverty and fear.

Get 'The Orphan's Rescued Niece' Here!

If you enjoyed this story, sign up to our mailing list to be the first to hear about our new releases and any sales and deals we have.

We also want to offer you a Victorian Romance novella - 'The Little Orphan Waif's Crusade' - absolutely free!

Click here to sign up for our mailing list, and receive your FREE stories.

CornerstoneTales.com/sign-up

Printed in Great Britain
by Amazon